ALIBI ISLAND

AN ILLUMINATI NOVEL

SLMN

Kingston Imperial

Alibi Island Copyright © 2019 by Kingston Imperial 2, LLC

Printed in the United States of America

Rights Department, 144 North 7th Street, #255 Brooklyn N.Y. 11249

First Edition:

Book and Jacket Design: PiXiLL Designs

Cataloging in Publication data is on file with the library of Congress

ISBN 9780998767499 (Trade Paperback)

PROLOGUE

Macy's lungs were bursting.

She crashed through the undergrowth, not caring about the thorns which lashed at her face and tugged at what was left of her clothes. Moonlight spilled silver across the wide-open fields all the way to the Enchanted Forest hugging the lower slopes of the mountain. The air was hot and sticky with a ferocious humidity, but inside she felt as cold as a grave.

Macy dared not look behind at the pursuing men. Any hesitation in her forward momentum would bring them even closer. She surmised they wouldn't risk shooting her with their hunting rifles from this distance, even though she knew some of them were good enough shooters to do so.

If there's one thing she knew about these men, it's that they would want to look into her eyes when they killed her. A bullet in the brain and a merciful release was no substitute for a kill made with your own hands, where you could taste the dying person's last breath upon your lips.

Macy also knew that she could never escape them.

Her biting Lobo Snelling's fat hand until he squealed like the pig he was, diving through the open window of his chalet, and running like her life depended on it, was in fact the complete opposite.

Macy's *death* depended on it.

She wanted to die. In dying she wanted to take away their ultimate pleasure. She was going to kill *herself*. Quickly. As cleanly as possible to rob them of the delight of seeing her die up close and personal.

She darted through the perimeter fence as a black patrol Humvee returned to the compound. It was precisely on time as usual. Every night. Like clockwork. She'd bitten Lobo's hand to coincide with the automatic gate beginning to slide open and pelted toward the opening before the complacent, black uniformed guards could even raise their weapons. Lobo hit the chalet's alarm stud almost as soon as Macy crashed to the ground and rolled away from the building. She knew she had less than fifteen seconds to reach the perimeter wall and get through the gate system before the alarm automatics kicked in and slammed it shut.

If she timed it right, she would go through as the Humvee came in, thus preventing the automatics from crashing the gate into the patrol truck.

Macy witnessed many other runners fail at this hurdle. They hid within the compound's grounds rather than heading straight for the outside, and that was their greatest mistake. Once the gates were closed, the dogs were released, and a runner would be caught in a matter of minutes, wherever they tried to hide.

But if you could make it through the wall, you had a chance...

Not of *living*...but of *dying* well.

Outside the perimeter fence was a well-maintained area of woodland, through which residents of the compound would take long lazy walks along wood-chipped paths, picnicking and enjoying the perennial sunshine on the island. There was an ornamental lake and an eighteen-hole putting green. Macy skirted the lake and sprinted across the green, heading for the area of shrubs and low trees that constituted the land reaching all the way to the island's central mountain, looming two thousand feet into the night sky. To the west it was all jungle. She'd never be able to run fast enough through that.

Someone, perhaps Lobo—in between beating her and fucking her—told her that this part of the island was all rainforest and jungle before the compound was built. The Owners brought in a team of Filipino workers to clear the jungle. When they finished and were taking a boat back to the mainland, Lobo and the others were granted the privilege of shooting the boat to pieces with the belly slung cannons attached to the island's two recreational JetRanger helicopters.

A red laser light beam lanced past her into the blue-black distance. Then a second, then a third. They were just trying to frighten her in an effort to arrest her run. So Macy continued at full speed. Let them shoot her if they wanted; maybe she would bleed to death before they reached her.

The sultry humidity reminded Macy of when she was taken seven years ago. She'd been walking home from school one summer's evening in New Orleans. She was swinging her bag, singing a snatch of a song her momma liked—a song that she sadly couldn't recall. It would have calmed her heart if she could remember it as she ran. It was a song her momma would hum whenever Macy was ill in bed, or when she was having difficulty getting off to sleep. Her momma, a beautiful but poor woman, waited tables during the day and sang jazz for pennies in the evening. She had a voice that could charm angels. Macy had often wondered in the time she'd been on the island if she inherited her momma's voice. She dared not try the skill out there, even if she did possess it. She wouldn't want to be found out. Having a skill that could be exploited for the sadistic and hateful desires of the permanent residents and visitors to the island was something that was imperative to hide. Any information could be used against you for the purposes of humiliation and degradation.

Macy had seen it happen too many times over the years that she was a prisoner. Girls who had phobias for spiders, made to sleep in a room with loose tarantulas for the amusement of the guests. Those who were afraid of fire, having their arms secured in locked boxes with glass sides, and their skin roasted while they screamed and the audience laughed.

Macy kept her phobias to herself, having learned that trick very early on. The less you gave, the less they could take from you.

The sound of a helicopter rising above brought Macy's thoughts back to the present and the reality of her situation. She estimated she was minutes away from her goal if she could maintain this pace. The helicopter would be used to track her but would not land to stop her. That was against the rules of the hunt, even an impromptu hunt like this one.

Only residents and visitors could take part in hunts; the security forces on the island were there just to provide safety from discovery or to ensure passions didn't get out of hand and visitors didn't start killing each other just for the fun of it. When there were so many drugs, alcohol, and absolutely no comeback, sometimes people might forget themselves. A resident would never do that; they knew how much they would lose. Visitors took a while to acclimate to the freedoms presented by the island.

The spotlight from the helicopter nailed Macy in a cone of the harshest white. It hurt her eyes, and she could feel the heat of it on her back. The draft of the rotors was getting nearer, so the pursuing hunters could range accurately where Macy was in relation to the far tree line.

If Macy made it to the Enchanted Forest the helicopter would no longer be able to track her, she figured, and the hunters—some in their late fifties or older—might just give up and leave the hunt to the younger residents. That would cut the number of men hunting her at least by half and increase her possibility of reaching her goal before they caught her.

Macy's chest felt raw as tenderized steak, her arms like cold lead, and her legs like her feet had been cut off and she was running on stumps.

She planned to escape tonight because she knew that Lobo Snelling would come for her in the auction. Whenever he visited the island, he would bid for her and had been doing so for a couple of years since he'd been allowed access to the tightly controlled island paradise. He told her he liked her coffee-colored skin and her green mulatto eyes —whatever that meant, she had no idea. He probably liked the way she lay there so that he could do to her as he pleased.

Inside she might have been aching, raging, and screaming, but her deliberately floppy body and blank face gave nothing away and took nothing back. It had kept her alive this long, and she'd gotten into the habit of flying her mind away to other places, to what she remembered of her momma's face, the kind teachers at her school, and her friends with whom she would play dolls or went lake swimming.

That made the things Lobo did to her easier to cope with, even if she was wracked with pain and tears for hours afterwards. She came to love those flights away from the island, oblivious of Lobo's fetid breath and fat sweaty body.

"Stay where you are! Do not move."

Macy was getting tantalizingly close to the tree line and the JetRanger pilot was using his PA system to communicate with her.

"Stand still or you will be shot."

"No. I won't," she managed to say through dry mouth and ragged breath. With that she seemed to leap the last twenty meters into the trees, making her prophesy come true.

In the forest, the moonlight was off her, and the JetRanger spotlight had lost her racing form. She ran for another thirty seconds, dodging tree trunks, and kicking through layers of brown autumnal leaves.

The Enchanted Forest was a lie too, like so much of the island.

When the jungle had been cleared, Lobo told her one night—after he had stopped working up his foul sweat over her body—that they'd brought in thirty thousand European trees to build an Enchanted Forest.

Girls had been taken there, forced to wear Princess Dresses, and subjected to the foul attentions of the residents. Visitors were only allowed so far into the Enchanted Forest, with its long twisting lanes, fat, gnarly oaks, secret dells, and clearings. Lobo had told Macy that one day he would become a resident and take her there to the Enchanted Forest, and he would become both the cause and savior of her distress.

Macy could still hear the helicopter, but it was muted by the fully-leafed oaks. A stream was running along a mulchy ditch in her line of sight, moonlight dappling through the branches, giving the man-made forest an ethereal beauty. Macy crept forward, the call of the water was too much to resist. Her throat was dry and scratchy from all the running, and she had the unpleasant taste of blood in her mouth. She crawled through the warm loam and leaves, feeling her heart thumping in her ears. There hadn't been the tell-tale crash of hunters entering this part of the forest; no flashlights beaming between the tree trunks. If it hadn't been for the clashing rotor blades, there would have been no fear and urgency in her body. The Enchanted Forest felt like another world: one where she could rest, grow strong, and...

She pushed the thought from her mind.

There was no living to be done. There was running and there was dying.

That was it.

Macy dropped her lips to the cool running water and drank deeply, hoping it would provide her with enough strength to get through the forest and out the other side.

She had been to this part of the island just once before, when she'd been taken on a hot air balloon trip with one of the residents. Arthur Bellows had a face like a craggy map and eyes that might have been transplanted into his face from a pig. That had been the hardest trip of her life. Not because of what she had to endure from the billionaire financier, but because of the phobia she'd managed until then to hide from everyone on the island.

Keep all information inside.

She'd been terrified they'd find out her phobia when they eventually landed. But because Bellows had gotten himself so excited over her anguish and terror, he'd given himself a heart attack. He got the balloon down to twenty feet from the ground before he expired right in front of her. She hadn't been blamed for his death. How could she when she'd been tied upside down outside of the basket?

The grip of terror from the journey stayed with her for

many days, and it had taken her a great deal longer to be able to review the trip in her mind. She had to because of what she'd seen on the far side of the Enchanted Forest.

It was what she had seen while suspended from the basket that had given her the idea for tonight's attempt to end the misery of her existence.

A way of escaping the island through death.

After Macy's thirst was quenched, she waded through the stream and climbed up on the other side of the bank.

That's when she heard the dogs begin to bark.

"That's not in the rules!" she hissed to herself. Suddenly she was losing confidence in her ability to outrun the hunters. If they were using dogs to track her, she had no chance of crossing the forest. When it was only men—rich, fat, ugly men with their guts wobbling and their jowls shaking—she had a chance. A narrow one, but the dogs were another matter. They were supposed to stay in the compound.

That was the rule!

Macy was consumed with the unfairness of the use of the tracking dogs. Her whole plan had been constructed around the idea that the rules of the hunt would be followed, and now she was not going to make it to the death she so desperately wanted.

She turned her head back as she ran, the barking spurring her on ever faster.

Macy never should have turned her head, because as soon as she did, her world became a thud of hard pain and enveloping blackness.

At first Macy thought she'd miscalculated and collided with a tree.

In her headlong rush to escape the hunters and their dogs, she knew that looking back while running was not the smartest idea, even when you weren't dashing through a moonlit forest.

She ached all over, and when she opened her eyes everything stayed black. Macy tried to sit up, but a hand pressed over her mouth and another pushed her back down on the shoulder.

"Stay quiet, don't move."

It was a woman's voice. Not like one of the harsh voices of the men ordering her to undress or to contort herself into muscle tearing positions; a kind and warm woman's voice.

"They're still searching and we're safe here as long as you don't move. Do you understand?"

Macy nodded.

Suddenly she could see, as the piece of material blindfolding her eyes was removed. The room was dimly lit by dusty old strip lights. The walls were rough mud, with roots and vines twisting through them. The hand over her mouth, belonged to a woman.

The woman was old, with grandma hair, a sweet mouth and sparkling eyes. She smiled down at Macy. And put her fingers to her lips.

Macy nodded and the woman removed her hand.

Macy had no idea where she was. It felt like it was underground, perhaps beneath the Enchanted Forest.

The woman got up and went to a ragged opening in the wall covered by a dank looking curtain. She moved the material aside and peered out into the night. Macy could no longer hear the dogs or the JetRanger.

"I think they're gone," the woman said, returning to Macy and sitting beside her. She smoothed Macy's hair back from her forehead. It was the first time in years—since perhaps New Orleans—that someone had touched her with what seemed like genuine affection. Macy felt tears welling up in her eyes.

"Where am I?"

"You're safe."

"Who are you?"

"I'm Rosa. And you're...?"

"Macy."

"Hello Macy. Welcome to my home."

"Are we still in the forest?"

"Yes. Beneath it."

Macy was surprised that she ran out of questions so quickly. But the underground room was warm and cozy, and even though she'd just awoken from unconsciousness she was so, so tired. A warm blanket of sleep was running up her body.

Rosa smiled, and soothed her brow again.

It felt so good to be there.

Macy had been aiming for the deep ravine she'd seen from the balloon that lay on the other side of the Enchanted Forest. She had known she would never make it off the island, so to throw herself over the edge—dashed and broken on the rocks below—was her only real hope of escape.

She'd thought for many weeks about doing it.

It was a fear she had to confront—her fear of high places that had so effectively been exposed by the balloon trip. Escaping the compound had been the least frightening aspect of her journey. The thought of standing on the edge of the ravine, looking down, and then forcing herself to jump had stopped her from escaping for so long. But another night with Lobo had convinced her that it was fear worth overcoming.

How wrong could she have been?

There was hope. There was a way out.

As she slipped back into sleep, she squeezed Rosa's hand. It was the most at peace she'd felt in her life.

So much so that she almost didn't feel the pop of skin as the stiletto in Rosa's other hand slid through Macy's ribs and sliced into her heart.

———

Rosa walked into the semi-circle of men; Macy's eyeless and opened body was draped floppily in her arms.

The men licked their lips, their eyes were wet with lust.

"You call yourself hunters?" Rosa spat.

The men shuffled uneasily, but didn't take their eyes off the body.

"Don't make me have to clear up after you again. Clear?"

"Yes, Owner," they intoned quietly.

Rosa threw Macy's body into the dirt, pulled a smartphone from her pocket in the waistcoat beneath her cloak, and took a picture of the girl's broken frame and dead eyes in her lolling head. She checked the picture, and uploaded it to the island's intranet. Then she addressed the men, her words hissing like snakes. "Make sure you cook her thoroughly all the way through. There's poison there that needs to be neutralized."

Then Rosa turned and walked back into the Enchanted Forest as the men moved in on Macy's body.

Macy was eighteen years old.

1

Passion Valdez was tired to the bone.

The huge Houston sky through the window of her hotel room was clear as the Pope's conscience and blue as Billie Holiday, Passion was rolled into a ball on the bed—naked and wanting the room to cool down and her head to stop throbbing. The air conditioning hadn't been triggered in the room before she checked in because of Global Warming or Earth Love or International Day of the Tree or something, and although Passion held no animosity towards the environment per se, should could have done without it turning her room into an oven that was cooling so slowly, she could have stuck a fork in her ass and shouted *I'm done* a good half an hour ago.

The shoot had lasted all night, and as she'd only landed from Manila yesterday—well, Istanbul in reality—the 34-hour flight had an eight-hour stopover in the Turkish capital. This dogleg to her journey had allowed no sleep, just a gritty bath in iron-colored water that had been the best the no-star hotel had offered. Passion didn't like to waste money on frivolities, and so as she'd booked that hotel herself, she didn't feel she had the right to complain.

She wanted to sleep. But the heat and the blue sky—combined with Houston's higgledy-piggledy skyline etched on her retina by the harsh midday light—conspired to keep her awake.

The shoot had been a bore too. The 'tog had been an oily fuck who was a throwback to another time. Too touchy, too feely, too full of himself. It would have been the work of a moment for her to have taken him out back to the warehouse where she was modeling a new line in street couture for Zing! Fashions. They were clothes that she wouldn't have been caught dead wearing in real life, which is why she resented so much being alive in them.

Yes, it would have been so easy to take the oily fuck out back on the promise of a blow job and then kick his fucking head in; but she hadn't, tempting as it was. Being a model, albeit a reluctant one, was an excellent cover for a woman in Passion's line of *actual* work, and so all she'd done was tear open his throat with her eyes.

The oily fuck had taken the look as encouragement, got down behind the camera muttering, "Mine tonight darlin'. Mine tonight."

God, how she hated the English.

Passion realized that she wasn't going to get any sleep at all today. There was no work tonight, so she may as well just battle through these hollow hours of jet lag and exhaustion until sundown and get to sleep then.

Passion sat up and wiped her mouth with the back of her hand. She'd already decided against a shower in case it woke her up more, but it seemed like a good idea for exactly the same reason.

She hadn't moved three steps from the bed when her cellphone rang.

Sighing like a teenager, she went back and picked it up. "Yes?"

"Do you have the TV on?"

It was Bryan.

"Bryan, I don't even have any clothes on."

"I know."

"If you have me under surveillance again..."

"I don't. Don't worry. Put the TV on. Any news channel."

Passion had to crawl across the bed to get the remote. She flicked on the TV to a channel that was apparently *Houston's News Leader*.

There was a media scrimmage on the steps of an official looking building, a man Passion half-recognized, who was then helpfully identified by the ticker chyron as Prospective Senator Huey Ralston (REP).

Next to Ralston was a woman identified as his wife, Brenda. Ralston was an early fifties politico clone with a good suit and even better hair. He was just about holding it together. Brenda, behind huge sunglasses and recently arranged hair, held herself as if she'd been emptied out by horror and tears.

As Ralston spoke, his voice was tight with emotion, and the wide angle on the news camera caught his fist flexing and relaxing, almost in time with his words. "Alaina, if you're watching this darling, please come home. You're not in trouble. Whatever happened can be fixed. We just want you to come home so we can be the family we have always been again."

The words stilled in Ralston's throat and Brenda just shook her head and buried her face in her husband's shoulder.

The moment of silence was then destroyed by a thousand foam topped microphones being thrust towards Ralston's face, followed by a thousand questions.

A shark-faced suit with slicked back hair and skin the texture of pages from an old Bible, side-stepped in front of the couple, holding up his hands. "One at a time ladies and gentlemen. One at a time."

The news chyron flicked from *Stephen Crane, PA* to *Huey Ralston*. The microphone onslaught calmed a little, and Crane—scanning the crowd of reporters—said, "Mary?"

"Mr. Ralston, do police have any idea when your daughter went missing or where she might be?"

Ralston leaned into Crane's ear and whispered. Crane nodded. "Prospective Senator Ralston and his wife last saw Alaina yesterday morning before they left for their offices. Alaina was due to spend the day at the residence before going to the Jantell-B concert at the Astrodome tonight with friends. At some point during the day—before Mrs. Ralston returned to the residence at four—Alaina left the home to go to an unknown destination. She left the house alone according to staff, and once she walked out of the compound her cellphone was turned off, and she was not picked up by any cameras in the vicinity. Garth?"

"That's all you need." Bryan again, in Passion's ear.

She flicked off the TV. "Same M.O. as Manila."

"Yup, exactly. Rich kid. Phone switched off the moment she left the home, not seen since. No ransom. Dead trail."

Manila had been a *bitch*.

Passion had been there three days before the family would even consider seeing her. In Timberland Heights above Quezon City, the mansion residence nestled beneath blue skies was backed by mountains and was on the surface all about beauty. But the stink of bad money infected it, and it had infected the people who lived there.

The father had more pies than he had fingers and wanted a piece of them all. So when his daughter Bianca went missing—an 18-year-old studious girl with hair the color of night, a complexion as fair as it was beautiful, and an attitude to match—he'd been absolutely reluctant to involve the authorities in case any investigation into the disappearance of his daughter led to exposure of his nefarious business dealings. That was Bryan's assessment, and Bryan was usually right about these things.

Bryan's intel was right on the money.

Passion—again undercover away from a hastily arranged modeling gig under her agency name Jennifer Durant—approached the father through his office in the city. Bryan had given her an in when he slipped her the contact info. The father, he said, liked...no...*wanted* beautiful women. Passion was, of course, entirely that.

When "Daddy" realized Passion was there to talk about his missing daughter and not to offer him a place in her bed, he had refused point blank to take the meeting.

It was only his wife, broken by the loss of their daughter, who had eventually persuaded her husband's secretary to give up the information that the Agency had been in touch.

"Can you find her?"

"I'll try Mrs. Andrada. I make no promises."

"You've found children before?"

"Yes, yes I have. Not just children, but we have the skills needed for this delicate operation."

"You look too pretty to be a detective."

Passion would normally dress down when she went on Agency business. But the meeting with Mrs. Andrada had come unexpectedly; Passion was made up, with hair to kill and a Rodeo Drive ensemble to die for. Her work uniform was jeans, a blouse, and long hair savagely back in a simple ponytail. To look at Passion, or "Jennifer the detective" on the runway, you would swear they were two different women. They say that cameras never lie, but that's exactly what they were for. Passion only modelled to keep the undercover part of her life plausibly mobile; to go where she was needed by the Agency.

"My associate Bryan Frain will transmit my bona fides to you immediately Mrs. Andrada. The organization I work for has a long track record in successful conclusions to these situations."

Two days later, in a backstreet Manila warehouse full of the stink of death and awash with blood, Passion had found Bianca's thin, broken body hanging by electrical wire from a crossbeam in the ceiling.

Passion had made good progress tracking down the men who had taken the girl. Timberland Heights was an exclusive area, and she'd got a break from CCTV from a neighbor's gate entry system. The footage revealed two grainy frames of Bianca being pushed into the back of a Ford Raptor.

Passion tracked the vehicle through Bryan's secret contacts with the Manila PD, to a couple of petty felons who were trying to haul themselves up a few rungs on the underworld ladder.

Only it looked like Bianca had gotten the better of them and hung herself in her warehouse room when the crooks were distracted.

Brave girl.

Stupid girl.

If she'd waited six hours, Passion would have sprung her from the clutches of her kidnappers.

The death of the girl was not the outcome anyone wanted, but what made it stranger were the kidnappers.

They were dead too.

One was still attached to a cattle prod by his penis. Both had their eyes stabbed out, their throats cut, and their intestines given the chance of a vacation outside of their bodies. Whoever had done a number on them had enjoyed their work.

When Passion reached the warehouse, the kidnappers' bodies were still fresh. Bianca had been dead a good few hours longer.

To Passion it seemed the girl's suicide had pissed off someone higher up the food chain. And when the discovery of the girl's death had been made, there had been a swift and bloody retribution for the amateurs' fuck-ups.

Passion had arranged for Bianca's body to be returned to her parents and sent the retainer she'd been given by Mrs. Andrada back too.

The Agency worked on a *No Find, No Fee* basis. Although that didn't apply to expenses, Passion hadn't felt right about taking the money, even though Bianca's father had behaved like such an asshole and was shady as fuck. Even assholes didn't deserve to bury their own daughters.

Passion hadn't yet had the conversation with Bryan about the retainer and would put it off for as long as she could. Certainly until she was over this jet-lag and had a least one good night's sleep.

The mystery about the dead kidnappers was what maintained her interest. Bianca's kidnap had been the fifth in the last year that Passion had investigated with the same M.O.

The police were nowhere on it, anywhere in the world. In most cases the families, shady like Bianca's daddy, hadn't wanted to involve the police anyway. And although Passion had many other successes, she hadn't yet managed to find a single one of the five girls. And now, right under her nose in Houston, it was happening again. Only this time the Ralston's had gone public, big time.

"Have you sent them a handshake?" she asked Bryan, sitting down on the edge of the bed, feeling her longing for sleep was getting sent further away down the tunnel of work.

"Yes. Your contact will be Crane. I'm sending you his details now."

The phone's email notification pinged.

"Got it."

"And he'll meet you at Ralston's office in...45 minutes."

The phoned pinged again.

"And that's the address."

"Christ, Bryan I haven't slept for nearly fifty hours."

"You want this case?"

"Yes, you know I do."

"Then it's yours. Oh and have a shower. I imagine you smell like a fox."

2

Lainey Ralston hated being Lainey Ralston.

Not the girl part; she enjoyed the girl part. She liked the way she looked, and pretty much loved her allowance. She didn't even find school too infringing on her preferred modes of partying: dressing in Hot Goth Chic, sneaking booze out of the house and making sure she lived the fuck out of her life.

No. All that was great. *Supercharged* fucking great.

It's just the Ralston thing.

Being the 18-year-old daughter of a politician, especially one as controversial as Huey Ralston, made being anonymous around town difficult. It made getting out *into* town difficult, and when she got there it made getting into places even more difficult, especially the places where one might want to be seen.

Being Huey Ralston's daughter was...*problematic*.

Huey Ralston had a reputation to maintain, he had an entourage of political hangers-on and style-setters who didn't need an 18-year-old kid fouling the pitch unless she was going to be completely tamed, civil, and on board.

As a kid, Lainey had been fine about "being on board." Being ten and going everywhere in a limo, walking out to explosions of camera flashes and getting whatever she wanted, had done wonders for her self-esteem. But as her mother Brenda had screamed at her during the last fight they'd had, Lainey *knew the price of everything and the value of nothing!*

Lainey had screamed back down the stairs, "They're the same fucking thing!"

Lainey had been grounded for that.

Not that being grounded meant much to Lainey. Jake was the one who suggested the best way to get around that particular restraint anyways.

"All you gotta do is wait until they're out. Then you can do what you like," he explained.

Lainey's parents being Houston Socialites, Charity Stalwarts, and Political Glad Handers were out *a lot.*

On the phone, Jake's voice sent thrills through Lainey that she knew would lead to pleasurable explorations of her own body in the shower or bath later. She was amazed that Jake's voice had the power to do that to her. Just his voice; they'd never met. It was an online and telephone thing. She'd seen his pictures on his profile of course. Jake had a face so sharp you could shave your underarms with it, eyes that spoke of distant galaxies, and skin the color of a warm pale dawn over the endless ocean.

Jake was 19 and lived in Dallas. As soon as he could, he was going to come to Houston and they were gonna meet and play. Lainey was determined to lose her virginity to him. She wanted it so bad. Even though in the four months she'd been talking to him, he'd never once mentioned sex. He was the perfect gentleman, and that reticence made her all the hotter for him.

The only time Jake had mentioned sex was to tell her

how to get out of the house, even though she was grounded by her mom.

"I can't do that!"

"Yes, you can!"

"But..."

"No *buts*, Lainey. You got this. Make it happen. If you wanna go out, you only have to say nine words to him..."

The *him* Jake was referring was the Ralston's butler-come-bodyguard Sven Wikström.

Sven was a mile high, and a mile wide. Ex-*Särskilda Operationsgruppen*—Swedish Special Services—and he was built like someone had glued five Thors together into the one body. Men like Sven, when they left the special services, had a particular skillset which made them extremely sought after by the rich and powerful. Anyone could learn to be a butler, but not everyone could learn to be Special Services. So as personal bodyguards—with a sideline in running the household servants like a well-oiled military machine—Sven and his ilk were a godsend to people like the Ralston's.

Lainey had grown up around Sven, and although the mile-wide butler could be an imposing presence, he knew where the lines in the sand were drawn with Lainey. He would never tackle her bad behavior head on—if he caught her trying to break into Huey's drinks cabinet or invited her friends over to party on a Saturday night when her parents were out of town—he wouldn't make a fuss or go blabbing to her parents. No, not Sven. Being ex-military, he was someone who worked *strategically.*

The next day, the lock on the drinks cabinet would be changed, and the key Lainey had managed to appropriate would be useless. When Lainey invited her friends over to party, the entry coder on the main gate would mysteriously break down and no one from the installation company would be available until the next morning to come out and fix it. In that time, Lainey would look like a complete spaz because her friends had been left hanging outside of the main gate, and Lainey hadn't been able to get out to join them.

Lainey was athletic and strong, but she wasn't going to be able to climb the compound's sheer walls, topped with broken glass and razor-barbed wire.

She never knew for certain that it had been Sven beating her at this game of domestic chess, yet she never got any heat from her parents. Plus, any time she pushed the envelope too far, things would happen that would put a stop to her plans.

"My dad wouldn't believe me, Jake."

"There's one thing a daddy will always believe about his daughter, Lainey."

"And what's that?"

"That every man who is alive and breathing wants to fuck her. It's like *baseline* dad."

So six weeks ago on a Saturday night, when her parents were out of town, Lainey played the ultimate move in this game of household chess with Sven.

She'd just made the full conversion to Hot Goth Chic. Her blond hair was cut back to a severe bob and dyed crow black. Her lipstick was black, and she'd stuck two black diamante diamonds to look like tears in the corner of each eye. Both eyes were almonds of Khol, and her eyelids were pure smudged charcoal smoke.

Her dress was more fishnet than actual dress, and her bra was working it for her until it sweated blood. The skirt was a piece of material that had been introduced once long ago to the concept of skirts existing as a thing, but that was about as far as it went. Her knee boots had tractor tire treads and silver buckles all the way to her knees.

Lainey marched down the stairs into the wine cellar, where she knew Sven would be making his usual Saturday night inventory.

Sven stopped what he was doing, put the bottle of something very red and expensive on the table, and looked at Lainey. He hadn't seen her dressed in this way, and as it had taken her breath away when she'd looked in her bedroom mirror herself, she could only imagine the effect it might have on members of the opposite sex.

"Ms. Lainey. Is that you?"

"You know perfectly well it is. I'm going out."

Sven was on more familiar territory now that he'd gotten over the breathtaking transformation in Lainey's appearance.

"I'm afraid your Mother made it very clear to me that you were not to leave the compound, Ms. Lainey. I'm sorry to have to inform you…"

Sven's English was heavily accented, and a little slow, as if he had to think about every word before he said it. Lainey didn't have time for this. The taxi would be here in five minutes.

Jake had prepared her well, as if it were a script he had used himself many times in the past to get out of his house and away from his father. Although Lainey had never told Jake who she really was—she wasn't stupid, as her fake profile in the name of "Pippa Graves" had just enough real information about her to feel authentic. It would in no way let on to anyone that she was Lainey Ralston. Her close friends new about the change and the deception, but no one else. She shied away from telling Jake the truth, not because she was worried what he'd do with the information, but because she was worried that it would put him off.

They'd first gotten in touch through Pippa Graves' Instagram account. She'd published a few selfies of trying on some Goth Gear, and he'd commented favorably. They had been the kind of comments that signaled the dead sure *I'm interested in you* giveaway vibe. The going back on her timeline deep-liking scads of posts from the last two years, was the clincher. After that, they'd got chatting. She'd looked at his Facebook profile with her eyes out on stalks because he was so damn pretty, and so the pretense stuck. She'd felt herself falling for Jake long before she'd felt compelled to tell him the truth of her identity.

"Sven, do you like your job?"

Sven narrowed his eyes. This obviously was not the question he was expecting. Jake had been right about that too.

"Put him on the back foot, make him unsure. He's the kind of guy who expects everything to be just so, and you asking him that will throw him. Once he's off balance then you can put him down and you'll never have to worry about him again."

"I do not understand, Ms. Lainey. Of course I like my job."

"Then you'll be wanting to keep it."

"Ms. Lainey, if there is some complaint you would like to make, or some issue you would like to discuss then I'm sure we can hold a meeting with your father when he returns from the fundraising event in Corpus Christi."

Jake had been right again. Sven would try to deflect and would subtly bring up the issue with her father. She still hadn't told Jake who her father was, just that he was in the oil business, that he was a very rich man and that he was a controlling asshole.

Lainey could argue until the cows came home with her mother. Brenda was weak and somewhat of a lush. The majority of the drinks that disappeared from Ralston's cabinet were taken by Brenda, and that's why Huey—

knowing her mom's problems—hadn't made such a fuss. He liked her quiet and drunk. It kept her out of his hair. If he'd known how much booze his daughter had been misappropriating in the last year, then the situation would be very different.

But Lainey never won an argument with her father. He was a bully and as stubborn as three mules with their heads up each other's asses. If she pushed him too far, he wasn't beyond putting her over his knee and teaching her a lesson with the flat of his palm. That was a humiliation she had managed to avoid since she was twelve. She'd managed to avoid it by not getting into fights with her dad. She knew her mom resented it because she got the brunt of Lainey's rebellion. However Lainey could cope so much better with her mom's half-cut screaming matches than she could with Huey Ralston and his old fashioned take on home discipline.

"There will be no discussions, Sven," back on script. "I'm going out now, and you're going to wipe the section of hard drive in the security system that records me leaving. And when I get back in the morning, you'll do the same. Am I being clear enough for you, or would you like me to repeat it for you more slowly?"

God, Jake was good. He knew exactly what to say because Sven's eyes blazed, but he kept his cool.

"Ms. Lainey I'm afraid..."

"And that's when you scream," Jake said. "Top of your lungs. He'll drop his lunch. No man wants to be trapped down the cellar with the boss' daughter screaming *rape.*"

And Jake had been right. The scream made Lainey feel infinitely powerful. Sven...mile wide, mile high Sven had held up his hands, his Swedish Special Forces Super Cool shattered.

"D...don't touch me! D....don't touch me! Daddy! Daddy!

Oh, Daddy! Thank God you're home! Sven tried to touch me. He made me meet him in the cellar and he tried to touch me!"

Lainey leaned forward and added a wrinkle of her own so confident that she felt it was working out for her now and nudged the very expensive bottle of wine by the neck. It teetered, turned, and fell, smashing against the tiled floor —sending a bloody spray of wine up Sven's trousers. "I threw a bottle at him, Daddy! It was the only way I could stop him. He's a monster! Call the police! Please, Daddy, call the police."

Lainey was breathing hard, Sven's mouth was gold fishing.

"Just wait thirty seconds. Say nothing. Let it all sink in. He will comply. He has no choice," Jake said, and so she waited every single one of those 30 seconds as the gravity of the situation sank into Sven.

He paused, and then he nodded, "I will do what you ask."

And from then on, Lainey had zero trouble from Sven. He got her a new key to the drinks cabinet, and the entry coding system on the front gate worked every single time it was needed.

Which is why, when Lainey Ralston disappeared for real, there was no CCTV of her leaving the house. Sven didn't raise the alarm for nearly 20 hours because he never knew when to expect her back. He just waited to clean up the digital files when she did.

Just before Huey Ralston fired Sven he told the Swede that he'd rather have heard the butler-cum-bodyguard tried to fuck his daughter, rather than just let her walk out of the building.

The irony was not lost on Sven as he walked out of the compound for the last time.

3

Huey Ralston loved being Huey Ralston.

There was no doubt about it. He loved Huey Ralston to the absolute max. 6'2", a tightly packed 210 lbs.—with the ability to fit into the same tux now that he could have slipped right into when he was 20—he often couldn't pass by a mirror without straightening his tie. He used a licked finger to push back a stray hair or feel that warm glow of loving himself so hard, he honestly couldn't understand why the rest of the world didn't find him so damn agreeable.

Ralston liked to tell the story of how he'd worked his ass off to get where he was, but like most apocryphal stories, there were only a couple of diamonds of truth buried in the bullshit of misdirection.

Ralston Oil was his Daddy's company, and Old Man Ralston—as even Huey's mom had called her husband—had done all the hard work. He'd been the one that had built the business up from the dirt: doing the surveys, digging the wells, losing two fingers on his right hand when a chain hauling a new drill bit into place had snapped and crushed them like jelly. Legend had it that Old Man Ralston had carried on working, leaking blood and gooey bits of flesh until the new bit was in place and the machinery could be started up again at the drill head.

Huey—breaking a nail when he'd flubbed picking up a hammer to pass to a drill head rigger when he'd been at the Santa Clara Well—didn't really have the authenticity or veracity of the Old Man Ralston tale. But over the years and true to form, Huey had augmented and embellished the story somewhat. Now the scar he had on his arm—from a drunken tumble down some stairs onto a smashed vodka bottle at a Frat party—became the story of how he'd saved the drill head rigger from certain death by shielding him with his own body, as the rig had been ripped apart by a whipping back drill string in a *heinous* well accident.

The fact that the particular drill head rigger had been sought out by Stephen Crane, given $50,000, and made to sign a handcuff-tight NDA to never talk about any incident, was beside the point.

Truth should never get in the way of good mythology.

Ralston had scraped through college with the barest grade averages and had fallen straight into the family business.

The myth stated that Old Man Ralston had made his son start at the bottom as the lowest of the low mail boy in the Houston office of Ralston Oil. A quick conversation from anyone back then (NDAs notwithstanding) would tell you that Huey spent much of his days not *delivering mail* to the girls in the typing pool, but instead just *delivering MALE.*

By the end of the first year, Daddy had paid for three terminations and paid off another girl who was threatening to go to the police for harassment. Huey had been kicked upstairs—kept to the executive level, away from the typing pool, to sit in an office twiddling his thumbs. He'd mainly play Solitaire on his computer while Old Man Ralston boiled about this "wastrel son" and got on with the serious business of becoming a multibillionaire.

By the time Old Man Ralston had died of a coronary so suddenly that he'd fallen face first into his soup at dinner and had been dead before could close his eyes, he'd surrounded himself with people who could run Ralston Oil in his absence like clockwork. No "wastrel son" who would inherit and become the putative head of the company would be able to "fuck it up," however dead Old Man Ralston was.

And so Huey had become the Chief Executive Officer of Ralston Oil at 40. Like any automatic system, he only had to be there on site occasionally to nod through what his advisors advised about the business. They would suggest which acquisitions and mergers were best placed to make more money for the company, which renewable technologies were best to move into, and when to couple that buy out with the increase in fracking businesses. He'd been told it was a good idea to have feet in both sides of the green divide. And who was Huey to argue? He knew fuck about fuck...all except for fucking.

Fucking he knew all about. Fucking and...other pleasures.

Even getting married to Brenda hadn't stopped the fucking and attendant activities. Huey had realized early on that money was the greatest aphrodisiac known to man, and the succession of cheerleaders, models, and starlets who had punctuated his marriage had been testament to that. Huey loved the power that kind of money gave him. Exposure to that many beautiful women ready to respond favorably to his advances made him feel like a god.

When Huey fucked them, he tended to do it from

behind' He'd seen too many fleeting looks of disgust flicker across the faces of the women who'd temporarily rented space to him in their bodies, but never in their heads. Huey didn't care. To him a fuck was a fuck, and where Old Man Ralston had made his first billion in the Texas Oil Business, Huey was well on his way to making his billionth mark on the bedsheets of the Texas Fucking Business.

Even when he'd grown jaded with the fucking and had moved on to different avenues of sexual gratification, he found more than enough women who would meet his particular needs for money.

Capitalism was a wonderful tool.

So with the business in the hands of people who could run it well, Huey was at a loose end. There were only so many parties he could go to, there were only so many secret and brutal liaisons to have, and there were only so many presents he could buy his wife to shut her the fuck up when his latest blond-haired bimbo had been found in their house by a maid.

What would he do with his days?

Huey had found politics as easy as he had fucking. In many ways, they were the same thing and came from the same place. The only difference being, that instead of fucking one airhead at a time, politics allowed you to fuck thousands—and both *fuckees* fell for the same shtick.

Money was the aphrodisiac that oiled progression in both spheres as far as Huey was concerned, and he was mightily successful at both. It was all about how you picked your bedmate in either circle. Huey would default to crazily beautiful, easily influenced, and available women. He did the same with the electorate—crazily populist platforms in the Lone Star State—tough on illegals, tough on crime, support for the NRA, reductions in welfare to boost the public purse. It's not that Huey had a political idea before he entered politics—it was fair to say the only ideas he had before politics were about promoting his brand and fucking and beating his way around Texas—but when smart political operators saw someone they could mold into a Titan of conservative populism, they would gravitate towards Ralston. Soon he had an automatic team around him who would do all the donkey work for him in campaigning: write his speeches, set him up with the best meetings to take, decide which special interests to listen to, and whose palms to grease.

Very much in the same way Ralston Oil had been run since his daddy had taken a dive into the pea and ham soup, *Ralston For Senator* pretty much ran itself. All Ralston had to do was turn up, miss the furniture, and sign the checks. It wasn't exactly taxing—but the hard-on it gave him for power was matched only by his hard-on for the next delivery of blonde submission.

Everything was on automatic until Alaina had decided to run away.

Huey was not a natural father. He'd realized early on in his marriage that having a child would look good on his public face. That was the face of a socially conservative family man with a great head for business, who believed raising a family was not only what the nation expected of its great and good, but also was God's work too.

Huey had been advised that appealing to Evangelists was precisely the constituency he should aim to have high approval ratings with. And so he went to church, he listened to sermons, and he spoke at gatherings of evangelical lobbyists. It occurred to him, as he watched the pastors struttin' and frettin' across their altars in their Mega-Churches—soaking up all that adulation and all that *money*—that perhaps he'd chosen the wrong pastime by entering politics. Maybe setting up his own Church in the future might be a nice side-line and a fine income diversification project...

You could find gullible people almost everywhere you looked—and the ones that voted for him would be the same ones who fetched up in their thousands to pay for their pastor's new Gulfstream. If Huey could find the right fire and brimstone speechwriter to work him up some sermons, there could be an even brighter future for him.

But of course Alaina was trying, in her typical way, to pour fresh Novocain into his Vaseline.

He'd left bringing up the child to Brenda. It seemed to be her forte—well perhaps back before she'd started the drunken screaming matches with Alaina. They were those "difficult teenage years" that Huey had heard about on daytime talk shows. Huey didn't know anything about difficult teenage years; he'd had everything he ever wanted and had pretty much coasted until puberty. That's when he learned what girls were for.

But as Alaina had grown from the family asset into a dyed-haired, torn-clothed punk, Ralston had ordered Brenda to *get the little bitch in line* because it was now impossible to have her at campaign meetings or rallies dressed like the Princess of Darkness.

Nothing happened, of course; Brenda was too busy crawling in and out of the next bottle, and it was as much as she could do to plastic herself up enough to not look like an embarrassment in front of the cameras or at charity functions.

Ralston didn't want to have to speak to the girl about her behavior; that wasn't his job, it was Brenda's job. But if things didn't change soon, he was going to have to intervene. They were hitting the campaign trail for the Fall elections soon. If Ralston was going to make it to the Senate in Washington—he'd already won the nomination at a personal cost of 13 million of his favorite dollars—then that girl was going to be blonde again, dressed for church, going to do what the fuck her mom told her.

Then of course the ungrateful little shit—who had an allowance most kids would die for, a bedroom suite as large as some of her friends' houses, every single piece of computer equipment, and audio visual tech to make her bedroom look like freakin' Mission Control—had gone missing.

When they'd returned the next morning—and Sven had been in the kind of panic that was usually reserved for Brenda when she'd run out of bourbon—Ralston had immediately realized the gravity and danger of the situation...especially to his political ambitions.

His first thought had been how this would look: Prospective Senator's daughter, so unhappy with her parents she's run away. *Not* the perfect family. Press digging —oh how those fuckers loved to dig—and knowing that if they dug deep and hard enough they'd find something. The lid had to be kept on this, especially when Sven confessed that Lainey had been blackmailing him to cover her tracks leaving the house for the last six weeks. How would that look on the cover of the Houston Times?

While the shit was turning to water in his bowels, Huey started making calls to his retinue; they had to keep a lid on this, they had to keep it quiet. They had to find the girl fast, and they had to employ someone good—*really* fucking good—to get this done.

There would be no police. There would be no press. This would be a silent operation.

So when the cop cars rolled into the compound, and the satellite trucks had parked at the end of the drive, and the news reports about "Missing: Alaina Ralston, Oil Heiress and Daughter of Prospective Senator Huey

Ralston" started to run across the TV, and the alerts started pinging on his cell phone, Ralston had tracked down Brenda in her dressing room. She sat, bottle in one hand and telephone in the other, just getting off the phone with her cousin Randal in the FBI. It had been all he could do to not set Brenda on fire and kick her down some fucking stairs after he'd done so.

After the press conference on the steps of the Federal Courthouse on Smith Street, Huey and Brenda went back inside. They went into a back office the Governor had put aside for them to use, and as it began to fill up with Crane and Ralston's staffers, he raised his hands.

"Thank you everyone for your support today, but if I could have a few moments alone with Mrs. Ralston...I think we'd like just ten minutes to gather our thoughts."

"No, it's okay..." Brenda began, but Ralston took her hands gently in his and stared into her eyes. He smiled, kissed her forehead, and then hugged her. As his mouth came into line with her ear he whispered, "Now we can do this the easy way or the hard way, clear?"

He felt her head nodding next to his, the hiss her skin made against his stubble—"Stay unshaven, it makes you look more *concerned*," Crane said—told Ralston of Brenda's supplicant assent.

Crane turned around and shooed everyone out of the room.

When they were alone, Brenda had the look of a puppy that had been found next to a chewed up pair of expensive shoes. But that look didn't give Ralston pause.

It never did.

He knew that she knew what was coming. Ralston

needed her for the press conference on the steps of the Court House; she wouldn't need to be seen in public for a good few hours yet.

"Please, Huey. I didn't think. I was just scared! I just want her back."

"If this fucks up my campaign, you will pay, Bren. You will pay. Do you understand? I wanted the Police out of this."

"I'm sorry."

Ralston punched her hard in the stomach. Always best to avoid the face, especially with the sunglasses. Brenda fell down onto her knees, winded, her shoulders drooping and hands knotting and twisting over the site of the punch. A tiny groan escaped her lips.

"Get up you stupid cunt, and sit down over there," he said, pointing to a green leather chair in the corner of the wood-paneled room. "The grown-ups have work to do."

4
_____

"Y ou come highly recommended."

Passion recognized the man who had met her at the side entrance of the Federal Court House as Stephen Crane, Huey Ralston's media wrangler and spokesperson. He was dressed soberly, but he still had something of the wolf about him. Passion noticed as they entered the cool marble innards of the building, and made their way along a gloomy corridor, that Crane's feet made no sound on the cold surface of the corridor. He knew how to arrive anywhere without telegraphing an announcement. That was a hard acquired skill that not many civilians could do.

A useful skill in Passion's business, but in a press secretary?

Crane led the way, walking two feet ahead of Passion. There was nothing friendly or welcoming or relieved about the way he had responded to her arrival, but it definitely had that "employer leading an employee to her desk" feel. Passion didn't know whether to be insulted or impressed. When there's a crisis going on, you need people around the place who cut briskly through the panic and slice off all the bullshit. Passion had a job to do, and they wanted her to do it.

"You have received my bona fides?"

"We have, Ms. Durant."

Crane called her by her cover name, not by her real name. The bona fides wouldn't have given away anything about her true identity. They would just indicate that she would arrive, listen, leave, and that she would transmit updates to the Ralston family every four hours until the girl was found.

"This way."

Crane turned sharply onto a smaller, shorter corridor. The doors were mahogany, with gold leaf numbering. The whole place had the sense of a solid, dependable edifice, where sober decisions were taken by old white men and where you didn't expect to hear a woman crying at any point in the proceedings. So that when Passion heard the sobbing, she was flicked back to the emotional engine that would be running Crane's professionalism. He was having to juggle a lot of balls—and the fact that his demeanor could be the same one he's displayed just showing a new secretary to where the office water-cooler was situated—spoke volumes of his abilities.

Crane double knocked on the door from which the crying was emanating and didn't wait for an answer.

Several things hit Passion as odd as the door opened on a small office that had tall windows overlooking the quad behind the Court House. Brenda Ralston was sitting on a green leather chair, holding her stomach and was crying freely. Tears were streaming down her cheeks and there was an unpleasant snail trail of snot hanging from one of her nostrils, swinging like a bulby pendulum as her shoulders shook.

Secondly, as she stepped in and Crane shut the door

with a secure click behind her—she still could not hear his feet—the room stunk of cheap food, like a cross between BO and a bad fart. It was comparable to the way fast food smells when some asshole insists on eating it on a subway train. There was grease and hot meat in the air. Passion felt her nose wrinkling. And lastly, there sat Huey Ralston—jacket off and tie off, shirt opened three buttons, and in his hand was a sloppy burger in the process of going to his mouth while blue cheese dressing slid out the rear of it like slime and coated the back of his hand.

The matrix of dissonance made by the woman—left alone to sob out her heart as her husband stuffed his face like he didn't have a care in the world, while in a room that smelled of a hobo's armpit—stopped Passion in her tracks.

This was *absolutely* not what she'd expected to find.

Usually when she met the parents or families of those who had been kidnapped, there would be tears, shock, or sometimes a stoic façade collapsing into a quivering heap of tears. Those displays of emotion wouldn't help the situation any for sure. But this? This was weird, not just unexpected. Like something out of a sick joke horror movie.

"Ms. Durant, Sir. From the Agency." Crane said, going behind the desk to stand at Ralston's side.

At the mention of the word "Agency," Brenda Ralston's tear-streaked face lifted, eyes sparkling with hopeful expectation. "FBI?"

Before Passion could even start to shake her head, Ralston made a swift movement with his hand, one that said *I'll handle this. Be quiet.*

"No, honey," he said in reality as Brenda sank back into the chair. The way he said *honey*, it could have rhymed with *cunt*. "This is Jennifer Durant. She's come to help us, but she's not from the FBI. She's from...a different agency. Please, Ms. Durant, take a seat."

Ralston's eyes were looking at Passion as if the next bite of meat conveyed to his mouth was going to be from her. Passion had acute *Slimeball Radar*. She prided herself on it. She needed it in her dual role as fashion model and undercover hostage locator. Like the 'tog at the shoot last night, there was always some guy—and more rarely women—who would see her availability to dress in any way they desired to promote their clothes or businesses as a form of sexual availability. Passion was happy to disabuse them of that notion. But the way Ralston looked at her now, there was zero subtlety and maximum slime. It was making the hairs on the back of her neck raise with distaste.

Ralston was a piece of work. Passion got that from the get go. Anyone who could think of food and the sexual availability of a woman like Passion, when their daughter is in the hands of kidnappers, needs to have a *serious* talk with themselves.

Passion sat down. She didn't offer to shake Ralston's hand. It was still smeared with blue cheese dressing.

"Sorry about the burger. Gotta eat on the go today as I'm sure you understand," Ralston said putting the half-eaten fast food back in a carton on the desk. He wiped his hands with a paper napkin, and then sucked on the straw of a soda. He swilled his teeth like someone about to spit out mouthwash, but instead swallowed. Then he continued, "Can you find her?"

"I'll try, Mr. Ralston..."

"Huey, please." Ralston slimed.

"I'd prefer to keep this formal and professional, if it's all the same to you."

Ralston's face flickered with annoyance, this was a man not used to being told no, especially by a woman. But he recovered well. He nodded and flipped the annoyance into a small smile.

"Has there been a ransom demand?"

"We've not received any communication at all, right Stephen?"

Crane nodded. Brenda sighed sadly.

Passion got up from the chair and knelt before Brenda, putting a hand over the older woman's own, giving the tiniest of squeezes. She could smell alcohol on the woman's breath, and close up could

see the broken blood vessels in her nose. The signs of drinking inadequately covered by make-up told Passion all she needed to know about the woman and her addictions. She felt a rising swell of compassion for the woman and a sense of understanding. Anyone who had to live with Huey Ralston would turn to drink to get through the day. That much was given. "Mrs. Ralston, our Agency is uniquely qualified to carry out the search and rescue of your daughter. We've done it many times before. I will work night and day to get this done. You have my word."

Brenda could only whisper "Thank you," before her eyes dissolved to tears again. Passion gave Brenda a handkerchief from her purse, and returned to the chair.

Ralston's eyes and Crane's uncomfortable shuffling from foot-to-foot indicated that the prospective Senator was not used to having the center of attention moved from him to anywhere else. Especially not his grieving wife.

Passion gave nothing away, but she felt herself enjoying the moment, noting it as a tactic for later use. She'd had clients before who felt they knew best, that they could shape the situation and maintain their control over everyone in their orbit. That was another notion Passion was happy to disabuse those clients of. The only way this worked is if she had the minimum pushback from the client and maximum control over her areas of expertise.

Ralston looked like he was winding up to make such

pronouncements, and so Passion held up her hand as he was sucking in the breath to speak. "If I may, Mr. Ralston?"

Ralston looked like he was about to throw up his burger, but said nothing. Crane's eyes looked like they had defocused with shock.

"Your daughter hasn't been seen now, by anyone for 26 hours. She left the family compound of your estate yesterday morning, but I understand that because of an *arrangement* she'd made with your security operative, the digital files of the surveillance cameras had already been reset so that there was no evidence of her leaving. Am I correct?"

"Yes." Ralston's voice was thick with discomfort.

"I also understand that Alaina had not been happy for some time. There had been many fights at home..."

"My wife...deals with...I mean, I..."

Brenda sobbed quietly.

"I understand, Mr. Ralston. It happens in busy families where both parents have high pressures in their work life impacting on their ability to spend time with their children. It's the modern way."

Ralston's Adam's Apple bobbed.

"I understand that six weeks ago, she cut her hair, dyed it black, and pretty much changed her appearance. But her Facebook page doesn't reflect that change. There are no pictures of her on social media under any of her accounts?"

"I don't...ummm...Stephen?"

"We monitor Alaina's social media footprint of course, for security and safety reasons."

"And you didn't think it odd, that an 18-year-old girl—who had completely changed her look—had not updated her profile picture and told the world that she was unhappy?"

It was Stephen's turn to look uncomfortable. "Well...we

assumed that she didn't want to embarrass her father or the family. The press can be very difficult when there's a campaign in the offing. They'll do anything to try to dig up..."

"I'm aware of what the press are like, sir. But no one thought to flag this up? I don't know an 18-year-old girl on the planet who would comb her hair a different way in the morning and not Instagram it to every single one of her friends."

"Well, I don't see..."

"It means she has accounts you don't monitor, Mr. Crane. It means that she probably has several phones you don't know about. It means that I need to talk to her best friend or friends, and I need to talk to them now. Who is her best friend?"

Ralston's Adam's Apple bobbed like that was all it was capable of doing and was trying to set a new world record for bobbing. "My wife...she ah...she deals with..."

"Mrs. Ralston?"

Brenda shook her head, "I...I don't know. I'm sorry."

Ralston recovered some of his composure and placed his hands flat on the desk. Passion was unsure if it was to recover some of the power dynamic in the room, or just to stop his elbows from shaking. He sigh and said, "Okay. You've made your point. I'm a shitty dad, and my wife is a shitty mom. You think we don't know that?"

Passion said nothing.

"But bottom line: You do this. You find her. And you do it before the cops or the press get to her, and you bring her home. None of this can get out. None of it."

And there it was. It was the Slime-Dunk.

"Surely it doesn't matter who finds her, as long as she's found."

"No, Ms. Durant. It does *not*."

Crane walked Passion out of the building. Ralston's recovery of the control in the room had not been total, but Passion knew in no uncertain terms what the priority was for him:

His reputation rather than his daughter.

Passion got the distinct impression that he'd be most happy if Lainey was found dead. A dead child, who couldn't show evidence to the world that not everything in Ralston World was all hunkies and dories, would absolutely help the Senatorial campaign, not hinder it.

For a moment she considered calling Bryan and telling him she didn't want this one, it was too dirty. Ralston made her skin itch and just being in the same room as him made her usual professional performance want to slip two notches and punch his damn lights out.

But no.

The M.O. was what kept her in the game.

The similarities to the other girls in the last year. The lack of ransom demands, and in four of the five cases, no bodies. Just an absence in the world where the girls had been was what gave Passion the hunger in this one. This one she wasn't going to lose on the table. This one was going to work out okay.

She was not going to get to Alaina Ralston too late to save her, and she was going to bring her home.

The midmorning heat of Houston hit her like a baseball bat as they exited the building, clipping down the stairs and walked to the parking lot serving the Court House.

Passion noted that Crane's feet had started to make sounds now. It was not just Ralston's sensibilities she'd ruffled.

"I want to speak to the bodyguard."

"Mr. Ralston fired him."

"Just forward me his cell and address. I'll do the rest."

"Of course."

"I'll need access to the house, to Alaina's bedroom, to all her tech, and all her passwords that you know."

"Already in hand."

They reached Passion's black Hyundai Santa Fe Sport. She'd rented it from the Hertz at George Bush Intercontinental Airport last night before the execrable shoot. The heat was starting to cook her now, and she wanted to get in the SUV and have a long blast of air-conditioning. It was not just to cool her down, she admitted to herself, but to blow Huey Ralston's actual and metaphorical stink out of her hair and off her skin.

"You'll make sure the staffers at the Ralston Home know that I'll be coming? I'll need to work fast, I won't have time to screw around with petty door-Nazi's shutting the stable door after the filly has bolted."

"Your credentials and ID have already been circulated. There will be no issues with access."

Passion punched the key fob with her thumb and opened the door of the Hyundai. "Then I'll bid you good day. I'll be in touch every four hours, if not sooner."

"Excellent. I really hope you'll be able to find Alaina...*Passion*."

Passion blinked at the unexpected use of her real name, rather than her cover name. Crane turned away and walked back to the Court House without looking back.

Only now his feet had gone back to making no sound.

No sound at all.

5

L ainey awoke in the dark.

Her hands were tied behind against her spine, and her ankles were bound together. There was something hard sticking into the small of her back, and it felt like there was thick plastic tape across her mouth. She could still breathe through her nostrils, and the prevalent smell in the hot black space was of old damp carpet and engine oil. The kind of oil from that which had burned on the metal of a leaking engine.

She recognized the smell from Gary's car.

She shifted forward a little, by snaking her knees and relieving the pressure of whatever had been digging into her spinal column. The wave of fear that rolled over her, fuzzed up her brain and made her start to tremble.

What was happening?

Why was this happening?

Her heart started thumping in her chest, and she felt a trickle of sweat move from her temple onto her cheek. At least she hoped it was sweat. She was in trouble. She'd been abducted. And maybe the liquid that was now moving down the side of her face was blood.

Oh, God. Please don't let it be blood.

Lainey hated blood in any form, which considering she dressed like the uber-est of uber-Goths, was somewhat of a drawback when exploring the internet for changes to her look. God those Goth chicks liked blood.

She felt bile rising in her throat. Even the thought of blood was nauseating to her.

Oil. Engine oil. *Burnt engine oil.*

Think about *that*. Think about anything except...

Gary was a boy on the outer edge of her social circle. Two years older—from a family which had some money but nothing like the Ralston's or most of her friends—Gary was a hanger on. He'd driven some of the others around in his four-year-old Camry. When Lainey had gotten into it the first time, she'd never been in a car so old before. It was beat up, there was a split in the dash, the windows needed a wash, but it was a ride. Best of all it was non-descript enough not to draw attention, when it was rolling into town.

Gary was not the smartest tool in the box, and he didn't realize that his constant chauffeuring would never lead to him dating Lainey or any of her friends. But while he was driving them around, they weren't going to make him think any different.

So good old dependable Gary would turn up when they wanted their own Personal Uber, and he would drive them downtown, or anywhere they wanted to go. He'd even wait with the car in the parking lot while they got themselves into the clubs with their fake IDs to dance and drink illegally. Gary never complained, because if he did there were a thousand other guys Lainey or her friends could use for the task.

Gary knew his place.

One night the Camry had sprung an oil leak. The smell of burning hydrocarbons on the engine and the thick gout of smoke from under the hood made Lainey and her friends exit the car toot suite, leaving Gary by the side of the road while they booked a real Uber.

It was a smell that had clung to Lainey's blouse and hair for the rest of the evening. They all refused to let Gary drive them again until his car was fixed and he could promise them it would never happen again.

Gary got the car fixed. He wasn't going to miss out on driving Lainey around.

It was that smell that filled Lainey's nostrils now. If she hadn't been so terrified about what had happened to her, she would have been incandescently pissed off that she had been thrown into the trunk of a car even older than Gary's Camry and left there.

That was *better*.

Although she was still scared and didn't know what was happening or why she was in the trunk of the car, her thinking was clearer. It helped to move her thoughts away from when the panic rose, back to stuff she could remember. Stuff that made her feel better.

Lainey didn't know how long she'd been in the trunk because after the men had bound her ankles and her arms behind her back they'd put a sharp-smelling pad of cotton wool to her mouth, and that was the last thing she remembered. They must have put the tape over her mouth to stop her screaming when she woke up.

It had worked.

The tape was so tight and she could feel it had been wound all the way around her head so tightly that she couldn't even move her jaw. It was locked in place, and it had been done by someone who knew exactly what he'd been doing.

And *who* had done it?

And there was the panic again.

The constriction of her breathing by the tape across her mouth meant her nostrils needed to work overtime to not promote the feeling of panic. But in the hot and confined space her nostrils were not coming up with the extra breath her anxiety was demanding.

No.

Think.

A tumble of images blossomed open in Lainey's mind. She remembered giving the nod to Sven that she was leaving the compound and that she expected him to deal with the surveillance cameras. She'd swapped out her family cellphone for the one she kept in the false bottom of her black leather handbag—making sure to not only turn off her family cellphone, but to crack the back of the phone and remove the SIM card.

She didn't want her father to speak to any government types who would be able to tell him where she was going that night based upon passive signals from the SIM card. It wouldn't have been so sensitive if she'd been busted going to a club in town, but tonight she was supposed to be meeting Jake for the first time. He had booked a room at the Sheraton, and they were going to spend the night there. Lainey planned to consummate the relationship they'd been having for the last four months, by putting the first score on the doorpost of her virginity.

It was not as if she'd been saving herself in the sense that she wanted to wait until she was older, finished college, and was ready for that kind of deal. No. There just hadn't been the right kind of guy yet.

Not like Jake anyways.

There were plenty of guys at school who would have jumped through fiery hoops to lay down with Lainey and be her first. In fact, she kinda enjoyed making them want to jump through the hoops so much that they'd have set fire to them themselves—but none of them had the poise, the strength, and the presence of Jake. Just the tone of his voice on the phone, or the endless hours spent on messenger meant Lainey had become more and more convinced she wanted to offer herself up to Jake.

She wasn't scared of losing her virginity, wasn't apprehensive about how she would perform, or concerned about what Jake would think of her. She had confidence in spade, clubs, hearts, and diamonds too. No, she just wanted it to be right, and she wanted it to be with *Jake*.

When Jake said he'd be travelling to Houston with his dad on a business-slash-pleasure trip, her heart skipped all the beats, and then started jumping over the other members of the band. Jake told her that his dad would be cool with him spending the night away. That night could be spent in a suite near the top floor of the Sheraton and that it would be *insane* to spend that time with her. There was no pressure he'd said; whatever happens, *happens*.

"But I want it to happen," she'd said, nearly breathless.

"And so it will, baby. It will."

The three days after they'd made the arrangements, and he'd confirmed the hotel booking, it had felt like time had broken down and stopped moving forward.

Lainey had been unable to concentrate on anything. TV bored her. Music didn't cut it. She didn't want to talk to anyone but Jake, and she had several fights with her mom about trivial and stupid things. In fact, everything that wasn't Jake related was trivial *and* stupid.

She planned and changed the plans a million times over about what she would wear. She flirted with the idea of changing out of the Goth look completely, having her hair return to blonde and going wholly for the naïve virgin look.

She got as far as booking the hairdresser to come to the house and complete the dye job, but then cancelled at the last minute. Jake had been the one to encourage the black and the fishnets and the *Nightmare Before Christmas* look. He'd told her a million times how much he dug it, so she'd decided that it would stay, but she ordered new boots, an even more micro mini skirt, and a savage bra that would lift her whole body to another level. When she finally tried it all on in the full-length mirror of her bedroom, she had absolutely killed it.

She was going to murder out there.

The day had been blisteringly hot, without a cloud in the endless blue, making Lainey's *Gothly* look even more incongruous anywhere except a graveyard on a winter's night.

She knew Sven would be watching her on the cameras, as she walked down to the steel gates that led from the estate onto the compound surrounding the house. As she approached the gates, they opened silently and she walked through them out onto the estate road. Jake said he didn't want his car to be seen by anyone. That made sense, considering there were servants, gardeners, and ranch hands who could have seen the car and who could have circumvented the deal she had with Sven, reporting directly back to her parents. The least information she allowed to get back, the better.

The estate around the house was basically a cattle ranch her father maintained for show rather than for any real sense of wanting to be involved in the production of beef.

There was a small herd that was tended by a farm

manager and ranch hands. Her father didn't get involved, other than occasionally, to put on a flannel shirt and muss up his hair some to have his photograph taken in front of a feed barn. Those pictures would be circulated on his campaign website to impress the voting farmers of the state. The Class One election was looming, and "Farmers are voters too," Huey Ralston would announce to anyone who would listen.

The walk off the ranch would take 20 minutes to reach the far gate on Luxor Street. It was called a street, yet it was nothing more than a tributary feed to the main Houston expressway. The only traffic it saw most days was the Ralston residence staff coming into work or Lainey's mother and father going to or returning from charity, masonic, or political events. Sometimes all three at once.

Lainey wished she'd taken a bottle of water with her, but she didn't want to mess up her lipstick that had been precisely applied—and removed and reapplied three times —until it was just right. It gave her mouth the fullness of a plum, with the sheen of ice. The only time she wanted to mess up her lipstick was when Jake slipped his tongue between those lips and kissed her deeply.

Lainey had imagined that moment a thousand times since they'd arranged the place to meet on Luxor. She wasn't going to say a word to him. She was going to reach up, put her hand on the back of his neck, and pull down his beautiful mouth to plant it on hers. And she was going to kiss him into the middle of next week.

It was that ambition that drove her booted feet along with mechanical regularity. The heat thrummed against the top of her head and stung the areas of skin exposed on either side of the straps of the fishnet dress.

When she reached Luxor, she checked her secret cell for messages from Jake. Disappointingly, as she stood by the scrubby bushes on the other side of the gate, she found Jake had not messaged at all. To add to her disappointment, he was not already there, waiting for that kiss.

Lainey thumbed open WhatsApp and sent Jake three question marks.

She waited.

There wasn't even a tree to stand under, offering shade in the killing heat. She could feel the track of a bead of sweat start to move between her shoulder blades, along her spine to pool in the small of her back. The sun beat down even harder as it moved towards midday. She started to wish she'd brought extra sunblock out with her.

And that drink.

Her brain was just about to boil over in her head when Jake's reply pinged through WhatsApp: "Two minutes."

And she was back in the room. Well, on the road.

Lainey stepped away from the brush towards the road, looking in the direction of the Houston expressway—the way from which she expected Jake's car to arrive.

But there was nothing coming. That was weird.

In the other direction, Luxor. Its grand name giving the impression it was more important that it was in reality—which in some respects made it the perfect name for a road leading to a Ralston property—led away in the opposite direction to Bumfuck, TX.

So when Lainey saw the approaching grille of a dusty blue 2011 Buick Lucerne, she was not so much weirded out as taken completely off guard. The sun was shining directly on the grill and the windshield of the Buick, making it impossible for Lainey to make out who was inside.

She remembered clearly the smell of it as it drew up, however.

That smell of burnt oil, the tang of hot metal, and the

aroma of cheapness that pervaded the Lucerne was now giving Lainey pause.

All of a sudden this didn't feel right at all.

Jake was the son of a rich businessman. His dad had a Ferrari, she'd seen it on Facebook. They lived in a huge colonial on the outskirts of Dallas. Those pictures dripped money. Jake dressed like money. He spoke like money.

So when a plethora of doors opened simultaneously and three men, all in their thirties and or even forties got out, the panic clapped in her heart like thunder. Their hair was messy, their chins were stubbly, their shirts grubby with dust and sweat.

Lainey took a step back, misjudged the brush at her ankles, and keeled over backwards.

The driver of the car—in his thirties with dark bushy eyebrows, a hooked nose, and a thick gold earring in his left ear— said, "Hello Pippa," in Jake's voice and reached down to pick her out of the dirt by the front of her blouse.

"I don't...who...?"

"You mean you don't recognize my voice?" The man who wasn't Jake said. The grown, ugly, sweaty, unshaven man—whose breath smelled of tobacco and garlic, whose eyes were quick and black, the man who had a thick network of old white scars in the side of his neck?

He was *Jake*?

Lainey was lifted up onto her feet. One of the men, a paunchy mustachioed Mexican with a squint, was unravelling thick silver duct tape from a roll in his hand. He was biting at it with gold-capped teeth.

Jake-Not-Jake pushed Lainey facedown onto the hood of the Buick. The metal was scalding through her clothes. Her arms were pulled behind her back and taped by one of the men, while the third—a bald heavy set white guy with neck tattoos of dragons—did the same with her ankles.

"Stop! Please! Stop!"

And that's when the cotton wool pad was placed over her mouth and the world went dark.

Lainey's heart was beating too fast again. The thing that was sticking in her back had shifted, or her body had and it was hurting again.

The heat inside the Buick trunk was unbearable. Her mouth was so dry she was unable to swallow and the liquid — *notbloodnotbloodnotblood*—rolling down her face was increasing in regularity with every passing moment.

The swell of panic would no longer be settled by thoughts of Gary's car or Jake-Not-Jake. There was a tide of fear rising in her now that had nothing to do with being abducted, but had more to do with the encroaching claustrophobia of the oven-like trunk, it's building heat getting ready to roast her alive.

Such was the smash of her heart against her ribs and the twisting agony of anxiety in her gut, that Lainey nearly cried with joy as the trunk lid was popped open and the sunlight flooded in, blinding her with its intensity.

If it hadn't been for the muzzle of the pistol being aimed at her face, Lainey might have thought that she had been visited upon by a welcome salvation.

6

The door opened, and Sven's bleary-eyed face peered out into the gloom of the corridor. When he met Passion, his eyes did the *fucking hell she's gorgeous* thing, and his face changed from indifference to intense curiosity without shifting a gear. The Swede had a good eight inches on Passion's 5'9 frame, and as he moved behind the crack in the door his sideways travel seemed to go on for longer than humanly possible.

This was a *big* man.

The door closed, and Passion heard the sound of two chains being unhooked before it opened again. Sven was naked from the belt of his shorts to his beard and long, dirty blond hair.

If Sven ever had trouble getting work as a butler/body-guard, Passion could totally get him work in her cover industry as a model.

Sven would get a lot of gigs.

"Yes?" he said with Scandinavian succinctness.

So Passion told him, and he let her in.

Sven had been living within the Ralston Compound for

the last two years since leaving *Särskilda Operationsgruppen*. The apartment where Passion had found him in was small, light and airy, and had no furniture. Sven had only moved in last night.

In the center of the living space—with access to two bedroom doors, an open plan kitchen, and a short corridor to the bathroom—were two open suitcases, a camouflage rucksack, an empty shoulder holster, and a tuxedo hanging from a hook above the door frame.

"I would offer you coffee, Ms. Durant, if I had any coffee, cup, or kettle."

Passion liked him already, and not just because of the way he looked. He carried himself like a man who knew he was hotter than a landing on the sun, but had the air of humility that goes with someone who knew they were also far from perfect on the inside.

"I was a fool. Oldest trick in the book, and I fell for it. She knew there were no housecams in the cellar, so she picked the only public place where she could pull her blackmail. I should have gone to Mr. Ralston immediately. Not to save my ass, you understand, but because it was the right thing to do for the family. Whatever the girl's faults and dishonorable conduct, if she has been abducted, and even worse hurt, I don't think I could forgive myself."

Passion could feel Sven's genuine concern for Lainey coming through loud and clear.

"It's just you hear so many stories of men overstepping the mark with young women, using their positions of power to get their sexual kicks—the story she would have taken to Mr. Ralston would have been all too plausible. But as I said, I've been a fool."

Passion pulled a Samsung Tablet from her bag, turned it on and started flicking through a succession of pictures. "These are from the friends list on Alaina's official Facebook account. We believe she's got another account, probably under another name. We haven't yet been able to find it. Can you tell me if any of the people she has as friends on this profile have turned up at any of the parties she held at the house?"

Sven crossed his arms over his chest, the muscles in his forearms rippling agreeably. As each picture moved past, he shook his head.

"I do not know. Some of them perhaps. Hold on. Go back."

Passion went back two pictures to a boy, thin faced, blond-haired. Gary Malcolm.

"Him. But not at any parties. He dropped her back at the compound a couple of times when she was legitimately out. He drew my attention because of the car: a beat up Camry. Not the kind of car you'd expect Alaina to come home in."

Passion clicked on Gary's profile. A succession of pictures flooded his timeline about his car—the beat up Camry— his buddies, and his nights on the town. After digging through 20 or so pictures, Passion found what she was looking for. It was a selfie of Gary in his car—with three girls in the back seat, holding bottles of Becks, looking like they were seat-dancing to something on the radio. Gary had the look of a boy who couldn't believe his luck.

Two girls were unknown to Passion, but the girl on the end—half a face obscured as if she didn't want to be in the selfie—was Alaina. The selfie had been taken before she'd changed to the Goth look, but it was definitely her. Everyone else in the picture had been tagged except Alaina.

Bingo.

Gary Malcolm had not been hard to find. There was enough information on his Facebook page, reading it from Alaina's legit account to cross-reference enough with Houston internet directories to find him and his family.

Gary's parents' house was on the approach to Houston along the expressway, five miles from the Ralston Compound. A modest detached ranch style property with a low roof, a garage with a baseball hoop above the door, and a small well-kept garden.

Painfully suburban. Painfully average.

The Camry was on the drive, and as Passion pulled the Hyundai to a stop, she saw that there was a police car there as well.

Shit.

She checked her watch. It was 30 minutes before she was due to make her first report to Ralston.

Working against the Police rather than with them was always a risk. It wasn't the first time she'd done it. In fact, the anonymity of the Agency and its secure working methods made it very attractive to the high end clients who could afford its services. But working against the Houston PD, or the State Police in the US was a much more difficult proposition than working against the police in a place like Manila. Bald corruption and a *laissez faire* attitude in the police of countries with a different set of priorities made doing her job a lot easier if palms could be greased, eyes suggested to look the other way. Here in the US the cops would be looking for Lainey as hard as they could. It was a *social* corruption Passion was working against here. Lainey was rich, white, and from a powerful family. It's not like she was a black kid from the projects, with a dad in jail and a mom bussing tables in the day and turning tricks in the evening to make ends meet.

Those were the kids society said could *stay* lost.

Passion was from somewhere in between those two worlds. Her family hadn't been rich, but neither had they been poor. Her father was Mexican, and her mother was from Canada. They'd met at college and made a life for themselves that was nearly as beautiful as the child they made.

Passion was a pleasing hybrid of both cultures—with naturally brown skin and auburn hair that would only be curled by chemicals or tongs. Left to itself it could have been used as a ruler. She was tall and thin, yet well-proportioned, and walked like she was riding a cushion of air and had an easy beauty which never bordered on heroin chic. She was blessed with a body frame which made any clothes hang like they had been designed especially for her.

Passion's mother Veronica had been recruited by the Canadian Security Intelligence Service when she was still at college. She was a fine mathematician and naturally gifted in code breaking. She's risen rapidly through the ranks and been spying successfully undercover in the Middle East and Europe by the time she was 26.

Joel, Passion's father, had been an athlete, boxer, and marathon runner. He was a man of immense competitive spirit, but also capable of great compassion.

At college, Passion herself had become known to CSIS, and they had toyed with the idea of recruiting her too. Veronica had been all for it; her career was going from strength to strength and could guarantee Passion a great trajectory within the service.

That dream had all gone to shit when Veronica had been burned in a sting operation that had gone wrong in Estonia. Passion's mom had ended up tied to a concrete pillar and thrown into the Baltic off the coast of Tallinn by a faction of the Russian Mafia who were trying to sell weapons-grade Plutonium to ISIS.

Veronica had managed to intercept and expose the coded transmission between the groups, revealing the potential sale, but in doing so had lost her life in the operation that followed. Russian Mafia didn't cut corners when it came to disposing of people who had crossed them.

Veronica Valdez had died hard.

Joel died a year later of a broken heart.

Passion was 21, and that was seven years ago now. When she made it clear to CSIS that she would not be interested in joining them even if they were the last intelligence service on planet earth, the *Agency* had come calling.

She was told the Agency was wet up, yet it was never confirmed. Bryan was her only contact with the organization—by ex-members of CSIS the CIA, FBI, MI5 and MOSSAD—the Agency was an Extra-Governmental private security concern, providing conflict resolution, hostage negotiation, kidnap protection and recovery, as well as cypher communications, bespoke security solutions, and bodyguard acquisition.

The Agency didn't advertise. They didn't need to.

They had more business than they could ever need—according to Bryan—and they only took the best.

Passion had spent two years being trained in personal combat, weapons skills, counterespionage measures, good old fashioned detective work, digital comms systems, asset acquisition, and how to be a model.

All the Agency's Field Operatives had cover jobs and cover names. And although Passion had never knowingly met any of the other agents, Bryan occasionally would mention names like The Surgeon, The Actor, The Journalist, The Parliamentarian, and even The Clown. At the mention of the last name, Passion said she'd really appreciate a set of tickets for *that* circus. Bryan, in whom she hadn't detected much of a sense of humor, had cut the call and told her not to be such a "twat."

The British were *so* good at swearing.

Passion checked her watch; ten minutes until the Ralston update was due. The Police Car was still sat on the driveway next to the Camry, and all was quiet.

Passion turned off the engine and opened the driver's side window. The afternoon heat radiated in from outside. Her lack of meaningful sleep was again in danger of creeping up on her. She needed a coffee or a cold shower— preferably both.

The door to the Malcolm house opened, and two uniformed cops came out. One was carrying a laptop, the other a case for a desktop PC.

Dammit.

That woke Passion up. She was hoping to get access to those computers *before* Houston PD.

What to do?

She'd still needed to speak to Gary. He was the only possible link she had between both of Lainey's profiles that she had right now.

The cops put the computer gear in the trunk of the car, said a few words to someone in the dark doorway who Passion couldn't make out, and then got in the car. Within seconds, it rolled backwards off the driveway.

As the police car moved past Passion's Hyundai, she continued pretending to fix her lipstick in the rearview mirror. From the corner of her eye, she saw the boy appear from behind a bush where he'd obviously been hiding. It happened so nonchalantly that she'd almost missed him climbing out of the shadows thrown by the harsh sun, down through the garden and onto the street. The boy walked quickly along the sidewalk away from the house, but towards the Hyundai.

It was Gary Malcolm.

Passion recognized him from the Facebook profile identified by Sven. He looked like he hadn't slept for nearly as long has Passion. His cheeks were hollowed and there were dark rings around his eyes. His t-shirt was damp with sweat, and his sneakers were smeared with mud. He'd been hiding in the trees by the side of his house for some time, possibly since the police had pulled up onto the driveway next to his car.

Gary obviously thought he had reasons to avoid the police right now and had done so. He walked nervously and furtively, looking at his smartphone in his hand as he moved, his finger hovering over the power button. His head was down, not seeing anything but the phone, and for all the world he seemed like a kid who wanted to be *anywhere* now except for here, and wanting it *badly*.

As he approached the Hyundai, Passion stopped pretending to put on make-up. She pressed the control that would lower the roadside window and leaned across the car.

"Gary?"

At the sound of his name, Gary stopped in his tracks; a look of pure shock on his face. He visibly flinched. This wasn't a boy who was just avoiding the police. He was terrified of anyone and everyone.

"I didn't speak to them!" he hissed. "I hid in the damn garden!"

Passion of course had no idea what Gary was talking about. "I'm not who you think I am, and I'm not the cops. But I can help you. And baby, you look like a kid who needs help."

Passion fixed Gary with her most convincing stare and then allowed the ghost of a friendly smile to pass her lips.

"I'm looking for Lainey. I think you can help me too. Shall we help each other out?"

Gary's forehead ran with sweat, his Adam's apple bobbed as he swallowed three times.

"I don't know who you are..."

"Get in the car, and I'll tell you."

Gary's eyes flicked back along the street to his house and the Camry, then back to Passion. What clinched the deal was a police interceptor—perhaps the one that had just left—emerging from a side road, and trundling back toward Gary's house. "Okay," he said, spit barring at his lips, collecting in a white paste of fear in the corners of his mouth. He scooted up to the Hyundai, and jumped in before the interceptor went past. The interceptor rolled past Passion's car, and then straight past Gary's house. Whatever the police were looking for, they weren't yet looking for Gary.

Gary's eyes were bulging, his chin set. Passion could see he was in no position to talk right now. So she started the engine, and pulled smoothly away from the curb.

Passion drove for three miles telling Gary to just try to calm himself, and they'd talk when they found a place.

"Who are you?"

"My name is Jennifer, and I'm looking for Lainey. I'm freelancing. I reckon there might be a reward for information leading to Lainey's return yeah? Ralston has big bucks."

The boy nodded, eyes darting, looking worriedly at the cars rolling past and people going in and out of the stores on the strip. "What do you mean by *freelancing*?"

"I'm a private investigator, and I want nothing more than to see Lainey Ralston safe and back home."

That information seemed to relax Gary enough for his

spine to slacken and for him to sit back in the passenger's seat.

Passion parked up in a lot adjacent to a nondescript strip on the outskirts of the city. There was a Denny's across the street, but the boy didn't look like he was in the mood to eat.

"I've been told not to talk to anyone about Lainey."

"Told? What do you mean?"

Gary held up his smartphone. There was one message from a withheld number, which indicated it had landed on the phone three hours ago. It read simply, "If you talk to the police, Gary, we will kill your family."

7

Pictures of Macy's dead and broken body—before it had become the main meal for some of the island's cannibal faction—had been circulated to the girls in D-Wing as both a warning and a reminder.

The guards and Owners did this often when one of the girls challenged the status quo, or tried to escape. Vengeance and execution were swift and terrible on the island. They had a small population to control, and the best way to do that was through abject fear.

Mary-Joy understood fear all too well.

For two years before she'd even reached the age of eleven, she'd already been scratching a living on the rubbish heaps surrounding Davao City. The Philippines, a country of huge contrasts between the mega-wealthy and the mega-poor, had wide and stinking slum towns crusting like scabs on the wounds of their cities. These squatter homes were backed against the stewing garbage fields and supported a population of rummagers. Mary-Joy, with her younger brother Benjie, worked the garbage for scraps of metal wire or anything else they could sell. It was their main source of income; without it, they would starve.

While other kids Mary-Joy's age in the affluent areas of the world would go to school, play with their friends, chat on social media, watch TV, and generally live lives of unimaginable privilege, she and her brother would be searching the piles of the city refuge for copper.

The privileged and unthinking throw away so much stuff. So many things that are still valuable to a child who has no meal to look forward to. That next meal was dependent on filling a bag with copper, reclaimed from discarded electrical goods. This waste was often thrown into the trash because the objects were the wrong color or their shape no longer matched the newly decorated room where they'd previously sat. These bits of tech could be snapped open or cracked with rocks, and tiny lengths of copper wire could be reclaimed. Electrical leads could be stripped with teeth and precious wire pulled out with bloody fingers. Once the bag was full, Mary-Joy and her fellow trash-sifters would sell the copper to the first sharks up in the poverty chain. The small amount of money she made went into food for her and her brother to consume in the dark, dank shack in which they lived. It stood on the edge of the garbage fields and landfill, next to an open latrine that served as a street. Occasionally Angel, their mother, would join them if she was too sick to work the streets in the nearest red light district. Otherwise they wouldn't see her for days on end.

Angel would call her condition *sick*, but what it was in reality was a lack of *Shabu* in her system. Enforced meth withdrawal—when Angel couldn't afford any of her drugs of choice from her street supplier, or couldn't find one who would fuck her for meth—was a body slam of crushing fatigue setting in like a hammer blow. Her mood would drop like a baby from a burning building. After that came the paranoia and the hallucinations. While Benjie cried confusedly in the corner of the shack, Mary-Joy would be holding her mother down, trying to stop her from howling like a wolf, or running naked to offer herself to anyone or anything who would give her enough money to buy the even the smallest wrap of *Shabu*.

Mary-Joy made damn sure she sold the copper to the hawkers before she made it back to the shack in the evenings, because if Angel showed up, the daily copper wouldn't be the first thing she would steal to feed her habit.

Mary-Joy couldn't say that she'd loved her mom anymore; there was too much broken between them now. But Benjie, whom she had become the de facto parent for in the stinking slums and landfill, still wanted Angel around. He wasn't old enough or educated enough to know any better.

Not that Mary-Joy had been educated beyond fifth grade. She'd had to leave school to work the rubbish heaps, amongst the fires and the violence, once Angel's habit took hold. When everything she had earned selling her body went to her drugs, Mary-Joy knew that unless she worked the hellish refuge glutted landscape, she and her brother would likely die in the dirt.

Mary-Joy could read, and sometimes that skill provided some relief. The constant search through the garbage— with bare hands, breathing in the foul stench of methane and chemicals rising from the layers of rotting detritus— would often lead to finding pages from newspapers and magazines. Sometimes when she was very lucky, she discovered whole books.

One day she found a torn and damp copy of *The Very Hungry Caterpillar*, and had slipped it inside her shirt. She managed to read it five times to Benjie, his face lighting up at the pictures, laughing at the words and hugging his sister tightly as she read to him. On the sixth night, Angel came back to the shack, sick and shivering, and had thrown the book onto the fire because she was cold.

That memory burned Mary-Joy way more than the tiny amount of heat that the book had made in the hearth.

D-Wing was home to 25 girls. Only two of them had been there longer than Mary-Joy's three years. At 18, she was thin yet not emaciated like some of the other girls. Her hair was cut short into a bob, with eyeliner and lip tattoos that had been designed to her face. These tattoos hadn't been her wish of course, and she'd been threatened with a severe beating if she didn't hold still while they were applied. So she sat there on the reclining chair, in the room they called The Parlor, and allowed the island's resident tattooist to work on her eyes and face.

Every two weeks the girls were forced to the Parlor to have their treatments—eyebrows micro-bladed, Botox injected for those who needed it, teeth whitened or other cosmetic dentistry, discussions about the best time for breast implants for the girls who were flat-chested, or those the Owners wanted to make grossly large for the customers who liked that sort of thing. Mary-Joy's chest seemed to be adequately proportioned...for now.

The girls in D-Wing—whose ages ranged from eight to twenty—were split every morning into their respective groups. Mary-Joy and those in her cohort would be sent to the gym for two hours of rigorous exercise to tone their muscles and increase their stamina. Another cohort was sent to the dining area to eat high-fat high-sugar foods. Eat or be forced to eat; the Owners and guards didn't seem to care. These girls were prepared for the clients who liked a bit of puppy fat on the children they abused, or liked their victims to be massively overweight. These girls were some of the unhappiest of all on the island, Mary-Joy had noted. No one was happy to be there, it was true, but those girls treated and fed like farm animals seemed to carry the most upsetting cloud of depression around them. Perhaps they realized that with their bodies blown up and their hearts strained, they would never have the strength or agility to escape—not just from D-Wing, but from the island itself.

Mary-Joy looked up at the picture that had been taken of Macy dead in the dirt. She and Macy had been bunk-mates in the dormitory. The broken girl, with the white sightless eyes, did not match her memory of the mightily smart tenacious girl from Florida who Mary-Joy had known. Mary-Joy imagined Macy would have been successful at anything she tried in the future—if she'd had a future.

Macy arrived on the island a year after Mary-Joy had been sold by her mother to traffickers for the price of six months' *Shabu*. Macy and Mary-Joy couldn't have come from more different worlds—Mary-Joy from the landfill life and Macy from the affluent upper middle class of South Florida. Mary-Joy had been sold openly to traffickers. They had come to the shack, given a handful of notes to Angel, tied Mary-Joy up, gagged her, and carried her out of the slums, past the shacks of her neighbors.

Macy on the other hand had been on her father's boat on a fishing expedition during a lazy Sunday afternoon. Macy had told Mary-Joy that another boat had signaled to them that they were in distress. Macy's father had taken his boat alongside it, and what initially Macy had thought was a robbery turned into something much worse. The three men on the other boat had drawn weapons and stepped

onto Macy's father's boat. They clubbed the man unconscious and tipped him over the side "for the sharks."

Macy had been tied, taken to the other boat, and stowed
in a cabin with a bag over her head. Her arms were tied
roughly behind her back.

Mary-Joy had made the journey to the island from the
Philippines, first chained inside a container on a cargo ship,
left in the dark with a barrel of brackish water. It was
enough to last the month of the trip, with boxes of candy
bars as her only source of food. She'd been in the container
with four other girls who had also been taken from the
slums at the same time as her. One had died three weeks
into the journey. Because of the dark, she and the other
girls hadn't been able to see the corpse they'd dragged to
the corner and covered with blankets in the dark.

But they had been able to smell her.

After the journey to a port of which Mary-Joy had no
idea of its location, they'd been released into the hot breath
of an intense summer heat. The light had hurt their eyes.
Living off candy bars and dirty water had not done their
health any good whatsoever. Their mouths were sore, their
skin broken and spotty. They'd been told by the three men
who seemed to have the run of this area of the cargo ship—
the same three who had taken her from the slums—that if
they made any noise they'd be killed on the spot. Mary-Joy
was so grateful to be out of the container that she readily
agreed. The Port was hot, colorful, and bustling with life.
All the faces around the dock were black African, and no
one paid any attention to the ship or the girls it was transporting.

The surviving girls were allowed to shower, given fresh
clothes, and driven to the airport, where they had been
flown for another six or seven hours. They landed at a
small airfield in a jungle, and then were transported to a

rusty old single funnel steamer, which then took them out to the island.

The boat was ancient and asthmatic, its decks weathered and unvarnished. It looked as if a derelict house had been placed on top of an iron hull and pushed out to sea. The hull had once been bright red, but was now stained with rust and crustaceans. Black smoke belched from the funnel as it steamed, and the girls—chained into the forward cargo space, beneath the poop deck—got no rest from the thudding and banging of the engine as it propelled the boat through the waves.

Macy had been taken in by her captors, who from the description, seemed to be the same three that bought Mary-Joy from her mother to a landing stage on a remote Caribbean island. They were then flown in a small luxury jet to the same jungle airfield where Mary-Joy had been taken, and then brought on the same streamer to the island.

Mary-Joy's inner strength, grown and nurtured in the most hellish environment ever created—the Filipino slums —had not exactly prepared her for life on the island, but it made her strong enough to cope. That resolve meant what happened on the island had not torn her down inside. Macy, however, had been the opposite. In the three years of degradation, humiliation, rape, and abuse—both physical and mental—she was driven to believe that being dead, getting to the rocks on the other side of the Enchanted Forest, and throwing herself onto them, was a far better option than trying to escape the island or waiting for a rescue that would never come.

She'd told Mary-Joy a little of the plan she'd concocted to escape the next time Lobo came to the island to abuse her. Mary-Joy had tried to persuade her not to do it. She wished she could have injected the younger girl with some of her strength, and some of her resolve. But it was clear that Macy was determined that she needed to die and that throwing herself onto those rocks was the best way to do it.

Mary-Joy sat on Macy's bunk as she heard the alarms, the dogs barking, the helicopters lifting off, and the commotion in the compound. She'd buried her head in Macy's pillow that still smelled of her skin and the perfume she'd been made to put on before she met with Lobo.

When the dogs stopped barking, the helicopters returned to the helipad, and the noises of the compound had returned to normal. Only then, when she knew it was over, did Mary-Joy allow herself to cry for her friend who she knew had escaped the island—but only to her death.

To have the sickening evidence, blown up and printed on a glossy picture and then pinned to the notice board in the D-Wing Dormitory, made those tears want to rise again in Mary-Joy's eyes.

But she didn't give the black uniformed guards the satisfaction of seeing how the picture affected her. While some of the other girls sobbed quietly on their bunks, or others purposefully looked away, Mary-Joy walked the length of the concrete-floored building and stood in front of the picture. She stood there staring at the body of Macy and looked at the shape and hollows of death in her stomach and her cheeks. She viewed the claws her fingers had become in pain, the pulled back grimace of her lips and then hard into the whites of the dead girl's eyes.

Mary-Joy was not going to end up like this.

She wasn't going to be dead.

She also had a plan of escape, and it was going to get her off the island and she was going to go home, find Benjie, and live happily ever after.

But not before she'd killed Rosa.

8

The message to Gary Malcolm about killing his family was the first confirmed contact Passion had seen from the people who might have kidnapped the girls—specifically Lainey—and so it immediately made her suspicious. This change in M.O. separated Lainey's disappearance from the others straight away.

"Why would they send you this message? How did they know you had anything to tell?"

Gary's eyes dropped from the anxious darting to something that looked very much like shame. "I...Christ...I'm in so much trouble."

"Gary, tell me what you know, because if you don't Lainey may end up dead. Do you want that?"

"No! Don't say that. They're not going to kill her! They're not!"

"How do you know?"

Gary shook his head.

Passion didn't have time for this, but if she pressed too hard the terrified boy might clam up completely. She could threaten him with taking him to the police—a thing in reality she couldn't do, because of wanting to keep her work as far from them as possible—but Gary didn't know that. However, that again might make him run.

Gary really seemed to believe these guys would kill him if he opened his mouth to the police. Or to anyone.

"I want to go. Please. Take me...take me anywhere. I need to get out of town. I need to go somewhere where they aren't going to find me."

"Gary...I can help you. I promise. I can get you some money, put you in a motel, help you keep your head down until this blows over and Lainey is back. But to do that I need to know what you know. Okay?"

"You can do that? For me?"

"Yes. One phone call and it's sorted. I promise."

Gary rubbed the sweat from his palms across his thighs, took another look through the Hyundai's windows to make sure they weren't being watched and said, "I cloned her phone. Her *other* phone."

This was massive.

If the boy had access to Lainey's secret smartphone—the texts, messages, keystrokes, and call log—that could be a huge leap forward for Passion, getting her much closer to the girl. Passion tried not to get ahead of herself in the excitement and spook the kid any more than he already was. "How?"

"Bluetooth hack. She accidentally left her phone in my car one night after I'd brought her back to the house. It had fallen out of her purse as she got out of the Camry. I saw it on the floor still unlocked."

Passion knew the procedure well. She'd used it enough times on active investigations herself. The software was easy enough to source on the internet. "So you turned on the Bluetooth, used the hack-tool, and then took the cell back to Lainey pretending that you'd found it and was just being a good friend. Right?"

His cheeks reddened.

"You were stalking her?"

"No!" His eyes were fiery, and a spray of spittle exploded from his lips hitting Passion on the cheek. Cloning a smartphone these days was a simple enough deal if you can get at the target phone when the password was unlocked. That was the key. Anything after that was gravy. You just change the settings so that Bluetooth will accept handshakes from unknown sources and switch it on. The cloning process takes a few minutes as data is transferred. After that, the software embedded in the target cell would transmit everything the phone does from that moment on to the designated receiving smartphone or computer. It could have been easily done in the time it took Gary to drive from the Ralston residence a few miles down the road, finish cloning the phone, and then return like the Good Samaritan to show what a stand-up guy he was.

The process is easy, the results always interesting, and it gave the spy access to everything the victim says or does on his or her phone.

"I'm not stalking her. I love her."

Passion buttoned her lip and didn't say a word.

"She would call me up all the time to get me to take her home from one of the clubs she went to with her weird friends. I was the only one she knew with a car. She couldn't use her allowance credit card for an Uber, because her Mom would see the bill. Her rich friends were the same, so I had a car, and I became the guy who ran her around when she wasn't out of the house for a legit reason."

"And you cloned the phone, why? I'm still not clear."

"I wanted to...protect her." It was clear from Gary's face that he knew how lame that sounded, almost before it left his mouth, but he nodded hard enough to convince himself it was true.

"Protect her from whom?"

"Jake." Gary spat the word out like it stung his mouth because the letters were made of razors.

Passion hadn't seen a *Jake* on the friends' lists of any of Lainey's legit profiles. So whoever Jake was, he was someone exclusively to the contacts on her dark profile. The way Gary spoke about Jake gave Passion a much greater insight into the mindset of the boy.

He was a stalker, pure and simple, consumed by envy and jealousy. Bitter and twisted inside. Jake had become a major figure of hate.

"She was always talking about him. How much she loved him, how happy he made her. How sexy he was. About how she was going to...going to...lose her..." He could not say the word. It was stuck in his throat. "How he was gonna be her first... She wouldn't shut up about it. Wouldn't stop!"

Gary thumped the dash of the Hyundai so hard, Passion thought he was going to trigger the passenger airbag.

"She talked to you about this? About Jake?"

"No! To the girls I drove around with her! To Marcia and Frankie!"

Two new names for the list.

"But you heard everything?"

"Yes! It was as if she didn't care I was there. I was just the driver. I was just the guy who hung on her every word, and did whatever she wanted, whenever she wanted!"

Gary was a confused kid, but that didn't stop Passion from thinking he had all the makings of a slimeball when he grew up. The typical entitled shithead who thought every woman owed him their minds and their bodies. And that sense of entitlement lead to stalking, bullying and in this case the cloning of Lainey's smartphone.

"The last dump of info I got from her account was her promising to meet Jake outside their house on Luxor—he'd come down from Dallas and he'd rented a car. They were going to the Sheraton. He'd booked a room and..."

His voice choked with emotion.

"I don't know how she could do this to me. Doesn't she get how loyal and loving and dependable *I* could be?"

It was all Passion could do not to reach across to the boy and shake the self-pity out of him until it made his eyes rattle. The boy needed a good hard slap and an injection of humility. But even with that in mind, Passion knew that getting to the information contained in Lainey's phone was absolutely imperative.

She could do all the slapping she wanted later.

"The cops took your home PC and Laptop. Was Lainey's cloned information downloaded there?"

He actually looked hurt at the mere suggestion. "Do you think I'm crazy? Of course not. The PC and laptop are shared with my sister. Dad wouldn't let us have one each."

Passion wanted to kiss Gary's dad.

"So, your phone?"

Gary nodded, holding up his S8. The gel case was grubby with fingerprints and maybe the splashes of tears. Gary thumbed through the menus to the Bluetooth app, which had a separate password to the phone and opened it up. The page was arranged in several sections. Text. Email. Social Media. Key Stokes. Passwords. Lainey's phone had been raped of all its information, and every few hours it would be dumped silently—at pre-arranged times if it was on, or when it was next switched on, or connected to a Wi-Fi. It was an insidious piece of software, created by assholes, and exploited by scum like Gary.

It was also Lainey's lifeline.

"May I?" Passion said, holding out her hand.

Gary hesitated, but eventually handed her the phone. Passion knew, because she'd used the very same software in the past, that there was a pop-open menu which gave the option to forward the information to another account. She typed in her email account, and copied in Bryan.

"I need the app password to forward the information from the cloned phone. What is it?"

Gary's face dropped, and his eyes looked away, the shame now burning in his cheeks, like the light from the summer sun.

"I didn't hear you Gary, what's the password?"

Another spray of spittle as Gary looked up and enunciated the letters like he was taking part in a Spelling Bee final: "L...A...I...N...E...Y...W...I...L...L...B...E...M...I...N... E...I...4...3..."

Spelling out the password didn't make it kick at Passion's anger any less. But she typed it in, and then threw the smartphone back to Gary.

Her own phone pinged to say the information from the Clone App had landed on her own cell from the Agency Cloud. Text, pictures, messages, and passwords were siphoning onto her own memory card now.

Ping. Done.

Passion had all she needed from the boy, and suddenly felt dirty just being next to him. All her life there had been a succession of boys like Gary who had grown into men like the on-shoot photographer.

Passion had gone past the shaking and slapping stage, and would have been quite happy to punch the boy square in the chops for behaving the way he did. It was not a psychotic obsession or a demand of entitlement due, which drove men like Gary and the photographer. It was their inability to blame anyone but themselves for their personalities and behaviors. Women were objects. Meat. A meal ticket. They were holes to be used and abused, and it didn't matter what the women thought. Sure they'd dress it up as love or harmless lust, but in reality they were predators. One step up from pond scum.

Passion shook her head, trying to dampen the rising anger there. She didn't have time for this. She had a kidnapped girl to find.

Passion reached across Gary, her elbow scraping against his chest.

"Owww!" Gary had never sounded more like the whiny toddler he really was.

"Get out."

The look of shock on his face was complete. His eyes immediately filled with tears.

"Get out before I kick you out."

She deftly unclipped his seatbelt and let it roll back into its sprung container. "You've got five seconds."

"But you said you'd help me! You said you'd get me a motel!"

Passion shrugged. "I betrayed you, Gary. Like you betrayed Lainey. Just be grateful that I don't pass that betrayal onto the Police. And I'm only doing it because the information I now have might lead me to her."

Gary got out onto the hot tarmac and looked around. "I don't even know where I am!"

"Ain't that the truth?" Passion said as she pulled the Hyundai away in a wide circle, using the forward momentum to close the car's open passenger door on its own.

The last Passion saw of Gary was him standing stunned in the middle of the parking lot, crying. His shoulders shaking and the look of a lost little boy on his face.

Passion didn't give one single damn.

Jake-Not-Jake shoved Lainey's phone at her face. "Who cloned your fucking phone, cunt?" She'd been pulled from the trunk of the Buick. They were standing in an underground parking lot. The place was deserted, apart from the car that had brought her here. Jake-Not-Jake put the gun back in the belt on his paunchy stomach then ripped the tape from her mouth so she could speak.

"I don't know what you're talking about."

Jake-Not-Jake slapped her. Hard. Because her ankles were taped together, she fell hard against the Buick. Mustache's arm snaked through hers and pulled her back into a standing position.

"I told you not to let this phone be touched by anyone else, cunt. So if it's been cloned, then either you've lied to me or someone has been spying on you. Is it your dad? Your mom? Who the fuck is it?"

"I don't know! Honestly, I don't! No one has touched the phone *ever*. It goes with me everywhere! It lives in a secret compartment in my bag that I put in there *myself*. I've never told anyone! I only use it to talk to you, or to meet my friends when I'm leaving the house to party. No one knows about the..."

Lainey stopped, as the memory came flooding back.

Too many drinks, too much dancing, a few tabs of ecstasy and getting Gary to come and pick her up and take her home. Too risky to use an Uber on her allowance credit card, so she always called Gary. Stupid, poor, ugly, dependable Gary. She knew he had the hots for her—how could he not the way she treated him like a doormat with wheels? But the only time the phone had been out of her hand or bag in the time she'd gotten it to set up Pippa's secret Face-book Profile, was when she'd dropped it in the back of Gary's scummy Camry. He'd brought it back to the front gate 20 minutes later. He'd made a song and dance about handing it to Lainey herself; he said because he didn't want Sven to know she had a second phone. But now it also made sense, especially if Gary thought Sven might check it for malicious software before he handed it to Lainey.

"Gary Malcolm. He had it for twenty minutes. I dropped it in his car, but Jake...or whoever you are...he couldn't have done anything in that time, could he?"

Jake-Not-Jake hit her again. This time Mustache let her fall as the third man just said, "Stupid cunt."

Jake-Not-Jake thumbed his cell and snickered at what he'd written. "This will fuck 'Cloning Gary' up. Fuck him all to hell!"

———

Thirteen hours later, they made Gary write his own suicide note with shaking hands before they hung him from the beam in the underground parking lot next to the Buick.

Once they had his name and cellphone number, he was easy enough to trace through their contacts. Gary had stupidly left his own phone on, desperately waiting for another clone dump from Lainey's cell, as he'd wandered through the Houston suburb's back streets. He dared not go home—hiding from the police and whoever had sent the threatening text that morning, not wishing to be found by anyone.

Finding a boy who didn't want to be found had been small potatoes, especially when they triangulated his cell signal and saw that he was wandering around a Home Depot trying to look incongruous and non-suspicious.

Mustache had put a gun in the boy's spine, and they'd walked out of the store leaving dots of pee from the bottoms of his trousers and socks from where his bladder had opened itself out of sheer terror.

But that wasn't the icing on the cake.

Jake-Not-Jake's eyes had widened with shock, when Gary called Pippa "Lainey."

"You shitting me?"

They'd sat Lainey against a concrete column and told her to watch. She looked up, and nodded. "You are in so much fucking trouble you have no idea, whoever the fuck you are."

Jake-Not-Jake laughed, his uneven teeth yellow in the half-light of the underground parking lot. "You're Huey Ralston's daughter?"

He didn't wait for an answer. "Hot damn. That's justice of the poetic kind. Rosa is going to love my ass from here to the middle of next week."

Gary said, "Can I go now. Please?"

Dragons hit him in the gut, and Gary went down onto his knees, vomiting messily. "No, you can't." Dragons said.

Mustache pulled Jake-Not-Jake to one side and hissed into his ear. It was an attempt at a whisper, but if Lainey strained her ear above Gary's sobbing, then she could hear the exchange. "*Fuck* man. Ralston's daughter. Are we sure this is a good idea?"

Jake-Not-Jake clapped the Mexican on the shoulder, "It's perfect. Rosa will dig it. No problem. We're made on this."

"I dunno man. It's..."

Jake-Not-Jake pulled the Mexican's forehead in and kissed it. "Trust me bro. Trust me. This is gonna take it to another level. All we gotta do is get the cunt to the airfield, and we'll be able to name our price."

Jake-Not-Jake ordered Gary to be brought to his feet and told Mustache to get a pen and notepad from the glove compartment of the Buick. When they were ready, they untaped Gary's hands and made him write.

What he wrote made Lainey sick to the very core. She couldn't believe what Jake-Not-Jake was making Gary do. It was the cruelest thing she'd ever seen in her short life. Every time she moved her face away from Gary's protracted sniffling and weeping, Mustache slapped her and made her look again.

"This will be instructive," he said to Lainey. "You'll learn not to fuck with us. We don't take *no* for an answer."

Jake-Not-Jake dictated. Lainey tried to concentrate on the voice of Jake coming out of the wrong mouth. Jake-Not-Jake's voice was so much younger than the body it inhabited. It screwed her up, knowing that she'd fallen for it so completely that she'd been played so comprehensively. And that deception had not only led to her capture, but would soon lead to Gary's death.

When the note was finished, Jake-Not-Jake took Gary to a small wooden box beneath the noose and told him to stand on it.

"What if...I refuse?"

"I wouldn't recommend it," said Jake-Not-Jake.

"You're gonna kill me anyway, so why should I help you make it look like suicide?"

"Because if you don't..."

The third man came over to Lainey, pulled a Glock from a shoulder holster, thumbed off the safety, snapped the rack back to put a round in the barrel and put the gun against the girl's temple.

Gary's eyes bulged.

Jake-Not-Jake indicated to the box. "Get up and put the noose around your neck. All that stands between Lainey's brains putting in an appearance, and her living to fuck another day is you doing the decent thing. You love her, don't you? You really do?"

"No...I..."

"Don't lie Gary. I've been through your phone." Jake-Not-Jake leaned in, his lips almost against Gary's ear. "I've read the poems."

Gary nodded.

The air of defeat around his body was all-encompassing. He climbed onto the box and put the noose of nylon rope, liberated from the Buick's trunk, around his neck.

"Any last words?" Jake-Not-Jake said.

Before Gary could say anything, Jake-Not-Jake kicked the box away from Gary's feet and he dropped eight inches.

"I hate last words," Jake-Not-Jake said to Lainey directly. "I'm an impatient guy. I like to get to the good part."

Lainey was made to look, as Gary slowly strangled on the rope. His eyes bulging, his tongue poking out of his mouth on a billow of thick foam. His feet kicking, then trembling and then becoming still.

That's when Lainey fainted.

9

Bimala longed for the Pink City.

She wanted the crush of bodies in the Tripolia Bazar, the growl of the *Tuk Tuk* rickshaws carrying tourists and their purchases, the street sellers with their trinkets, the waves of life running across the surface on the rivers of commerce.

There on the island, there was an awful quiet. It was a quiet that crushed the spirit and hollowed the soul. In E-Wing, the girls were all in their first year on the island. It was where Rosa and Carla put the newest arrivals, and it was where the girls were broken in by guards then trained by Rosa's three Madams. Their lives were planned for the bedroom and fetishistic skills they would be taught to please the men and the women who came to the island.

Bimala had been told this on her first morning on the island, four months prior. She was told by Rosa's deputy herself, Carla, who personally inspected the new arrivals, checking their bodies and their potential.

Carla, the tall blond-haired Colombian—whose hair was the color of platinum, body was like cast bronze, and who walked with the air of a Queen—told Bimala that she was pretty enough and would do well for the *Straights*. Those were the men who valued the idea of a romantic, faux consensual, liaison with the girls they abused. Bimala at eighteen was forming into a striking young woman, and Carla marked her for the Exercise and Make-Up cohort.

Carla had told her the training would begin immediately.

Bimala didn't know why she expected her training, in whatever form it would be, to take place in the classroom of a school. She hadn't been prepared at all to be dragged onto a grubby mattress in a guard room of E-Wing and subjected to two hours of terror being passed from guard to guard.

When they returned her to her bed, she ached in every part of her body; there was blood and there was internal pain. She hadn't slept and cried into her pillow, not wishing to draw attention to herself—not wishing to comment when other guards came for the next newest girl to begin her education on the same mattress stained with Bimala's blood.

Bimala survived by thinking about her life in Jaipur, though not the life before that. She had nearly no memories of her earliest life; her real parents were killed in a car crash when she was two. She had a couple of dog-eared photographs of her mother and father plus the ghost impressions of long ago memories, but that was all. In actuality, she'd been raised by her Aunt Chaaya and her Uncle Bharat. They were childless and unhappy about that, with the shame and humiliation brought upon a barren family. So the death of Chaaya's brother had been both a terrible tragedy, but also a blessing in disguise.

Destroying one family and making another.

Jaipur was a wonderful place for a young girl to grow, especially one born into Hinduism and readily willing to take on the beliefs, tenets, and rituals thereof. One of the first prayers she had learned as a young girl was the one used in the morning purification ritual. The prayer was part of a meditational ceremony to Govinda: the Cowherd, the Protector. The prayer *"Govindethi sada snanam Govindethi sada japam, Govindethi sada dhyanam, sada Govinda keerthanam."* became a constant in Bimala's life on the island. The need to purify herself from the dirt and pain of the Owners and their guards meant the ritual and the words were soon a way for Bimala to take her mind off whatever was being done to her body and leave it to the men and their ministrations for as long as was needed. Repeating the words over and over again, the feeling of purity would return to her bones and wash across her skin.

Bimala was pure, despite whatever they might do to her body for the purposes of her training.

There was no provision made on the island for dietary needs for those who were already following a particular religion. In the dormitory were girls from Jewish families in London, Catholic families in Ireland, Muslims from the slums of Syria and Turkey, as well as Russian girls brought up in the Orthodox faith. There were also girls who came to the island too young to know what faith they were or how they should observe it.

Everyone was served the same food, and they chose to eat it or not. Bimala wasn't a strict vegetarian—there was no instruction in the Vedic texts that forced a Hindu to be one. But like many of her faith and like that of the people who had brought her up, she would avoid meat and eggs where she could—swapping her meat with girls who wanted more in exchange for extra vegetables. The guards didn't seem to mind this internal market in food to bond the girls together. As Carla said to Bimala one day when she'd come to take a look at how her "flock" was coming on,

"It's not like you're going to be here long enough for it to matter. When we think you're ready for the permanent wings, then you'll be moving on."

The rest of Bimala's training consisted of instructional videos on the techniques of pleasure. Bimala pretended to watch, but really was away praying to Govinda, purifying her thoughts.

The attacks from guards continued but with less frequency, and they didn't seem to care if she was reciprocating their assaults. In the end she was able to completely disassociate herself from the present while the guards did to her the most terrible things; things beyond her imagination or comprehension. The fact that she had no idea what was happening to her could be even held up as an example of what people might consensually call pleasure. It seemed to be a poor imitation at best, and an annihilating travesty at worst.

"Govindethi sada snanam Govindethi sada japam, Govindethi sada dhyanam, sada Govinda keerthanam," she whispered beneath her breath or in her mind. Eyes closed, or if they ordered her to open them—as they would more often than not—she would focus on a spot on the wall of the dirty little room which smelled of sweat and depression.

She would focus on a blemish in the wall plaster that was almost the shape of the Ghost Lake of Ramgarh. The man-made lake itself had dried up before Bimala was born. But the picture she had of her parents, dog-eared and stained was taken there. Her parents had visited eight years before Bimala had been born when the lake had still been full—before the vagaries of local government had caused it to become poorly maintained and ultimately dried out. To Bimala, the lake was a real world spot where she knew her parents had visited. But the ghostliness of it, the absence— the water having gone years before—meant that no one again could have that memory of standing by the water to have their photograph taken. Bimala's parents had become Ramgarh Ghosts, and that spot on the wall in the plaster—where the white skim had fallen away to expose the rough brickwork beneath—was a shape that pretty much mirrored the one of Lake Ramgarh. And it was that shape Bimala fixated on as the guards did their worst.

She longed for the Pink City, and so she would travel to the Ghost Lake in her mind.

On the evening of the fourth month of her captivity, Carla came for Bimala in the dormitory. Carla brought with her a golden sari covered in intricate stitching, silver threads, and printed with the patterns of a rising sun over deep water. It was the most beautiful garment Bimala had ever seen.

"Put it on," instructed Carla.

Bimala did as she was told, wrapping the cool material around her body and over her slender shoulders where it hung like a heavy sash.

Carla reached into the bag she carried and passed Bimala a pair of diamante and brocade covered slippers with red silk uppers and soft canvas soles. Bimala slipped them on her feet, and they fitted as if they'd been made for her.

Bimala didn't need to ask why she was being given these incredible clothes. She had seen similar rituals in the past four months, as girls were lavished with gifts, and taken away by Carla—never to return to the E-Wing dormitory.

It was now Bimala's time.

"You have done well, Bimmy," said Carla, running her fingers through Bimala's hair smoothing down any strays that weren't already tightly bound into the rope of black hair that hung in a braid over the nape of her neck. From there the braid curled over Bimala's shoulder to hang like the end of the sari across her breast.

"I didn't think you'd be ready for months yet, but you have completed your training already, and the guards tell me that you have stopped screaming when they are with you. You've stopped crying when you come back to your bed. This is a good sign. Girls who respond like that stay alive on the island. Those are the girls we value, those are the girls who do as they're told, and give us no trouble. Girls like that are worth a million Macy's."

Bimala hadn't known Macy, but the picture of her dead body had been hung as a warning in the E-Wing notice-board. It was only captioned as "Macy." No one needed to have it explained to them. What they should take from it was the fact that it was there.

"You're not going to end up like Macy are you?"

Bimala was half here, half at the Ghost Lake saying her prayer in her mind. She shook her head.

"Outstanding," Carla said and led Bimala by the hand out of the dormitory.

Bimala had not been outside the one story cinderblock E-Wing since she'd been brought to the island by the steamer. Nothing much had changed from what she could remember. Six containment wings around a central mansion, a helipad, a staff wing, and control towers. This was the service area of the island, and to get to it from the main gate, you would have to drive or walk past the timber-framed guest chalets.

The evening was sultry and hot. Muggy with clouds as if the sky sweated into the atmosphere.

Carla led Bimala toward the chalets.

Bimala could see out of the compound toward what she knew to be The Enchanted Forest, and beyond it the mountain—black and craggy rising up above the mist. Beyond even that, the sea.

The sun was setting, casting long shadows below the cloud layer which glutted the sky from horizon to horizon. The air had the same feeling Bimala had at the start of the monsoon season back in Jaipur, but the air wasn't thick and hard like India.

Her journey to the island had taken many hours. Two or three days in fact, even before reaching the jungle port where she had been chained into the hold of the steamer with three other girls. Bimala couldn't be sure where in the world she was now, but all she did know was it was tropical and very hot.

They passed three chalets, and came to a fourth set back from the cinder path. It was bigger than those around it: a two-story construction with a veranda on both levels, dark windows in the failing twilight and just a sliver of yellow light sliding through a screen covering the front door.

Carla looked down on Bimala, pushing her chin up with her crooked index finger. Bimala concentrated on the Ghost Lake and the ritual of purification.

Govindethi sada snanam Govindethi sada japam, Govindethi sada dhyanam, sada Govinda keerthanam Govindethi sada snanam Govindethi sada japam, Govindethi sada dhyanam, sada Govinda keerthanam

"Do as you're told, and I'll let you keep the slippers. If I hear back that you've gone beyond the call of duty then I'll let you keep the sari."

Govindethi sada snanam Govindethi sada japam, Govindethi sada dhyanam, sada Govinda keerthanam

"But if I hear things that I don't want to hear, I'll cut you open from throat to cunt and feed you to my dog."

Govindethi sada snanam Govindethi sada japam, Govindethi sada dhyanam, sada Govinda keerthanam

"Carla? I'm sure we don't need to use threats."

The voice was American; husky and yet kind. Bimala looked to the veranda. There were three men standing there now. She'd been so intent on the ritual and the memory of the Ghost Lake, that she hadn't noticed the men come from within the chalet.

Two of the men were in black suits, with white shirts beneath and sporting black ties. Both were wearing wraparound sunglasses and had curly transparent wires coming from their ears. The wires disappeared into their jackets. They were looking everywhere except at Bimala. They surveyed the compound, heads swinging like RADAR dishes. Constantly scanning.

The third man was in a shadow, but she could make out that he was tall and broad. An expensive blue suit fitted him perfectly. A green tie hung down the front of his pink shirt. He was made of color. He reached out a hand towards Bimala.

Bimala's feet didn't move.

Govindethi sada snanam Govindethi sada japam, Govindethi sada dhyanam, sada Govinda keerthanam

Carla nudged Bimala forward, "Go on, Bimmy. There's nothing to be afraid of."

"Quite so, Carla," said the man. "Come Bimmy, let's go now."

Bimala took the offered hand. It was warm, soft, and transmitted nothing of the threat she was feeling.

"If there's anything else I can get you...?"

The man gently guided Bimala onto the veranda and took her towards the door. "No thank you, Carla. You have already exceeded all my expectations with Bimmy here. So I'll wish you a good night."

As the chalet swallowed them up, Bimala dove into the Ghost Lake. Its cool waters rushed over her mind's skin, filling her hollows with its fresh purity, washing the fear from her body to leave it empty of thought and terror. The last thing she heard before the door closed was Carla replying, "And a good night to you, Mr. President."

10

"Okay, Bryan, what have you got?"

Passion was back at the hotel. She'd showered, taken four hours to sleep, but no more, and although didn't feel fully refreshed, the sense that she'd rubbed off some of her exhaustion that morning was a welcome one.

"My God. Teenage girls. We should create a virus and have them all eradicated."

"You don't have children do you, Bryan?"

"Not if I can help it, no."

"I haven't had time to go through all of the logs and messages. What have you got?" Passion could feel the antsy-ness from lack of sleep rolling back into her speech—coupled with the fact that sometimes Bryan was an infuriating asshole. It was an unfortunate combination.

"Jake doesn't exist. Well, not in the way Alaina thought he existed. He reached out to her Instagram account and the rest, as they say, was grooming. He was very good."

"Doesn't exist?"

"Nope. There's no one called Jake Whymark in Dallas of that age who matches. No father who matches. The pictures on his profile, seem to have been lifted from this account: a Mark Sendon."

The screen of the Samsung tablet flicked from the Jake Whymark account to that of Mark Sendon. The pictures were the same, but not in the same order, and the lead post was a pronouncement from Mark's parents that although he was dead, he would be forever in their hearts, and they were leaving the page up as a tribute to their forever loved son, Mark. The rest of the profile had been lifted wholesale to create Jake.

"Mark was killed last year in Atlanta. Good kid by all accounts, bright future. Stumbled onto the wrong side of a gas station hold up and got himself shot. Whoever has been grooming Lainey—or Pippa Graves as she was known on her secret profile—was very good. I mean, *really* good. Professional. Definitely not nineteen, and definitely not Mark Sendon."

Pippa Graves' profile replaced Jake's.

Lainey in all her Goth Glory as "Pippa."

"How *much* Goth is the surname Graves? I'm almost impressed."

Passion shook her head, but didn't answer Bryan. She flicked through the Pippa profile. It couldn't have been more different from the Aliana profile—the transformation from blond-haired 18-year-old cheerleader to Goth ingénue, partying and excessing her way through a series of selfies and shots from her Goth friends. The clubs looked dark and sweaty. Lainey's eyes looked strung out and her clothes left little to the imagination.

There was rebelling against your parents, and there was a full-on civil war. The fact Lainey had pulled on the shield of Pippa's maturity disguised the bald fact that Lainey was still naïve and vulnerable. Jake—or whoever he was—would have seen that in a heartbeat and seized on it. To groom in this way, you have to have an ability to spot the weak and those open to having that weakness exploited. Was this same method this guy had used on the other girls the Agency had failed to find? Those girls who had slipped through Passion's grasp?

Was Passion now closer to this man?

"Is it possible the girls we've not found before were groomed by the same man and in the same way?"

"It's possible. Without knowledge of their fake profiles and logs it would be difficult to say for sure. We were lucky here that Gary Malcolm cloned Lainey's phone. Without that we wouldn't have known any of this."

Passion was skimming the chat logs between "Pippa" and "Jake": two people who weren't who they said they were, talking as if they had been lovers for eternity.

Passion scrolled and scrolled the streams of text.

"Jake doesn't know who she really is."

Passion's speakerphone made a snort. "I was wondering how long it would take you to notice."

"I've had four hours sleep in nearly three days, Bryan. Give me a break."

"But yes, correct. He doesn't know—well certainly none of the logs would indicate it. Her Instagram account as "Pippa" was public, he could have found it by random and played her along until he was ready to take her."

"I don't think we're dealing with a serial killer here. I think there's something more to this."

"Well it's clearly not random. Other than the one body, a suicide in the Philippines we have no other bodies. What's happening to the girls, I have no idea. But unless he's very very good at disposing of corpses, I think we can only assume the girls are still alive."

"That doesn't bear thinking about."

"Indeed. I've never been able to watch *Silence of the Lambs* a second time. Or think about body lotion."

"Bryan!"

"Yes, well. We're working on out finding anything we can about Fake-Jake. "Pippa" never called Jake when they spoke on the phone. He always called her at a pre-arranged time and his number was withheld. He said it was because his father was heavily into family security. How *ironic*."

"Okay, let me know when you find anything."

"We have a record of Pippa receiving a call from a withheld number the night before she disappeared, and that was the last dump of info that was sent from the cloned phone to Gary. So that's where the trail ends. When she walked out of the compound, we don't even know if she was met at the gates or went on down the road a ways before meeting up with Fake-Jake. Sven did his job all too well with the CCTV. He didn't even review it before he wiped it."

"So the trail is cold?"

"Not quite."

"Oh."

"Pippa's phone was turned on after many hours and dumped a fresh set info to the clone app. No messages were sent, no chat logs, no new pictures. If someone had the technical knowhow to check to see if a phone had been cloned then..."

"They would know, possibly, that the cops or someone like us may have all the information we need to find them."

"Yes."

"And that might make them careless?"

The speakerphone made the noise again.

Passion didn't realize how careless Fake-Jake would be until she heard about Glen Malcolm's suicide on the car radio as she drove away from the hotel.

His body had been found hanging from a beam in the underground car park of a yet-to-be-opened shopping mall. He'd written a suicide note confession to the abduction, rape, and murder of Alaina Ralston. He said he'd dumped her body in the river, and that he was sorry, and that he was taking his own life because he didn't deserve to live.

The media expected a statement from the Ralston's in the next hour, as the feeding frenzy was growing.

Passion made two calls. One to Bryan, and then one to Stephen Crane.

───────────

"And in an amazing twist, reports are reaching us that Gary Malcolm, school friend of missing Alaina Ralston— the 18-year-old daughter of prospective Texas Senator Huey Ralston—has confessed to the abduction and murder of the girl in a suicide note. The note, which the Police have yet to confirm, is an accurate account of the death of Alaina Ralston. They say his body was discovered by security at the site of the new Mall of America site in Fleetway Village this morning. Police report that there will be an autopsy carried out to ascertain the cause of death, but are not releasing any further details at this time. A spokesman from Mr. Ralston's office say that the prospective Senator will be making a statement in the next few hours."

Jake-Not-Jake laughed as Dragons turned off the radio.

Lainey had been taken out of the trunk of the car again, especially to hear the news report. The Buick was parked in a huge, empty metal-framed building that was open at one end before the bright Texan sky. There was a vast expanse of concrete outside the building, and Lainey could hear jets taking off and landing somewhere out of sight.

She was in an aircraft hangar.

When they'd opened the truck, Lainey was stiff with cramps, as her hands and feet were almost blue from the cut off circulation caused by being bound. The first thing she told them was that she needed a pee. Jake-Not-Jake rolled his eyes, and Dragons cut the tape around her legs. It still clung to her fishnet stocks and flapped against her ankles as she walked.

Jake-Not-Jake led Lainey to the end of the hangar, where there was a small office, a tool shed, and a small rest area for the ground crew to do one's business when on shift. Jake-Not-Jake took her into the stall, but did not untie her hands. Lainey looked at him.

"Do you want me to pee through my underwear?"

"Where you're going, doll, that's exactly what some of the sick fucks will want you to do. But, hey I want to deliver you in prime condition, so let's cut the chances of diaper rash, huh?"

The garlic stink of his breath was in her face as he leaned in. As she had expected, instead of Jake-Not-Jake releasing her arms, he hugged her close, pushing his chest against hers. She felt the stubble of his cheek against her temple, saw the light dancing off his earring. He was hot and humid with sweat, and as he pulled her in tighter, she could feel a hard lump in his pants against her thigh.

"Gotta admit you got me hot, Pippa. All those texts all those promises of what you were going to do with me in the Sheraton. Are you really a virgin, I wonder? Really? Shall I check?"

With rising panic, Lainey felt his rough hand moving down her belly toward her groin.

"Please...please...don't" she pleaded. "I don't know

what's happening with all this, but I won't cause you any trouble I promise. I'm scared. I can't...I don't...please..."

Jake-Not-Jake's hand stopped, then in one quick movement flipped under her skirt, slid a thumb through the top of her underwear and yanked it down to her knees, burning her thigh in the process.

"It's okay, kid. Only playing with you. Rosa's gonna want your virginity intact. That's an ultra-sellable commodity right there."

The words chilled Lainey, almost as much as watching Gary slowly strangling as he dangled from the rope.

Commodity?

The idea sucked her insides so hard she honestly felt that she would never pee again. Jake-Not-Jake removed his hot hand from her cold thigh and pushed her back onto the toilet. His toe caught onto the flapping duct tape on her ankle, and it ripped away from the fishnet-covered skin painfully.

"Oww!"

"A low pain threshold, huh?" Jake-not-Jake laughed, as he flicked the tape off the sole of his boot. "Some guys pay extra for that too."

Lainey looked up at Jake-Not-Jake with terrified eyes. He blew her a kiss. "You've got thirty seconds. After that, you're gonna be pissing yourself in the trunk, and we'll just hose you down before we put you on the plane."

"Plane?" Lainey said, trying to keep the tremor in her voice under control.

Jake-Not-Jake looked at the watch on his wrist. "Yeah, it's about an hour before wheels down. Just enough time to see what waves we've caused in the surface of the pond. Now, pee!"

Back at the Buick, Dragons re-taped Lainey's ankles,

just as tightly as before, but let her lean against the car instead of folding her back up into the trunk.

Mustache fed her some mineral water from a bottle he'd been drinking from without wiping the top first. Lainey didn't care. Her mouth was dry and her thirst was raging in the heat of the hangar. She had peed long and hard in the restroom and now she was feeling even more dehydrated.

The news report shocked her down to her guts.

The world and her parents would think she was dead. Did that mean the police would stop looking for her? And did it matter if they did? They were here waiting on a plane to land in the next hour that she assumed was going to take her far away from her family, friends, and her city.

It was going to take her to a place where her virginity and pain threshold were a sellable commodity. She had no idea what that might entail as a reality, but she knew it wasn't going to be pleasant.

Jake-Not-Jake clapped his hands, bringing Lainey out of the terrible things she was imagining about her immediate and long-term future.

The white nosecone of a small private jet—a Gulf-stream, like the one her father owned—was rolling into the view at the open end of the hangar.

Jake-Not-Jake was applauding. "That's my girl. Right. On. Time."

11

The Ralston residence was full of screams.

Huey sat at the wide expanse of his desk, his hand on the green leather top, surrounded on all sides by the red leather spines of books he'd never read.

Detective Myer spoke his piece, and Huey listened with a rising tide of chilly shock climbing from his belly—washing up over his head, cooling his thoughts, locking them in ice. Myer was Crane's connection to the Houston PD. Crane told Huey that he'd had many dealings with the young detective through his perfectly calculated connections with the Houston Police Benevolent Fund, which Myer's father—a grizzly ex-detective, who'd passed his tenacity onto his son—was still the patron. Robert Myer Jr. conveyed the lie of incorruptible freshness of a man who wanted people to think he was doing God's work. And as he told Huey and Brenda the news of the suicide of Gary Malcolm and what the boy had written in the note, he'd offered to kneel and pray with the family in their hour of greatest need.

The only time Huey knelt was to worship at the temple

of the Pussy. So he had politely declined, saying that he and his wife needed some time to process the information that their beloved daughter might be dead; heinously murdered by stalker scum.

Brenda collapsed into a hysterical fit on the carpet in front of Huey and Myer. She beat at the carpet, screamed for her baby and kicked her legs like a toddler having a tantrum. Huey and Myer stood by, both unsure how to handle the situation. In the end, Huey called on Marcella the housekeeper to help Brenda up to her room and to call the Doctor immediately.

Marcella hadn't been able to get Brenda to stand, and so Huey had to intervene and help as Myer stood back, his face a mask of cool evangelical compassion.

As Huey helped the plump, middle-aged Marcella— who he knew Brenda had engaged precisely for those attributes—to put him off fucking her, he realized that this was the first time he'd laid hands on his wife, other than to punch her in the gut in the last two years.

Brenda didn't stop screaming as she was brought to her feet and hung her arms around the plump and unattractive housekeeper. She continued screaming as she was led from the office. Huey and Myer heard her screaming all the way up the stairs to the master bedroom. Even with the door shut, and the office door closed, there was still a background scream underpinning everything.

It was like being irreversibly trapped inside an Edvard Munch painting.

Myer told Huey that everything would be done, God willing, to find Lainey alive or to bring her back to her home. "It'll be Houston PD's number one responsibility sir. No question."

After that, Myer had left, giving Huey the first opportunity since he'd been told the news of Malcolm's note to address the elephant in the room. Although he was shocked, saddened, and angry that the life of his daughter could have been taken so egregiously, there was also the *Political Math* to consider.

Huey checked himself at that, surprised that political ramifications and the political *advantages* of a dead daughter, could be in his thoughts.

A succession of future images tumbled through his mind. A press conference. Stoic and statesman-like. Perhaps a tear. *I'm sorry but I'm sure you understand why my wife isn't here right now.* An interview for the *Post*, no...*60 Minutes.* A sofa sit down with *Fox.* The funeral, high summer and high drama. A flag-draped coffin, a sea of mourners all in black; women in veils. Brenda stumbling on his arm. Huey holding her up. Did the Marines offer gun salutes for the children of politicians? He made a note to ask Crane how they would get that done. And then the election in the fall. *Of course I'm not pulling out. I owe it to the people of Texas to stand for them. To stand with them against the tide of crimes sweeping up from the South. I have been touched by the same tragedy as you, my friend. I feel your pain. I know your hearts. You wouldn't want my personal grief to rob you of my support in Washington, would you? Thank you. Thank you. I accept the nomination. Thank you! Thank you! I will work for all Texans! Even those who did not vote for me. I will be a Senator for all!* Huey's ears were full of cheering. His eyes full of people. Balloons falling from the ceiling of the office. The fireworks in the fireplace! The music! The book deal...the *Presidency*...

Huey shook his head again, reaching off the table with his right hand, to adjust the front of his pants, where his erection was pressing painfully against his fly.

His heart was beating. His mouth was dry. His body throbbed with possibility, and that made him horny as hell.

He reached for the desk phone and dialed a number he'd never seen written down. One that he'd never written down himself. One that he had been instructed to commit to memory.

Rosa answered at the third ring, but Huey could still hear Brenda screaming.

"My name is Carla."

The blond-haired woman pulled the seatbelt across Lainey's lap as the Gulfstream taxied toward the runway. Jake-Not-Jake had thrown Lainey over his shoulder, deliberately flashing her backside at Dragons and Mustache. "Eyes on the prize, boys."

He slapped one cheek of her ass smartly, the sting making Lainey's back arch with shock. "And what a prize, huh?"

The Gulfstream had rolled to a halt. Dragons and Mustache pushed the steps up to the door as it opened. The uniformed pilot and co-pilot, all aviators and slicked back hair, descended and began connecting a fueling rig to the aircraft. They did this with practiced hands, as if it was a journey and a ritual they had completed dozens of times.

Jake-Not-Jake then pulled down Lainey's skirt to cover her underwear and taken her towards the plane. "Word of advice kid: if you think I've been a horror, you ain't seen nothing yet. These people play for keeps, and you're just meat to them. I like your spirit, and I enjoyed reeling you in. It's not like I don't have a conscience, but the money kinda gets in the way of one. But, if you're going to get through this, just do as you're told. Trust me, it'll make it all a whole lot easier on you."

Lainey felt close to tears again. She could feel the links

in the chain that held her to everything she knew snapping one by one. Her head bobbed away from the Buick as Jake-Not-Jake carried her towards the aircraft.

The hangar was rapidly filling with the smell of kerosene, and Lainey's eyes were stinging with it, making her feel like she was crying even more. "Please," she said to Jake-Not-Jake's back and near skipping feet. "My daddy is rich. He'll give you more than these people will. He'll double it. You could say you found me in a car somewhere unconscious. I won't tell anyone the truth I promise. Please, Jake, please!"

Jake-Not-Jake patted her backside again and gave it a squeeze, "Honey, I love it when you beg."

Inside the Gulfstream, no expense had been spared in the custom conversion. It was all cream leather, deep pile carpets, and panels of beechwood, polished and highly varnished. It was less a luxury airplane and more a luxury yacht.

"Just one?" said the voice of a woman.

Jake-Not-Jake slid Lainey off his shoulder into a cool leather seat and for the first time Lainey could see the woman who was speaking. Striking, tall, platinum blonde and looking at the teenager as if she'd just stood in something the dog had left in the yard.

Jake-Not-Jake smiled. "Yes, just the one for now. We have five more operations ongoing, and we'll reel them in. But this one is special, and that's why I called you in ahead of schedule."

The blonde looked Lainey up and down in the seat, her expression not changing. "Pretty I suppose, well-proportioned, but special? How?"

Jake-Not-Jake paused for dramatic effect, and then announced his surprise like a ringmaster in the circus.

"Carla, I give you... Huey Ralston's daughter. She was

using a fake ID. I thought she was just another crazy little rich girl wanting to get her freak on. But her smartphone had been cloned..."

The woman's eyes blazed. "What? And you still took her? Are you fucking *insane*? Remember what happened to the Philippine's crew, Daniel. Rosa just has to wave her finger and..."

"Chill, baby, chill. We dealt with the clone and the cloner already. He saw the error of his ways, and decided to take his own life. It was tragic."

"As will your demise if there's a security breach."

"It's done. We have the cloned phone, the boy's phone and we've wiped everything from his iCloud. It's over."

Carla put her hands on her hips. She looked like she was trying to contain her anger, but it was still spilling out of her eyes. Lainey felt it pouring out of the woman. A small muscle twitched on the woman's cheek. Lainey had the impression this was a woman who walked a line between calm and simply *astonishing* expressions of violence. And that it didn't take her a lot to flip from one to the other.

Lainey resolved to take *Daniel's*—now she knew his real name—advice and play along. Feeling like a commodity and piece of meat to be bought and sold, gave a new precariousness to her situation. She threw possessions away all the time, once they had outlived their usefulness, and that was something right now she was not willing to become. Not trash.

Daniel bent down, and kissed Lainey on the cheek, "There's also something that puts the icing on the cake?"

"Oh?"

"*Jake* was gonna be her first."

The blond arched an eyebrow. "Oh, really? Dressed like that and you were going to be the first in?"

"It's all a front, isn't it Lainey?" Daniel ruffled Lainey's hair and smiled like he was telling a child she could have a pony. "She's just playing at being a grown up. Not the real thing. Not by a long shot. Kinda dumb, when all is said and done, to have fallen for Jake so hard. I'm almost sad not to have followed through."

"I bet you are. Okay, I'm still not convinced the security on the island hasn't been compromised, but I'll get the comms team to look into it. I'll need the phones."

Daniel reached into his pocket and pulled out Lainey's Pippa iPhone and Gary's Samsung. They'd been taped together with the same insulation tape they'd used on Lainey.

Carla took the phones and tossed them onto a seat.

"All that leaves…" said Daniel.

"Yes, yes." Carla's irritation was still there on show. She pulled her own phone from the breast pocket of her jacket and thumbed the screen.

"And…a…bonus for such a worthwhile catch?"

"I'll need Rosa to authorize that, but the baseline should be in your account now."

Daniel was already looking at the screen of his smart-phone, his eyes lighting up at what he saw there.

"Bingo."

And that was that.

Lainey had made the fall from independent teenager with a life she controlled and a lifestyle any one of a million other girls would have killed to have lived just for a day, to simply a piece of property. Bought and sold for money.

———

"I said pay attention."

Lainey snapped out of the cold repulsion of her situation and focused on the woman. "I just want to go home."

"You are. To your new home."

Lainey felt her bottom lip trembling. She didn't want to show this blond-haired monster in an expensive suit, that she was scared. She didn't want to give her the satisfaction. *But I am more scared than I've ever been in my life,* she thought to herself. Her heart was fluttering in her chest, and she was sure that vibration would be transmitted up to her neck for the woman to see.

It had all moved so fast. It was so incredible she almost expected to wake up from a nightmare of epic proportions. But it wasn't a dream. This was all too real. They had groomed her over weeks, they had killed Gary in front of her, and they had 'five other operations ongoing.' There was a succession of girls, just like Lainey, out there falling for Jake—keeping it from their parents and inching blindly toward their doom.

Their professional set up—with its gangs of men acquiring victims, a Gulfstream Jet, and a *comms team*—felt nothing other than massive. A conspiracy that stretched from Houston to the Philippines and all places in between. Lainey felt less than a commodity now. The realization hitting her was just a tiny part of a voracious machine throwing girls like her into its jaws at a constant rate and chewing them up. What happened to the girls they had already taken? What happened to those which they needed to be replaced?

A dark depression hit her.

It wasn't just the call for tears; it was the sense she'd become entirely inconsequential. That her dreams, ambitions, needs, and desires were now secondary to the people: this Rosa and her *teams* who now owned her.

Carla sat in the seat next to Lainey, buckling herself in

after smoothing down her suit where it had wrinkled up against the leather.

"I can see the sheer hopelessness of your situation is sinking in, Lainey. I may call you Lainey, may I?"

Lainey could do nothing except nod. There were no words she could put into her own mouth that could decode the utter collapse into grief and loss she was feeling.

Carla patted her knee. "Of course, I've seen it dozens of times, that which you are now experiencing. Sometimes it takes a while, sometimes not until we reach the island, or even then beyond that. The *very* stupid, the ones lacking the very basics of self-awareness take the longest. But I find those young women who *appreciate*...if you will, who *embrace* the complete hopelessness of their situation early on, have the advantage. The island can be survived. You'll never leave of course, but you can survive if you have the pragmatic mindset to accept what is happening at the earliest juncture."

Carla was saying all this like she was reciting a shopping list, or ticking off items on her to-do planner. She smiled again, down at Lainey. The smile of an aunt taking her niece on a trip to the zoo.

"Don't see it as losing your life, Lainey...see it as gaining a rapist."

12

"There's no way he killed her."

"Isn't that your guilt talking, Passion?"

"I don't feel guilty, Bryan. Gary Malcolm was a stalkery little slime ball with way too much time on his hands and an unnatural interest in spyware, but he was *not* a killer."

The speakerphone made the noise of disapproval. Passion sat back in the Hyundai's driver seat and drummed her fingers on the steering wheel. "Perhaps I shouldn't have gotten angry with him and over promised. So maybe I feel a little guilty. But there was nothing stopping him going to the police after he left me and fessing up. Nothing at all."

"There was nothing stopping you from suggesting it to him either."

That stung.

Bryan continued, "I must also update your staff profile to include your immense ability to self-justify almost any screw-up."

"I'm going to off you, Bryan." Passion cut the call.

The Hyundai was parked about three miles from the Houston suburbs. Passion had stopped to gather her thoughts before going to see Huey Ralston. Stephen Crane had given her the go ahead to come over, but she had to "prepare herself for the immense grief being suffered by both parents" and "not do or say anything that would make their situation worse."

"Don't worry, I won't, but I do have information that will be of great interest."

"Unless it leads to the body, I doubt it will be of any interest," Crane had said before hanging up. Passion thought about calling him straight back and demanding to know how Crane had known her real name yesterday at the Court House. It rattled her more than she'd realized now that she thought about it. With the full-on pace of the investigation of Lainey's disappearance, she hadn't given it any time at all. But now it was itching at the back of her mind.

Certainly Ralston had not let on that he thought she was operating under an alias. Very few people knew her real name. In fact, she could count on the fingers of one hand who called her "Passion" or "Ms. Valdez" these days. Saying "Jennifer Durant" was so second nature to her now that she almost introduced herself by the name, even to people who knew better. It was ingrained.

There had been plenty of traffic going back the Court House as Crane moved away; perhaps she'd misheard him in the rumble of traffic.

Maybe.

But still it *itched*.

Back to the present.

Gary's suicide and note would have sent police down the wrong path. It wouldn't be the first time, and conversely it might help Passion's investigation. While the police were using their resources for dragging rivers and trying to find the murder scene of a killing, Passion was absolutely sure it never happened. At least while their activity moved in the wrong direction, it gave Passion a chance of digging deeper into the Pippa Graves profile.

There may be messages in the clone dump which reveal where the rendezvous between Lainey and Fake-Jake had taken place—where most certainly the teenager had been kidnapped. But Pippa may have told someone; a girlfriend perhaps. Maybe she'd been excited and bursting at the seams about meeting her new love? It was a long shot, but Passion made a mental note to look at the Pippa profile after her meeting with the Ralstons to look into who the most likely subject would be based upon messenger and phone logs.

Passion drove the last three miles to the Ralston residence with her head full of possibilities and conjecture.

Lainey was still alive. She was sure of it.

The jungle simmered in the equatorial heat of summer. It was heat that slapped Lainey in the face and drenched her in sweat as Carla led her from the Gulfstream, down the steps onto the blistering concrete. Carla had cut the tape around her legs an hour into the three-hour flight so that Lainey could get up and walk around, returning some feeling to her legs.

"It's not like there's anywhere for you to go."

Carla had also unwrapped the duct tape from around Lainey's wrists, replacing it with handcuffs. This time her hands were secured in Lainey's lap, so that she could sit back in the chair, rather than having to lean forward the whole time.

Feeling had come back slowly into her limbs, but there had been pins, needles, and cramps. Carla rubbed Lainey's wrists and ankles. "Just because I'm the bad guy here, doesn't mean I want to see you suffer," Carla said with a smirk. "Well not yet anyway."

Lainey was used to Houston heat, but that was nothing like this on the edge of the jungle. The air was thick with moisture, as if it were already raining, yet it was just humidity. The runway had been cut out of the virgin rainforest and had the half-finished look of something that didn't need to be used that often, or one that was many years old. The strip was cracked and full of weeds.

There was a refueling rig under a rusty corrugated shack, and a large tank of fuel on wheels that was attached to a Dodge truck, almost as rusty as the shack. There were a few people in grubby uniforms milling around in the heat —putting chocks against the tires of the Gulfstream and getting ready to refuel.

"Wait," Carla said, as the heat from the runway began to seep through even the thick soles of Lainey's boots. Carla gripped tightly to Lainey's arm above the elbow. "Let them come to us. That's what we pay them for."

From behind the Dodge, an ancient Jeep painted army surplus green growled into life and pulled into view. The driver turned the vehicle towards the Gulfstream and trundled towards it.

If she was going to do it, Lainey figured she'd have to do it now.

As the Jeep pulled alongside them, she took advantage of the first time in over 24 hours that she didn't have her ankles and knees taped together and exploded into movement. She crashed her shoulder into Carla. With a surprised yelp the tall blond crashed into the hood of the Jeep, her head bouncing back comically. Carla slithered to the concrete with a soft thud.

Lainey took off. Her legs pumped and the soles of her

boots thumped on the concrete. She expected to hear shots, or hear shouting, but there was nothing.

Perhaps the slapping of her boots on the concrete was drowning out any other sounds.

Perhaps she was too valuable of a commodity now to be shot.

She didn't care either way.

As the sun beat down, and the humidity drenched her body she passed the corrugated shack and the fuel tank with ease. Lainey worked out every day in her gym. She had stamina and she had strength, even after being cooped up in the trunk of the Buick with her limbs tied. That hadn't diminished those powers.

The jungle was just another forty yards away as Lainey pelted towards it. She didn't have a plan or a strategy. There hadn't been time to formulate one. All she could think of doing from the moment Carla had freed her legs, was getting away.

In the jungle she'd be able to hide. Maybe she could get to a village, raise the alarm. Maybe even get to a road. *Anything*, as long as she was away from the madness.

Twenty yards.

She could hear voices shouting. Lainey couldn't make out the words, but the voices didn't sound commanding, like they were ordering her to come back, they sounded panicked. Scared even.

No matter. She had to get away. She couldn't stay with Carla and be transported to wherever the final destination was. She was getting to the jungle and she was going to...

Lainey ducked as the treetops head of her exploded with bullet fire. Branches shattered, leaves flew up. It was if there was a giant among the trees, and he was shaking the trunks with his mighty hands.

The bullets were being fired from behind her, over her head. Warning shots.

That sealed it. She was definitely too valuable to kill.

Lainey had a chance—a *real* chance—of getting to the edge of the airstrip and jumping up the slope into the trees.

Another barrage of shots from machine pistols. Some flew into the trees, some into the dirt on either side of her full-on pelt towards the thick greenery of the jungle.

And that's when Lainey saw the deep ditch, the sharp spikes and heard the dogs.

She staggered to a halt and raised her hands, the breath still hot and rapid in her throat, her mouth dry. She let out an aching whine of defeat that keened and wailed like a snake of sound between her lips.

The airstrip was surrounded by a twelve foot deep concrete-lined ditch.

The floor was dotted, every two feet or so with razor pointed iron spikes at varying angles. Among the spikes were German Shepherds that roamed and snarled. Their muzzles were slick with foam, their eyes dulled by a furious hunger. It was clear to Lainey that the firing over her head and the shouting hadn't necessarily been to warn her, but to bring the pack of dogs to the area where someone was trying to escape.

If she'd been running at night she would have fallen into the ditch in the darkness, more than likely to be skewered on one of the spikes and then eaten by the starving dogs.

As it was, if she tried now to ease herself down the slope into the pit, the dogs would have been on her in seconds, and her handcuffed wrists would have not been able to put up any defense against the fearsome animals. They jumped and barked at her, eyes fixated on her, with their ears back and foam shaking loosely in huge white gobbets from their muzzles.

"Cute aren't they? I have them fed once a week. It's just enough to keep them hungry without eating each other in the meantime. I think that one wants your guts."

Carla was standing beside Lainey now. She was holding a handkerchief against her forehead where it had bounced off the Jeep. There was blood on her cheek, and some had dripped down onto her cream suit.

"Now do you get it, Lainey?"

There was no fight left. Not one piece of it in Lainey. They'd managed, in just a few hours, to kick it all out of her.

"Come on, sweetheart. Let's get you to the boat."

Carla gripped Lainey's arm, turned her around and walked her back to the Jeep.

———

Huey's hand wouldn't stop shaking.

It had been over a day now and the tremor had not abated. He couldn't hold a glass to his lips with his right hand without it rattling against his teeth.

Brenda hadn't stopped screaming until the Doctor had come to sedate her, and even then, she would wake every few hours and her sobs would travel through the house like a ghost in an old castle.

In the end, once he'd gotten a handle on his own panic, Huey had to get out of the house. He walked stiffly down to the white fence of the pasture and stood there as the day fell toward night, shaking with an unaccustomed mix of fear and fury. Those two emotions met in a confluence of red hot anxiety in his guts, then flared behind his eyes, turning his thoughts into jagged shards of shame.

The breeze off the farm was warm and sweet with the tang of hay and grass. In the distance the cattle were eating, their oblivious nature accepting of whatever befell them. Huey could have gotten his shotgun, gone over there and killed ten of them. And the others, spooked for a while, would still come back to him if he held out some sweet grass for them to chew on.

Everybody in his life until now had been like those cattle. Whatever he did, whatever terrible things he had visited upon them, they would still come back and feed from his hand.

Brenda was the prime example. However much he humiliated her, scorned her, punched her or reviled her, she knew exactly where her bread was buttered.

Huey was used to having the drop on everyone, and now in the space of one phone call, every table had been turned.

Huey was cattle now: big and stupid and willing. However much he was beaten or humiliated—and he could sense what was coming—he would always have to return to the place from where his bread was going to be buttered from now on.

Rosa made everything clear to him.

Rosa spelled it out.

She hadn't even given him time to tell her that he needed to book a visit to the island. She'd cut him dead and told him to shut up.

No one told Huey Ralston to shut up, and that was his first inkling that his world was about to fall apart.

When she told him the rest, he just wanted to die.

Huey knew he was too much of a coward to check out that easily, but even if Huey wasn't dead, he knew his life was over.

13

Getting out of the dormitory on D-Wing was a more difficult challenge than getting under the wall.

Sliding out of the sleeping quarters unnoticed was in many ways the more critical part of the escape. It relied not on clever strategy, but on the actions of others within the system who ran the island, specifically the guard Parrish.

So it wasn't a case of D-Wing having a vulnerability that could be exploited. It's a very rare thing that a building fails. For the human systems within, however, it's another matter entirely.

Mary-Joy knew that Parrish—who worked the night shift on alternate nights to Schmidt and Karpov—was not only a creature of habit, but one of dark and terrible desires. She had noticed him many months ago, letting himself into the dormitory sometime between three and three thirty a.m.

On the surface, it looked as if he were checking on the girls in their bunks, counting heads and making the rounds. But Parrish—fat, balding, and flabby-faced, with eyes that looked like thumbs had been pressed into old

dough and a sheen on his top lip that was always there—
had an ulterior motive to be moving stealthily through the
rows of bunks, like so many other guards.

Guards on D-Wing did not have the same rights and
privileges to break new girls in as those on E-Wing. That
was the first point where the system broke down in a way
that Mary-Joy might be able to exploit. The girls on D-Wing
had been deemed ready to go out to the clients and be used
and abused by them and so guard activity was entirely
supposed to be just that. Guarding.

Whether Parrish would rather be on E-Wing where his
sickening desires could be fed to his heart's content, or if he
enjoyed doing the things he did illicitly and hidden on an
island where everything illicit and evil was permitted,
Mary-Joy didn't know. But she had suffered from many
nocturnal visits from Parrish—dreading the shift in the
mattress when his weight had been lowered onto it, the
snake hiss of his breath and the oily squirm of his hands
moving beneath the covers.

For Mary-Joy, the relief that Parrish's attentions had
moved on from her to other girls in their bunks after a time
was tempered by knowing that someone else was suffering
in the same way. That hurt Mary-Joy's heart, but she knew
that to intervene and help the other girl would lead to her
being taken to the punishment cells in B-Wing. She had
only tasted the horrors of that place once, a year after she'd
come to the island and had slapped a guard who had
cornered her against a wall as he was reaching out to
touch her.

The punishment cells were cubed cages.

Clothing was denied, as were the most basic rations of
food and water. Mary-Joy was beaten hourly—visited by
the most sadistic clients on the island. These clients were
given almost free reign to act out whatever perversions they

could imagine. Mary-Joy's arm had been snapped at the elbow—deliberately and within extremely slow precision. It was only the medical facilities and the ministrations of Doctor Driessen and his team of nurses who saved the movement in it. Mary-Joy's arm still ached in the rainy season on the island, and when it did, she would be back in the cage in her mind, screaming, though not loudly enough to cover the crackle of a snapping joint.

It was enough to make Mary-Joy stay in her bed when Parrish moved through the dormitory at night, but she didn't hate herself any less.

The click of the door opening came at 3:15 a.m.

Mary-Joy had not allowed herself to sleep, keeping her mind occupied with images of Benjie and his beautiful face when she had read *The Very Hungry Caterpillar* to him. Even though she had lived in a shack in a slum and made a living digging with bare hands through the detritus of Davao City, it was still better than this life. It was still more secure, and the thought of it brought a warm nostalgia to Mary-Joy's thin body even on the coldest nights in the unheated dormitory.

Mary-Joy heard Parrish's feet moving across the bare concrete floor. He was trying to move as silently as he could. It seemed his thing was reaching beneath the covers of girls who were either asleep or pretending to be asleep, not daring to say anything. Mary-Joy shuddered to remember those hands moving over her body. Gentle and caressing at first, and then growing ever more insistent and painful.

Parrish moved past Mary-Joy's bunk. For his last few attempts at twisted nocturnal pleasure, he had concentrated on Judith, two beds down from Mary-Joy.

Judith was barely eighteen, a Jewish girl snatched from a settlement in Gaza two years before. She and Mary-Joy had struck up the nearest thing to a friendship that could happen in captivity. Judith tried to observe the tenets of her faith whenever she could, and would swap out pork or seafood from her plate in exchange for vegetables from Mary-Joy's. Judith would sleep with her head covered by the sheet to observe a tradition she was denied observing during the day. She was a gentle-minded and kind young woman who Mary-Joy would have felt naturally drawn to in any situation. So when Parrish's attentions had switched to Judith one night three months ago, Mary-Joy had explained to Judith—because she felt she could trust her—what she had found at the base of the compound wall, and what she intended to do with it.

She'd been honest with Judith from the start, telling her she would not be able to follow Mary-Joy out of the compound. It was only a fifty-fifty chance that Mary-Joy would make it out anyway, but Judith's larger stature and chunkier frame made her escape from the camp impossible.

They had learned from Macy's attempted break that any further attempts involving guards, helicopters, and the Enchanted Forest would end in failure. Even if Macy's avowed intention was to die and she'd achieved that at least. But Mary-Joy knew that Macy had been caught way before she'd reached the ravine. It made getting out of the compound by stealth, at a time when the guards were otherwise occupied, imperative to the success of Mary-Joy's mission.

So Judith agreed to help in any way she could, even if it meant a trip to the punishment cages.

Through the corner of the only eye she dared open, the one nearest to the pillow on which her head lay, Mary-Joy held her breath as Parrish reached Judith's bed and sat his considerably-sized backside down on it. Judith would have been keeping herself awake in the same way as Mary-Joy. She shifted dreamily on the bed, and began to snore in the prearranged moment.

The snoring would have two outcomes Mary-Joy had planned: it would keep Parrish interested, as the more asleep a girl seemed to be to him, the more it drove him on to concentrate on expressing his black-hearted desires. The second outcome was that Judith's snoring would cover Mary-Joy's footsteps.

Not towards the door, but towards Parrish.

She moved quickly as Judith's pretend snoring snuffled and caught in her nose. Parrish's hands were already under the blanket. His head was bent, his eyes intent on the sleeping girl.

Mary-Joy hit Parrish on the back of the head with the rock as hard as she could. There was a popping sound that was not unlike the crackle of her snapping elbow, and a spray of blood. Parrish fell face first onto the bed. Judith, eyes open now, head out from under the blanket, helped Mary-Joy lower the fat guard's body onto the floor. His eyes were half closed, the pupils had rolled up to white, and his eyelids were fluttering as if there was activity in his brain that was confused and random.

The rush of adrenaline in Mary-Joy's frame was shattering. Her heart was leaping and she couldn't believe the sound of it would not wake the other sleeping girls.

But it didn't. Or if the girls were awake, they didn't show it. Understandably the other inmates of D-Wing would know that any sense they were involved in this break out would lead to punishment and even death. Those who *were* awake, Mary-Joy reasoned, were laying paralyzed by fear or indecision. That suited Mary-Joy's plan too. A mass break out would raise too many guards and security in the compound. Mary-Joy wanted to get to the wall unnoticed.

Blood continued to pump from the shattered wound in Parrish's skull. Mary-Joy reached down to the guard's belly strained belt, pulled his pistol from his holster and lifted the bunch of keys from the hook where they hung, glinting in the moonlight coming through the high, barred window by Judith's bed.

Mary-Joy felt a hand on her shoulder and the shock was enough for her to turn savagely, with the rock she'd used to poleax Parrish held high.

Judith smiled.

The hand was hers.

She leaned forward, kissing Mary-Joy on the cheek and then whispered in her ear, "Go. I'll give you ten minutes to get clear then I'll raise the alarm. I'll say I just found him like that. I'll tell them he slipped. Hit his head on the floor."

"Thank you."

"Come back for me."

"I will."

Mary-Joy knew she had to. There's no way she could kill Rosa if she did not.

Mary-Joy saw the island pig's burrow from the closest chalet window in Charlotte's room, yet Charlotte took no notice of Mary-Joy now that she was already finished with her. Charlotte was laying on the bed, breathing hard, still in the throes of orgasmic aftershock. She was 58, thin and bony, her ribs showing through. She'd lost a breast to cancer at some point in her life and there was a livid mastectomy scar across her chest. Her fingers were long, bony, and cruelly tipped with witch nails. Mary-Joy was forced to spend hours between Charlotte's legs, wrists pulled painfully as the thin disfigured woman used the

Filipino's position to grind and sweat on her. Mary-Joy could spend that time floating away back to Benjie and the book, or once she'd noticed the island pig's burrow, plan for how she would use it.

She didn't know how long it would be before the Owners and their guards found the island pig's breach—so her plan would have to come to fruition very soon. She couldn't risk drawing attention to the burrow during the day by going to it, so would have to risk a onetime opportunity to go there after escaping the dormitory on D-Wing.

That evening, the last of Charlotte's on the island, she requested for Mary-Joy to join her at the chalet. Mary-Joy had almost yelped in happiness at the call. She knew that once Charlotte had finished with her, she would get a chance to see that the burrow was still there in the scrubby weeds growing up against the wall.

And it had been.

Using Parrish's keys to get her out of D-Wing was easy enough, but carrying the unfamiliar weight of the pistol was not. She had no idea how to use it for real, but figured she'd need it once she got to the landing stage and the steamer.

The compound beyond D-Wing was quiet at 3:30 a.m. — there was enough moonlight for her to move in the shadows it cast, but it was still dark enough to provide cover.

She skirted E-Wing and jogged in a deep well of shadows toward the guest chalets. Lights were on in some windows, and she could hear music playing from a few of them, where partying long into the night was not unknown.

The silhouette of a man standing with his back to an open window was talking with animated ferocity into a cell. "I don't care. I wanted that girl. Not a different girl. That girl. Egypt got in the way – for the last time. Find them both, and kill them both. I want to see Egypt's dead face. Make it happen."

Mary-Joy continued past the window, ducked down to the grass. Death was a constant companion on the island, and it didn't surprise at all it was reaching its chill fingers back to the mainland.

The edge of the perimeter wall behind the chalets was fully in shadows and providing excellent cover. Mary-Joy moved on, keeping low, the gun heavy in her hand.

"Hey!"

She froze. Dropped. The dry grass digging into her eyes and nostrils.

"Who has the gak?"

The accent was British.

A man, in his late '40s maybe, stripped to the waist. With his belly draped over the belt of his pants, lilywhite and bloated, he strutted towards Mary-Joy.

There was a black liquid smeared on his chest that in the dark Mary-Joy couldn't tell was gravy or blood. He would be on her in seconds if he carried on and she bunched her muscles, ready to get up and run. But without warning, he jumped up onto the veranda of another chalet and approached the door. He hammered on it with his fist with a furiousness that was bound to wake everyone up, and might even bring guards to investigate. He was no more than fifteen yards from where Mary-Joy was laid, hand shaking on the butt of the pistol, heart yammering, knees trembling.

"Come on y'fuckers! I want the gak. We've run out!"

The chalet door opened, and a woman in her '30s, her hair awry, and her body naked except for stiletto heels, appeared in the slice of red light from within.

"Fuck's sake, Phil. Why do you always use more fucking

gak than is humanly possible?" British too, and pissed off to the max.

She slapped a small plastic packet in Phil's hand.

"Now *fuck* off. We're busy."

"Cheer's babe," and with that fat Phil turned with his prize and waddled back to the chalet next door, opening the door with a rebel yell and running inside like someone doing a lap of honor after a race, holding the packet aloft like a sports trophy.

When she had calmed enough to make her legs move, Mary-Joy got to her feet and ran toward the back of Charlotte's chalet. The windows there were pleasingly dark. Once Charlotte had finished her activities with Mary-Joy, she always fell into a deep sleep. Mary-Joy would, like tonight, get dressed and turn off the lights in the bedroom. She would then call the guards from the chalet telephone, as she was ordered to, and then they would escort her back to D-Wing.

Mary-Joy thanked whichever god was looking over her now, keeping those windows dark. The same gods who made Phil unable to see her hiding in the shadows.

She jogged past the chalet to the place by the scrubby bushes where she knew the island pig's burrow was hidden.

Moving forward, she inched between the branches on her hands and knees. So close now. So near to the route of escape that would take her out of the compound, onto the island and the short journey across the fields to the dock.

She was so nearly out she could almost taste it.

And that's when the world exploded.

14

The island pig hit Mary-Joy at full force, its tusk digging into the flesh of her shoulder, ripping the skin apart as its trotters beat at her chest and she went down.

The pig trampled over her, its back legs kicking down on her forehead, the sharp toes ripping out her hair and scratching deeply into her skin.

The gun had been spun from her fingers by the smack of the impact, and she was winded. But it was clear she wasn't being attacked; the spooked animal was just getting away from her. She hadn't seen it hiding in the bush, and faced with turning its back on her to go into the hole, the pig had chosen to squeal and rush at her.

She could hear its diminishing trotter beats under the sound of partying from the chalets, and she could still smell its hot animal aroma in her nostrils, ripe with fear and panic.

Still laying on her back, trying to regain her breath, Mary-Joy explored the wound in her shoulder which was starting to throb and ache.

The wound wasn't deep but it was jagged, and the blood was coming freely. She could feel it running down her arm and pooling in the scars around her elbow.

Mary-Joy applied pressure to the wound and sat up. She had nothing to cover the wound or protect it. Even if she tore material from her pajamas she had no way of holding it in place. She had to hope that in the heat the blood would coagulate quickly and hold until she had an opportunity to find a bandage.

It occurred to her, as the breath returned and her heart reduced its frenetic drumming, that she was lucky the wound wasn't so savage that she would have had to give herself up to the guards to save her life.

Small mercies.

Very small mercies.

Mary-Joy reached out, picked up the gun and held it tightly, then tighter—trying to blank out the pain in her shoulder, but squeezing the warm metal as hard as she could. As a distraction it worked for a time. She got back onto her knees and pushed on through the undergrowth at the base of the wall. There was enough loose earth around to suggest the pig had been doing more burrowing that evening. The air was rich with the smell of disturbed earth, and Mary-Joy felt the fragrance spurring her on.

The entrance to the hole was just less than a shoulder width, but Mary-Joy wasn't going to let that stop her from diving head first into it. If she shifted one shoulder then the next, she made progress down into the darkness. Her mouth and nostrils were clogged, she felt fresh mud digging into the wound on her shoulder, but even that pain was not going to stop her. Sharp stones scraped into her side as she wriggled. Her knees barked against the edges of broken rocks which felt like broken glass.

She pushed forward, banging her forehead against low

hanging roots, where the bloody scratches caused by the pig's feet stung and protested.

The bottom of the burrow was slick with pig dung and urine, but she squeezed on, elbows digging in, knees pushing and her belly scraping.

When the blessed moment of relief came, as the tunnel started to turn upwards on the other side of the wall, Mary-Joy felt like yelling like Phil going back into his chalet with his prize of drugs.

But instead she struggled on silently, pulling with her hands, laying the gun down and pushing it along with her chin. In many ways this was another journey that her time on the garbage field had prepared her for.

Often she would have to dive down into the filthiest holes to retrieve a circuit board or a broken phone. She'd had to put up with the slime of rot and the stench of human bodily waste covering her skin with no facilities to wash until she got back to the open sewer outside her shack. Crawling through a hole dug by a pig was a happy holiday compared to the humiliations and survival necessities of the garbage dump.

First one hand, then a shoulder, then the other hand and then her head made it out into the open on the other side of the wall. She threw out the gun, hauled herself up and out.

She'd made it.

This side of the wall was well lit by the moonlight now. Anyone passing on the way to the Enchanted Forest or any Guard Patrols in their Humvees would see her without question. Mary-Joy hauled her exhausted frame up and crawled beyond the line where the edge of the jungle on this side of the island began.

It was only when she lay down again among the vegetation, and felt the wave of listlessness overcome her, that she realized that the injury to her shoulder was worse than she'd initially thought.

The blood loss it had caused was also about to rob her of her consciousness.

It was still dark when she woke.

The moon was still high in the sky, and there was a mist rolling from the fields that have been cleared between the compound and the Enchanted Forest. The mist was bringing tendrils of fog here to the edge of the jungle.

Mary Joe's shoulder hurt to high heaven. Her head was woozy, and the roils of exhaustion that were still washing through her body, told her gently to put her head back into the soft earth and to drift off into blissful sleep again.

What could be so urgent that she couldn't sleep? At least for a few more hours?

Mary-Joy sat up with a start.

She didn't know how long she'd been unconscious, but the way her body felt, it could only have been minutes. Perhaps she hadn't noticed the mist when she'd crawled out of the hole and collapsed. She'd been so intent on getting to the jungle that her focus had been totally in another direction.

The siren started then.

Spotlights from the control towers came on, scanning the interior of the compound, blasting above it. Mary-Joy got to her feet. There was no time to give into the pain or the exhaustion. She must get to the dock, now, or all was lost.

The dock, such as it was, was a metal-framed, timber-covered jetty that ran from the rocky beach out to the deeper water of the bay. At the beach end it led up to a cinder path which joined the twisting road leading up through the jungle to the compound. Mary-Joy's journey through the trees and undergrowth had been swift, although it might have been faster if she wasn't in so much pain or with a head woozy from blood loss.

The tear in her flesh from the island pig's tusk had stopped bleeding now. The wound was filled with dirt which fortuitously had decreased the coagulation time of Mary-Joy's blood, operating as a kind of cap over the wound. Occasionally fissures would open in the surface of the plug. Dots of muddy blood would seep up, but there was never an extensive repeat of the original flow. Mary-Joy wondered if her time on the garbage fields had exposed her system to all of the infectious bacteria the world could throw at her, and that she would be able to ward off infection better than someone who hadn't grown up the way she had?

Mary-Joy almost allowed herself a smile at yet more evidence that her horrific and awful life before coming to the island had prepared her for this moment, in more ways than she ever could have imagined.

The jetty was empty. No guards. No one.

There were some rusty oil drums at the beach end, and a small open shack that would have provided shade for the guards if they were there.

When Mary-Joy had arrived four years ago, the dock had looked much the same, except that it was bustling with guards and crewmen from the steamer. The boat was a large rusty hulk of a thing, the name on its bow obscured by years of neglect. Rust stains streamed from the bilges over the once, long ago, firetruck red hull. The central smokestack belched black fumes as it had made the 12-hour journey from the mainland. There were only five or six crew. The Captain had looked down into the hold just the once to see that the manacled girls were still alive and well. As he had done so, his peaked cap fell off his head into the water that ran around the girls' legs.

A crewmember, hard-faced and unshaken in a dirty, stained once white uniform, had splashed down into the hold to retrieve the cap. He'd belted Mary-Joy a sharp back-hander across the chops for the sheer hell of it before taking the cap back up to his Captain. That had been their only interaction with the crew before arriving at the jetty and the island.

Once tied up, Mary-Joy and the other captives had been herded down gangplanks, manacled together by their wrists. After that, they'd been made to walk the mile and a half to the compound in the midday heat, not given drinks or rest. The road up the compound was steep and exposed, offering no shade until it got near to the compound. There, the road wound through a section of jungle before arriving at the gatehouse.

Mary-Joy had been stronger than all the other girls combined, and had all but carried the ones manacled to her. The thin girl from Manila was on the verge of collapsing from malnutrition and being made to walk in the heat.

Mary-Joy had never learned her name and never saw her again within the compound. Perhaps she'd expired not long after arriving. Mary-Joy never found out, and in those initial months had been too afraid to ask.

Mary-Joy left the cover of the trees at the edge of the beach and walked down to the jetty, the pistol still hot and heavy in her hand. She assumed the area wasn't permanently manned because it didn't need to be, once everyone was up in the compound security was tight enough—or so she reasoned was the Owners' collective thought. That made keeping a guard patrol at the jetty a waste of resources. Also, any passing ships or boats would assume the island was deserted. The Owners obviously didn't want to announce their presence.

What Mary-Joy's plan needed was a place to hide until the steamer came in with its latest batch of slaves. She didn't yet know how, but she'd then find a way onto the steamer, and insert herself into one of the two life boats or below the decks until it went back to wherever the airstrip was on the mainland.

What she would do then, she had no idea. At least now she'd made it here, and the steamer would be due tomorrow morning. She just had to wait out twenty-four hours and take her chance. It was massively risky, but looking at the gun, she thought that at least she might be able to defend herself if discovered.

What she would do after that was anyone's guess.

Mary-Joy jumped down below the jetty. It was cooler out of the sun, and the water looked inviting.

She never had the opportunity to learn how to swim in her short and difficult life, but even so she only had a slight wariness of water. She waded out confidently, to where the seaweed-draped iron piles of the jetty were sunk into the seabed. The metal frame was encrusted with barnacles and other crustacea. The shells bit into the skin of her hand as she hauled herself forward, keeping the gun out of the water, kicking her legs and making progress with just one hand.

Seawater bit into her wounds, washing the plug of earth from her shoulder, but the bleeding was over for the most part, and the saltiness of the water soon became a soothing balm. Mary-Joy hoped the water would wash its salty anti-septic powers throughout the torn wound.

She carried on like this until she reached the end of the jetty. The gun was still dry, her feet no longer touched the seabed. If she had nothing to hold onto, she'd have to learn how to swim pretty fast. Luckily there were enough barna-cled iron spars to grab for.

There was a small metal ladder reaching down from the frame above her head. As the swelling but gentle waves bobbed her up and down, she thought the ladder would make it easier to get up towards the steamer when it came in tomor-row. There was also a small iron ledge three feet from the surface of the water. Reaching up, she was able rest the gun on it, and then have both arms free to cling to the iron spars.

She hooked her leg through one, and her arms over another, wedging her backside into the triangle between two spars. She was hot, thirsty, and exhausted, but exhila-rated by her progress.

Mary-Joy had given herself a fighting chance.

She fell asleep with the ghost of a smile on her lips.

———

Mary-Joy awoke at dawn. She'd jammed her body well enough between the spars to have stayed still all night. The gun was still on the ledge, and she had not been discovered. There was, however, a huge rusting wall of metal heading towards her, the sound of a clanging ship's bell and the steady THUB THUB THUB of the steamer's engine.

The exhaustion was still the most prevalent feeling in her body, but she knew she needed to wake up fast. The steamer was coming alongside the jetty, and already the waves from its bow were more frequent and powerful. As it came in to dock, the waves it pushed might reach all the way up to the ledge where the gun was resting out of the water.

Mary-Joy pushed herself forward in the wash. Where the top half of her body had dried out already, the shock of dipping the wound back into the salty water sent a white bolt of pain through her frame. Mary-Joy ignored it. This would be her only chance, and she had to take it. She hauled herself up the ladder until she was again well clear of the water. She reached down to the ledge to retrieve the pistol. She climbed up, hooking her gun arm around a rung and pulling up with the other.

The wall of rusted metal was almost alongside. She could hear shouts and feet running about on the wood above.

The realization she hadn't been woken in the night by guards searching the jetty slammed into her hard. Perhaps the Owners thought she *couldn't* have escaped the compound. Perhaps they thought she was still hiding within the compound. Maybe they hadn't found the hole outside of Charlotte's chalet...

This notion flooded her with a sense of freedom which swelled through her heart.

If the guards weren't looking for her out here, then maybe there would be an even chance of getting onto the steamer, offering a real chance of getting off the island.

Gangplanks were crashing down above her. More feet. Shouts. "Get up! Walk now!"

And then a female voice. Full of anger and hate. "Fuck. You. I'm Lainey *fucking* Ralston and you do not treat me like this you worthless cocksucker!"

Mary-Joy winced as she heard the slap, the snarl of a man and the terrified scream as the girl who had been hit, tumbled off the jetty and fell straight into the water.

15

"We believe our daughter is dead. We thank you for your service, Ms. Durant. Mr. Crane will deal with your invoice. Thank you again."

Passion sat in Huey Ralston's office, trying to keep the shock leaping out of her face and slapping the political aide across the chops. She scrambled internally to batten down the hatches and stop her contempt from leaking. Ralston looked hollowed out, gray and thin.

"Mr. Ralston, you can see from the messages on the cloned phone used by Lainey in her Pippa profile that she was being groomed by Jake. She'd agreed to meet him on the day she disappeared."

Crane put a hand on Huey's shoulder and said, "That was obviously Gary Malcolm too," as if that explained everything.

Crane squeezed Ralston's shoulder, then walked to the office door. He opened it swiftly, the implication clear. Passion was to leave, and she was to leave *now*.

"I spoke with Gary Malcolm twelve hours before he died..."

"Committed suicide. From remorse." Crane's voice was steely and the subtext was that he would brook no disagreement.

"That boy was gotten by the people who took Lainey. I'm sure of it. The operation to take your daughter, Mr. Ralston..."

The other man in the room, Detective Myer, sat quietly in the corner, brushing invisible lint off his pants. He stood up. "Ms. Durant, Houston PD takes a very dim view of outside agencies like yours working towards your own ends, cluttering up an investigation. We're satisfied that Gary Malcolm committed suicide; the autopsy is conclusive. The suicide note is genuine, and now that we have a *body*..."

This hit Passion like a whip crack on a frosty morning. "You have a *body*? When...?"

Myer indicated to the door, Crane coughed and Ralston, rubbed at his eyes. There were tears there.

Myer continued, "We're keeping the details out of the public domain for the moment. We want to ensure a correct identification, and we're aware how grief stricken the Ralston family is at this time. We understand why you were engaged and do not blame Mr. Ralston for his attempts...his *understandable* attempts to keep his family issues out of the media, but your work here is now done. Please leave this to...the professionals."

This news that a body had been found continued to hit Passion with rapid thuds to the heart. Blows that brought her straight back to the warehouse and the girl Bianca, who'd hung herself rather than be the subject of whatever depravity her captors had planned for her. Then *someone*— some unknown vigilante—had gotten to the kidnappers first. Torturing and murdering them was still a huge question mark over the death of the girl in Manila. Added to that the disappearances of four previous daughters of rich and powerful men that Passion had investigated to no avail in the last year, and it made her feel a sudden rush of vertigo at the loss.

Not *again!*

But this time, none of it added up.

None of it.

Passion was sure that Lainey had been spirited away by Fake-Jake. Gary had been forced to write that note. He *must* have.

The evidence, circumstantial though it was, pointed in that direction. Any fool of a detective could see that; anyone with a brain in their head. And yet now, she felt like she was in a meeting with the Stepford Husbands. The father, the PA, and the Detective all telling her that they were convinced Lainey was dead and the case was closed.

It didn't make any sense.

Myer pulled a smartphone from his belt holster and thumbed the screen. He held the device up to Passion, but ensured the screen and its upsetting image couldn't be seen by Ralston or Crane. "Ms. Durant, I took this picture myself last night. I'm sure you'll understand why I haven't shown it to Mr. Ralston yet."

The screen was an image of horror.

A body, bedraggled and dressed in black fishnet-covered clothes, with huge Goth boots on its feet. The dyed black hair full of wet weeds. The pale, waterlogged skin across the face and neck puckered and chewed by what looked like machinery. The flesh opened up to the elements in ragged chunks of red, the pearls of bone breaking through as the jaw exposed beneath.

The girl had died hard.

"We're waiting on DNA and formal identification from

clothes and possessions. But initial indications are that this is Lainey Ralston."

A brutal sob shuddered from Ralston's lips. His head fell into his hands, and tears began to trickle down his nose falling onto the blotter on the desk. This was a broken man.

Stephen Crane pulled the door wider. "Leave. Now."

Outside in the corridor, once the door was closed, Passion rounded on Crane, who had followed her out. "This is bullshit, and you know it."

"Ms. Durant..." Crane's eyes burrowed into her like black lasers, "...*née Valdez*. Let me be very clear. You were brought onto this investigation to assist the family to maintain its hard-won privacy. The discovery of the body has transmuted that desire to a sadly moot endeavor. We thank you for your efforts."

It hadn't been a fluke then.

Crane did know her real identity, her real name. Did Ralston? Did Myer?

Passion made the quick calculation that it would not be political to either confirm or deny that Crane's information— wherever it had come from—was correct. To do so felt amateur and would give too much away. Perhaps there was a simple explanation. Perhaps Ralston's prominence in the political sphere gave him access to information held by whatever NSA, CIA, or FBI files there were on the Agency and its workings.

Or perhaps it was more complex and she would do well to keep her powder dry until she had more information. Perhaps Crane was the kind of man who enjoyed wielding power, loved showing that he knew more than the person he was dealing with. Perhaps he'd made the mistake revealing his hand so early. Maybe this was a chink in his armor, not one in Passion's.

She smiled, "Okay, I'm sorry. I'm just as shocked as

anyone that Lainey is dead. I really thought I had a chance to find her."

Crane's smile was like that of a wolf singling out a lame deer. "We're all terribly shocked too."

His words had no connection to the expression on his face.

"Please tell your superiors to invoice at the earliest opportunity, and we will ensure a swift payment, for the time spent on the case. Whatever it was you did, which I gathered from your reports, was very little."

Again, he was trying to make her rise to the bait. Passion wasn't playing. "We didn't really have time to build up the momentum needed, I apologize if our service was less than satisfactory."

Passion could see that Crane was enjoying watching her turn onto her back, put her paws up and offer her belly in supplication. Men like Crane loved winning. Men like Crane hated losing.

It was something that she might be able to use to her advantage, because if anyone thought she was giving up on Lainey Ralston, then they had another thing coming.

Driving away from the Ralston residence in the Hyundai through the raging Texas heat, Passion drove without purpose in a random direction—mirroring the thoughts in her head. She was heading towards the city, yet she didn't have a direction in mind. She didn't know where she was going to go next, or who she should speak to.

Passion needed to get her thoughts in order, and she needed to do it fast. Only with that in mind could she make a plan of action that would keep the investigation on track until she was certain Lainey Ralston was either really dead, or could be found alive.

Passion reviewed what had just happened. Her anger boiling, to the point where the world outside would need air conditioning just to stand next to her.

The result of that meeting was not how Passion envisioned it.

She had initially assumed she'd been called to the residence to give a face to face update. Her remote updates had been passed to Ralston through Crane. She'd assumed the politician was the kind of hands-on guy who would occasionally want to have a same-room meeting. It wasn't unusual. Once the shock of a family member going missing subsided, typically the father started to recover his sensibilities. The commanding, business-focused side of his personality overcame the acute grief and shock. When that happened, they invariably would start to think they could direct the operation better themselves.

Passion understood perfectly well where that notion came from.

These men were used to leading and making decisions. They wanted to be useful, to contribute. They really thought they could, when in reality, they were taking Passion from the vital investigative work to come to their offices and service their egos. It would only take a few face-to-face meetings to placate them, make them feel their suggestions were worthwhile and that they were getting their money's worth by employing the Agency.

Passion thought that this is what Ralston was doing, but when she'd been presented with the broken man sitting behind his enormous desk and tried to reconcile that with the image of Ralston as a strong, confident businessman and politician, the two personas couldn't have been further apart.

Ralston now had the look of a man from whom someone had unscrewed the cap of his resolve and had allowed it to leak out all over the floor. Crane and Myer had been the leaders in that room.

Ralston had just been a bit player.

Could that really be because of the news of finding a body? A body with no face? Passion's RADAR was spinning and blipping—there was something about that whole situation that didn't ring true.

Crane and Myer thought they could play her for a fool.

Gary Malcolm was *no* killer.

And if Malcolm was no killer, then that body need not be Lainey. It just needed to be *a* body to end the investigation. That body could have been anyone, any missing runaway girl that no one cared about—dressed up, strangled, de-identified with a boat propeller and dumped in the river for anyone to find.

It was *all too neat*.

What would Ralston and the others gain from ending the investigation in this way? They had to be sure the real Lainey Ralston wasn't coming back from the dead.

And who the hell was Fake-Jake? Why had he spent months grooming the girl if it was just for a one night kill? That kind of investment in time and energy for a single murder just didn't add up.

Passion could feel the tectonic plates of something huge below the surface of all this rumbling and creaking. She couldn't as yet guess the cause of it, but the shape of it was there—black and jagged.

Perhaps Fake-Jake had targeted Lainey to get to Ralston, and that had caused them to agree to close the operation down. It had to be a high level conspiracy if Ralston could get Myer and Houston PD to either be involved at an intrinsic level or be so stupid as to buy the "dead girl without a face" thing...

Passion's smartphone rang, and she thumbed the steering wheel control to instruct the Bluetooth to take it to speaker.

"I have something for you."

It was Bryan.

Passion decided against telling Bryan that she'd just been kicked off the case. Well not until she had the information he was about to give her at least.

"Our people have traced the cell number Jake was using to communicate with the girl."

Our people was the cozy euphemism The Agency used for their contacts within the NSA and FBI, occasionally those links would come up with gold dust; and it seemed like now they had.

"Since the day of Lainey's disappearance, the telephone has been switched on twice and connected to local cell towers. Not for long, but enough for us to triangulate a fix. The first occasion was in the vicinity—well a couple of miles from the Ralston residence. Possibly, the phone and Jake were on their way to the rendezvous with Lainey, and they were communicating. Those particular logs from the cloned phone, as you know, have not been downloaded to Malcolm's cell phone, which is why we don't have them."

Passion drummed her fingers on the steering wheel at Bryan's annoying propensity to beating around the bush. Bryan, she was sure, would call it thoroughness, but Passion just wanted him to cut to the chase.

"Yes, figures."

"The other time it came on, was yesterday morning at 9:37 a.m., and it was on for 24 seconds."

"That's not long enough to get a fix..."

"Normally no, especially out in the badlands of South

Texas...they are Badlands aren't they? I used that correctly, didn't I?"

"Whatever, Bryan, did we get a fix?"

"Oh yes indeed, Passion. The phone lit up cell towers like a Christmas tree."

"And?"

"Well, in some ways it's good news. Good, in the sense I have a location for you to investigate, maybe get some CCTV perhaps, maybe ID Jake and his accomplices. I mean, that's all very positive."

Passion felt her heart sinking.

"And the bad?"

"It was at the Roman Field Private Airport and Executive Transport Facility to the north of the city. From their website, they say they're the busiest Business Travel air facility in the Houston area. Thirty to fifty executive arrivals and departures a day."

"So if Lainey was taken there. She could be anywhere now?"

"That's about the size of it."

Shit.

16

The President had not been pleased with Bimala.

She had been returned to E-Wing by the guards. Her nose was bloody, her shoulder ached from the way the President had forced her arm so far up her back that she had feared at one point it would snap out of its socket.

Govindethi sada snanam Govindethi sada japam, Govindethi sada dhyanam, sada Govinda keerthanam

If it hadn't been for her prayer, then Bimala might not have been able to respond in the ways the President had complained to Carla about. He shouted into the chalet telephone that the girl was "Fucking useless. She's just lying there like a fucking doll! I paid for a willing girl, one who wanted to enjoy herself with me, not a lifeless piece of shit! I'm not a monster. I'm not a rapist! I want one who likes it!"

Carla had come to the chalet, and was full of apologies to the tall man, who stood in the corner of the room, his white shirt open to the waist, showing the paunch that was well hidden by the cut of his suit. His tie, hanging around his neck in two thin strands, his hands shaking with rage.

"I am so sorry, Mr. President, I will bring you a replacement immediately. I think Desiree has sufficiently recovered from your last visit for you to see her again."

"I've had her! I wanted a new one!"

"I can authorize a 50% reduction in your fee sir, if you'll see Desiree tonight."

The President ran his fingers through his sweaty hair. "Okay, okay. I'll see Desiree. Get this useless slut out of here."

It had been Carla who had bloodied Bimala's nose. Not in front of the President, but as soon as they'd gotten outside of the chalet.

The blow from the blond woman's fist had exploded with a bright cloud of pain and a red spray of blood, stunning Bimala and propelling her to her knees.

"I see my trust in you has been misplaced, girl. You need more training it seems. Training in looking like you're enjoying what they're doing to you. And your training will begin tomorrow. I shall take personal charge of it myself!"

Bimala was pulled to her feet by two guards and dragged back to the accommodation block where she was thrown onto her blanketless bunk. Once there, she sobbed herself to an uneasy and uncomfortable sleep.

"Bimala! Bimala!" called someone in the dream.

At first she had trouble placing it. It was like a ragged memory that tugged at the thoughts without becoming clear—as if it were something she'd tried hard to forget, but only came back in nightmares.

Aunt Chaaya. It was Aunt Chaaya.

Aunt Chaaya's voice was always too shrill and too harsh, Bimala had grown used to it over the years she'd been living with her and Uncle Bharat. Bimala tolerated Aunt

Chaaya, but she loved sweet Uncle Bharat as if he had been her own father.

Where Chaaya was cold and shriveled, Bharat was warm, forgiving, wise, and hilarious. Many evenings while growing up, Bimala would spend time in the Mumbai garden of the Professor and his wife—laughing, playing, and talking to Uncle Bharat. He would tell her about the flowers, their scientific names, and their medicinal qualities. "The pippali," Uncle Bharat said holding the small green, elongated cone between his fingers, "good for coughs, colds, and asthma."

He moved on to the small greenish brown berry-sized fruit on an amla bush, "A good rasayanam. Rasayanam means to purify and develop the seven constituent tissues of the body. The texts of the Ayurveda tell us amla is good for many ailments that upset the body. It will promote the healing of wounds and can even help with the symptoms of diabetes."

Bimala could listen to Uncle Bharat teaching her for hours. She never grew tired of his gentle voice, nor his measured tones. The knowledge spilled from him in generous waves. He was Bimala's most favorite person in the whole world.

Aunt Chaaya on the other hand would always break the spell when she saw Bimala in the garden with her husband. She would call from the veranda, bringing Bimala to the house to do her chores in the kitchen, or in her bedroom. Chaaya would stand over Bimala while she did her homework, and whenever Uncle Bharat would come in to see what Bimala was writing, Aunt Chaaya would say: "Do not interrupt her in her studies, you old fool. She doesn't want to listen to your nonsense!" And she would bustle him away from Bimala, as if she were jealous of any time they spent together.

"Bimala! Bimala!" In the dream Aunt Chaaya's voice floated though the memories like the smoke created when all of your favorite things were burned by someone who hated you.

Bimala's Aunt and Uncle never had any children of their own, and Bimala often wondered if that had been for the best. Aunt Chaaya treated her as nothing more than a house pet, and Uncle Bharat was often so busy with his work in the University faculty—where he was senior a Professor on the Board Of Studies in Education—that she wouldn't see him for days on end, especially as he became more senior and more esteemed and took on more responsibilities.

This left Bimala with school and home. As Bimala had gotten older, Aunt Chaaya had allowed the girl very little time outside her chores and studies to visit school friends or develop friendships. The house was in a suburb of Mumbai that was not necessarily one with a high crime rate, but not one where Aunt Chaaya thought a young girl "should be playing in the street with urchins. Who knows what might happen?"

So as the years rolled on and Bimala grew, her time with Uncle Bharat became more precious, and her much more intensive time with Aunt Chaaya more problematic. Whenever she did get time with Uncle Bharat, Aunt Chaaya would redouble her efforts to pull them apart. It was almost as if she were jealous of their relationship in some way. This possibility played on Bimala's mind so much, that on the day before her twelfth birthday, while Uncle Bharat was away at a conference in Europe, she approached her Aunt in the living room and asked, "Auntie, may I ask you a question?"

Aunt Chaaya sighed, and taking off her glasses, looked with piercing intensity at Bimala. "What is it, child? Can't you see I'm busy?"

All Bimala could see was that her Aunt was sitting down on the enormous patterned sofa, in front of their enormous TV, eating sweets while watching reruns of the supernatural drama *Naagin*.

If that was busy, then Bimala hated to think what being relaxed might entail. "Auntie, please, there is something I do not understand. When I was younger, Uncle Bharat would spend time with me in the garden, teaching me about flowers and the plants. He would read me stories, and we would watch TV together when we could. But now, it does not happen."

Aunt Chaaya tutted, "He is a busy man. He doesn't have time to waste on you, especially when you should be doing your chores or your homework. Now run along and clean the kitchen. I'm trying to concentrate."

"But I've cleaned the kitchen."

"The stairs then!"

Bimala's worlds came out in a rush. "But Auntie, please. I know Uncle Bharat is a busy man, but even when he does come to see me, or ask to take me to the garden, you say no. You send me off and keep us apart. Why is that? It is almost like you are jealous. Like you do not like us spending any time together. I miss my Uncle, and you do everything you can to keep us apart!"

Aunt Chaaya exploded from the sofa, shaking her hands in the air, muttering words Bimala could not make out. Her Aunt stalked towards her, face consumed with rage. She then did two things which Bimala was not expecting. First, Aunt Chaaya reached out to the front of Bimala's sari and squeezed the chest beneath.

Since Bimala had been eleven her breasts had been starting to swell. She knew all about puberty, and what to expect from the changes that would come to her body. The developing of breasts was just a part of growing up. They just existed. Bimala didn't really pay much attention to them, or the fuzzy, wiry growth of hair that was starting to spread across her groin. Just puberty. Just life. Nothing to worry about.

No one had ever touched Bimala's breasts before, and the shock of it happening was almost as upsetting as how hard her Aunt squeezed them, sticking her nails through the fabric of the sari and digging into the flesh.

The second thing Aunt Chaaya did, once she'd stopped sticking her nails into Bimala's breasts was she slapped the girl hard across the face.

Bimala spun away from the crack of the blow, falling against a metal framed occasional table, knocking over a vase of yellow and white Gerberas. The vase shattered, and the flowers scattered in a puddle of sugar water.

Bimala reflexively put her hand up to her cheek and raised her other arm in an attempt at protection as her Aunt stepped forward another pace. "Your Uncle is a man! You are no longer a girl! Young sluts like you cannot be trusted with older men! I've seen the way you look at him! I've seen the thoughts you have, girl! It's written all over your face. I'm not having his career and my life here threated by a disgusting jezebel like you! You keep your eyes and your titties to yourself!"

Bimala's overriding memory of the encounter was that she would have to look up the word *jezebel* when she got back to the dictionary in her room. She didn't know what it meant, and judging by her Aunt's use of it, it was not at all complimentary.

"Bimala! Bimala!" Aunt Chaaya's dream voice was coming closer, pushing its shoulders against the closed door of terrible memories, inching it open.

A hungry, ravenous voice. Getting to the meat of the dream.

Aunt Chaaya never mentioned the incident again, and

the Gerberas were cleaned up by someone else. That particular flower was never seen in the house again.

Bimala's twelfth birthday was a cold wretched affair, lightened only by a Skype call with Uncle Bharat. Bimala didn't tell him what had happened the day before, but she found herself involuntarily averting her eyes from her Uncle's direct gaze, just in case her Aunt was watching through a crack in the door or had found a way to hack into her laptop.

Finding out what jezebel implied hadn't improved Bimala's mood at all, and she spent the next few weeks keeping her head down—doing her chores, homework, and wishing she could tie her sari tight enough to flatten her breasts back to the original line of her chest.

They were the reason she was being kept from her Uncle according to her Aunt. And so, even though on a conscious level Bimala knew it was nothing of the sort, emotionally the young girl came to despise the shape of her growing body. She hated the hair, and the smell of herself —which also seemed to be changing—was ever present, however much she bathed.

Aunt Chaaya kept very much out of Bimala's orbit, as long as Bimala didn't try to spend any time with Uncle Bharat when he was home from conferences or from work. Whenever he joined Bimala to chat, she would make excuses and go before Aunt Chaaya could intervene.

Then one night, as Bimala lay in her bed in the sultry Mumbai heat, she heard her Aunt and Uncle fighting. Their words were clear on the still, sluggish humid air. There was no attempt for them to hush their voices; perhaps they'd been arguing for some time, but now it had spilled over into something much more serious.

"Have you not seen the way she looks at you?"

"Don't be ridiculous, woman!"

"I'm not being ridiculous! She's a snake! A snake in our house, and she wants to take you away from me!"

"For a woman so disinterested in sex, you certainly spend a lot of time thinking about it. For god's sake, woman! Listen to yourself!"

"And I've seen you. Don't think I don't know what you're thinking, you dirty beggar!"

Another vase smashed.

A door slammed.

Uncle Bharat's car started on the drive and drove away into the night.

Seconds later, Bimala's bedroom door opened, and silhouetted in the hall light was Aunt Chaaya. She didn't say a word, but Bimala could feel the green eyes of envy burrowing into her, right up until her Aunt shut the door and stormed back downstairs.

"Bimala! Bimala!"

In Bimala's island dream, Aunt Chaaya was calling her down from her bedroom.

Usually Aunt Chaaya's voice would be tinged with scorn and disrespect, like someone calling a cat that they didn't like, begrudgingly, to their food. But now there was a different tone to Aunt Chaaya's voice. It was gentle, beguiling even. She'd come to the bottom of the staircase to call up, instead of hollering from the living room.

Bimala got up from her desk where she was awaiting a Skype call from Uncle Bharat who was in America on a lecture tour, and went out onto the landing.

Aunt Chaaya was indeed at the bottom of the stairs, and in the dream Bimala remembered that it had struck her as odd Aunt Chaaya was smiling—it was not a facial expression Bimala was used to.

Now in the dream she was screaming at her other self. Yelling at her, banging on the glass of the dream world, separated from herself by two years and thousands of miles wrapped in the fabric of the dream.

She watched herself going down the stairs. She watched as Aunt Chaaya held out her hand and beckoned the dream Bimala down.

There is still time, Bimala called to herself. *Go back up the stairs! Lock yourself in! Wait for the call from Uncle Bharat; tell him about the man!*

But the Bimala on the stairs was not listening, she was going down to Aunt Chaaya, suspicious of the smile but not scared, not scared like her dream counterpart was.

In the hallway was a man Bimala didn't recognize. He was not someone who she had seen visit the house before. Not that many people visited, Aunt Chaaya saw to that.

Run, Bimala! Run! The dream girl yelled to her other self. But the Bimala at the bottom of the stairs could not be reached.

The man was tall but podgy.

His white linen suit was crumpled, and the sweat on his brown face made his skin shiny. He had a thick moustache, and his hair was wild and uncombed. He gave Bimala the impression of a street vendor, or a restaurant waiter. He carried himself on nervous prissy footsteps, fingers moving nervously around the brim of an ancient Panama hat held against his paunch. As he moved toward Bimala, both the dream girl and the past Bimala could see his fat pink tongue moving across his fleshy, cracked lips, like the tongue of a lizard.

Govindethi sada snanam Govindethi sada japam, Govindethi sada dhyanam, sada Govinda keerthanam.

His eyes were sparkling with lustful avarice as he pulled the handcuffs from his pocket.

"Oh yes, Chaaya, she is everything you said... and more," his voice stuffed with desire.

Too late. Bimala realized she was in danger, so as she turned, she heard...

Run! Run! Run now!

Aunt Chaaya was too quick for Bimala. The older woman grabbed the younger by the shoulder with one hand and by the pony tail with the other, pulling up harshly and lifting the girl's feet off the ground.

As the man approached with the open handcuffs, Bimala began to scream, and the dream girl banged on the dream glass, until her dream palms bled and the morning light claimed Bimala's sleep from the night and transported her from that hell to this one.

17

The Roman Field Private Airport and Executive Transport Facility was a modern, well-proportioned facility to the north of Houston—with one low, grey main administration block, a wide parking lot dotted with high-end sedans, limos, and SUVs. Gaggles of drivers were smoking or chatting to each other in clumps having just dropped off their charges, or in the process of waiting for people to fly in. There was a central control tower just a few hundred yards away from the main building. Beyond that, a row of three modern hangers set back from the airstrip—on which a smooth looking Lear jet was just touching down as Passion rolled the Hyundai through the gates at the entrance to the airport.

Passion noted a small glass-fronted concrete building next to the gate, where a security guard was watching the arrivals and departures, writing on a clipboard he held propped against his belly.

Passion parked up and putting on her best investigator's face ambled over the guard building, proffering a wave and a smile to the guard.

The name tape on his uniform told Passion his name was Clayton Morris. He was in his late fifties and reeked of ex-cop. He put the pen behind his ear and set down the clipboard as Passion reached the door. You could have used his grin to scoop shit out of the toilet and sell it for a profit at the county fair. He eyed Passion's body for an age before he raised his attention to her face. "Yes, ma'am?"

Passion wasn't fooled by Morris' surface level civility. It was just your average baseline creepy. She'd seen it honed to perfection in many cops and ex-cops over the years. They could say the words, but only one in a hundred would imbue those words with any genuine authenticity. She flicked open her purse and showed Morris her Texas Licensed Private Investigator shield which Bryan had waiting for her at the hotel. Morris' back stiffened and he straightened his shoulders, obviously unhappy this wasn't a damsel in distress call which might necessitate some serious down blouse action. "This is private property, ma'am. I'm gonna have to ask you to leave."

"You don't know why I'm here yet." Passion gambled that the two $50 bills that her fingers slid out from behind the shield wallet would catch Morris' attention as deeply as had the contents of her blouse.

"Well perhaps you don't have to leave just yet."

"That's what I was hoping," Passion said, passing one bill across, swiftly deposited into Morris' uniform pants with the practiced hand of a man who was used to taking the cream off the top of the milk.

"I'm investigating some matters related to the disappearance of Lainey Ralston."

This was another huge gamble.

Myer had indicated that Houston PD had kept the news of the discovered body out of the public consciousness so far. But being an ex-cop, Morris would know that if this had become a homicide investigation, then the last thing the cops would want muddying the waters would be a private detective, and so he'd be more likely to clam up. But the news of the body, if it had been released, hadn't reached yet reached Clayton Morris.

"A terrible business. Ralston has my vote for senator, that's for sure. A good man."

Cut to the chase. "I noticed when I drove in, you were taking note of my license plate. Do you do that for every car that comes into the parking lot?"

"I guess they'll have a machine to do that for them soon enough, Miss...?"

"Durant. Jennifer Durant."

"...Durant. Everything becomes mechanized in the end. But yet, we keep a record."

"Have you been working here all week?"

"Yup. I do seven days on, seven off. Then seven nights, alternating with Jim and Zane."

"We have reason to believe that a car was here some-time on Sunday morning at around 9:30. Would you have been on duty then?"

Morris nodded and eyed the other bill between Passion's fingers. "Would you be willing to tell me which cars came in here at that time, perhaps an hour before which left afterwards, say during the next hour?"

Morris flicked back a few pages in his logs on the clip-board, but didn't show the page to Passion.

"There were three cars in and two out in that time."

"May I see?"

Morris was taking his own gamble and Passion could see the greediness in his eyes wasn't just financial. She unbuttoned two buttons on her blouse, exposing the generous depth of her cleavage. "My goodness, I do declare it is hotter than hell today," she said in her best Southern belle accent.

Morris' eyes narrowed. He liked what he saw.

"The only car I didn't know was a 2011 Buick Lucerne, shit brown and dusty as fuck. Three men. They met at Gulfstream, arrival at Hangar Two. Three men in, three men out."

He showed Passion the log for Sunday morning, and she took her smartphone from her pocket and snapped a picture.

"Here's your other $50 for the information."

She handed over the bill and reached to do up her blouse.

"Oh you could undo a couple more buttons," Morris said his tongue moving dryly at the corners of his mouth and his eyes focused on the dark skin exposed between the fold of Passion's blue silk blouse.

Passion clicked the side of her smartphone. The whole conversation they'd just had—including Passion handing over the $50 bills—was recorded and filmed. "I wasn't taking a picture of the log sheet Clayton, the video was already rolling, it just allowed me to take the film of you accepting a bribe for your information."

Morris' face was red with anger, sweat was beading across his forehead.

"It was only when you started to look at me like I was a piece of meat that I decided to fuck with you, Clayton. Men like you really need to find a different way to operate."

"What are you going to do with the film?"

"Nothing. Nothing at all. Because you're going to let me drive over to Hangar Two, and you're not going to write about it in your log. Is that clear?"

Morris sank back into his chair nodding, arching his neck, with his hands shaking.

"The Gulfstream it met...who owns it, and where did it fly in from? Can you get me that information?"

Clayton didn't bother to nod. He just turned to a computer terminal, put in a password, and called up the records he needed. "A private company, Enchanted Holdings. Flying in from Nicaragua."

"A regular flight?"

"Yeah. Twice a week, sometimes more."

"Always met by the Buick?"

Morris moved back through the sheets on the clipboard. "No. Different vehicles and drivers. No pattern."

Passion shot video of the terminal screen and then—with the practiced hand of a woman who'd pulled this stunt on many oily creeps who thought they could ogle her for their own kicks—reached down, slid her hand inside Morris' pants pocket and pulled out the crumpled fifties.

Morris didn't say a word, and he didn't look at Passion again as she went back to the Hyundai to take the service road out to Hangar Two.

Passion parked the Hyundai around the back of the hangars so to not arouse suspicion. She walked in the killing heat, shielding her head against the sun, before entering the dusty shadows between hangers one and two, and made it around to the entrance. Hangar Two was dusty and hot as an oven in the afternoon sun. There were no ground crew in the back office, and no sign of cameras or security.

Planes continued to take off and land behind her, as she walked into the hot space. The concrete was covered in the dusty trails of tire marks. Some from cars, others fatter and more defined from the wheels of an aircraft.

The office at the back of the hangar was big enough for two people to sit and wait, with two office swivel chairs, a filing cabinet, a desk, a cold coffee maker on a ledge by the window.

Passion pulled the drawers of the filing cabinet out, but they were all empty, squeaking out on rusty runners. The drawers below the desk were empty too. Either the office had already been cleared of all paperwork, or the people who operated it didn't like anything put down on paper.

There was a calendar on the wall that was two months out of date, showing a picture of Miami lit up at night, but other than that the office was as anonymous as could be.

Passion came out of the office and went past the padlocked tool shed and through the rest room door. The stalls were empty, even the containers where someone finishing up at the sink would throw paper towels, had only three or four pieces of scrunched paper in the bottom of it. This was not a place that was used on a regular basis, which made finding the two thick clumps of silver duct tape laying on the floor of the middle stall all the more interesting.

Passion bent to pick up the chunk of tape.

It was still sticky, not covered in dust four layers thick, and when she turned it over in her hand she saw her first real clue of Lainey Ralston's fate.

Stuck to the inner adhesive surface was a raggedly torn piece of fishnet stocking. It looked as if it had been ripped straight off the leg it had been wrapped around.

Lainey had been here, Passion was sure of it.

She reached into her purse to pull out her smartphone to get to Bryan, when she heard the nearby whine of a jet engine in taxiing mode.

It echoed the length of the hangar. The acoustics changed at the sound of an aircraft rolling into the space outside the restroom, making the thin walls surrounding her vibrate.

Passion dropped the phone and the duct tape back into her purse and slammed her back against the wall, next to the door. The engine was still winding down; there was a hiss and clank as something within the engine stopped moving.

Passion edged the door open with a nervous finger.

Through the slit between the door and the jamb she saw the nose of a white Gulfstream.

The plane and its engines were still in wind down mode, and Passion figured it was probably better to make a run for it now, rather than try to brazen it out. Whoever was in the Gulfstream, if they were connected to Lainey's disappearance—and the subsequent conspiracy to fake the school girl's death—then they might know all about Passion. And that was an argument she didn't want to have right now.

Discretion being the better part of valor, Passion tensed her muscles and made ready to burst out of the door. She would run for the hills hopefully before the plane crew finished their post flight checks.

Best laid plans...

There was a muffled gunshot, and a bullet hole followed by a spray of blood exploding out of the cockpit window. Passion ducked, thinking that perhaps they already knew she was here, but the shot and the blood had come from *within* the plane, not from without.

There were three more muffled crumps as more shots were fired inside the fuselage.

Someone was doing some serious shooting in there. Another shot and another hole appeared in a window. Passion couldn't make a run for it now, not with the hangar turning into a weapon hot zone. She figured that whoever was shooting up the plane was mightily pissed at something. The first shot might have been an accident, but the four that had followed were most definitely not.

The door on the side of the Gulfstream hissed and opened; someone behind it operated the emergency inflatable exit ramp which blew out like a dashboard airbag and whumped to the floor of the hangar.

A man's voice said, "Please! Don't shoot!" Just before there was another shot and a spray of blood, bone and brains messily hit the ramp. Then a body in a pilot's uniform crashed out through the door, pitched over the side of the ramp and fell face first to the concrete. The pilot was already dead, but the fall killed him a second time, breaking his neck with a crack that shook the hangar.

Passion expected a seven foot, camouflage bedecked action hero titan to emerge from the doorway.

But it was a girl. A thin Asian looking girl, with a spray of blood across her chest and a SIG-Sauer in her shaking hand, was standing the doorway of the Gulfstream. Passion had to almost close her eyes and shake her head like a cartoon character recovering from a blow to the skull. The image was just too crazy, the gun looked so large and ludicrous in the girl's hand. The blood covering her looked something out of a creepy kid horror movie. Passion checked to see if it was coming from any wounds on the girl. It was not. That was all the blood of other people.

Oooookay.

The pint-sized hijacker had taken out someone in the cockpit, at least one other person in the cabin, and the guy in the pilot's uniform who'd done the face slam on the concrete below the plane.

The girl was looking in every direction, seemingly trying to make up her mind if it was safe to slide down the Day-Glo orange, brain-smeared, inflatable safety slide.

The girl got onto her backside in the doorway, and holding the gun up out of her way—as if it had been a practiced maneuver—slid down to the concrete.

She got up, and pointed the gun at the dead pilot just in case. But the next time he was going to move would be into a coroner's bag.

Passion then watched with mounting discomfort, as the girl wiped at the blood starting to congeal across her chest, and looking up, seeing the door to the restroom, jogged towards it.

Passion was in such an off the grid state of mind by what she'd witnessed she was not ready for this development at all, she spun away from the door, and headed for one of the stalls in a blind panic. The girl was homicidal and she was going to kill anyone and everything that got in her way, especially a witness watching her from the restroom.

But the girl was too quick for Passion, she'd already reached the door before Passion could close the stall and climb up onto the toilet.

"Stay there. Do not move." The girl's voice was accented and confirmed the Asian heritage of her eyes and skin. Passion raised her hands. Her own weapon was in her Ops bag in the back of the Hyundai. She cursed herself for being so careless and not bringing it into the hangar.

But this was no time for self-recriminations. *It was what it was.*

Passion turned just in time to see the girl raise the gun, point it at Passion's face and coolly, with dead, emotionless eyes, squeeze the trigger.

18

They were in a hole in the ground.

Thick tree roots moved across the rounded ceiling. The walls were dry mud, and the floor flagged with grey stones that were covered in spirals of dirt.

There was a bed on which she lay: a table, a chair, and a thick green velvet curtain hanging over the doorway. There was a hearth, but it was not for a real fire. In it was a radiator of thick enameled iron. There was a dial on the side, with two small lights, neither of which were lit. That was a good thing because this hole in the ground was already stiflingly hot.

The woman, who had a cumulous of grey white hair floating around her head, was dressed like something out of one of those stupid Tolkien movies Lainey's mom loved so much. She had a cloak. *A freaking cloak!* Thin leather boots and a waistcoat running with gold brocade above the sturdy corduroy britches covering her stick thin legs.

The sound coming from the woman's hands as she sat at the table was the first thing Lainey had noticed as she came out of the deep sleep, she'd been put into.

The last thing before this she remembered was being pulled from the water, back onto the jetty from which she'd just been propelled by a mighty slap. They pulled her to her feet, sodden and gasping next to the rusting steamer, hit her again for her insolence. Then one of the crew reached around from behind and put a cotton wool pad over her nose and mouth.

It had sent her into a dreamless, silent sleep. And although that sleep had probably lasted many hours, she did not feel rested at all when she woke up. It felt like the aftermath of a sleep brought on by a fever, as a gritty, out of focus consciousness seeped back in. Lainey felt dirty, sweaty, and thirsty.

The noise coming from the old woman's hands was the sound of steel on leather. Lainey blinked, trying to get her eyes to work properly on what was going on in the old woman's hands. As the images resolved, Lainey wondered if she was still dreaming and had woken up in a lame Renaissance Fayre, and the old woman was one of the idiots working in the craft tent. There was a leather-sharpening strap attached to the leg of the table, and the old woman was working a thin blade up and down in methodical strokes.

Lainey's father used a blade and a strap like that. He would swipe the blade back and forth on the leather until the straight razor sang with sharpness. When Lainey had been a little girl, she remembered watching her father sharpen his blade and then shave his lathered skin with the razor. She remembered the hiss and the swish, and the crackle of the whiskers as they succumbed to the cut of the blade.

The old woman didn't look up, she kept sharpening. Kept stroking.

Lainey tried to sit up, and that was when she discovered

her legs and arms were chained to the bed on which she lay. She looked down her body, at the silver shackles pinioning her ankles, and the thick cuffs around her wrists. There was a chain rattling beneath the bed as she moved her right hand, and she felt the pull of it on her left. She was chained to and *through* the bed. All she could do was raise her head and perhaps lift a shoulder, but that was the full extent of her movement.

The old woman didn't even look up as the chains rattled, as if the sounds didn't matter to her at all. The old woman knew that Lainey was entirely secure, she could get on with working on the blade. It didn't matter what Lainey did.

"Where am I?" Lainey's voice was thick with fear and felt trapped in her throat by the dryness of her mouth. She tried swallowing a couple of times, but it felt like the saliva in her mouth had fully dried up within her skull.

The old woman stopped and held the blade up to the electric strip light hanging incongruously from the ceiling of the dry, hollowed out hole. The blade glinted, sending shivers of light bouncing over the walls and ceiling. The old woman seemed satisfied, and put the blade down on a metal tray on the table, next to a wooden rack of test tubes.

The old woman got up, her face wincing with a sudden pain, breath escaping her lips in a hiss like a chill breeze through dry grass. She rubbed the small of her back and hobbled out of sight behind Lainey.

Lainey could feel the terror clapping in her heart as it panicked in her chest. Not being able to see the old woman was worse than watching her sharpen the razor. Lainey tried to bring her head around, but there was a tall wooden headboard, ornately carved with centaurs and unicorns, which her body was too close to see over. All she could hear was the old woman shuffling and the sound of her breathing.

Then something started to drag across the floor, and Lainey could hear exertion in the old woman's breathing. The definite sound of her straining to pull something into Lainey's field of vision.

Slowly, and with rising horror, Lainey watched with terrified eyes as the old woman came into view, dragging a chair as she hobbled backwards. The chair had been tipped over onto its two back legs and screeched over the stone floor, setting Lainey's teeth on edge.

The chair had a fat man tied to it. He was dressed in a black uniform. There was dried blood caked to the side of his head from a sizeable wound which Lainey, with rising bile in her throat, thought had signs of exposed bone in the center.

The man was conscious, his mouth covered in the same kind of duct tape which Daniel had used to bind Lainey's ankles and wrists. The man with the head wound had his arms taped to the back legs of the chair and his legs taped to the front legs. His eyes were swiveling in his sockets, and the terror broadcasting from his face entirely matched that which Lainey's guts were feeling.

The old woman seemed relieved that the chair and its cargo were now in a position for Lainey to see. She ruffled the top of the fat man's bloody head, and rolled her eyes as they came away sticky with blood.

She wiped her fingers on the man's shoulder until they were clean, and then in one swift movement pulled the tape from his mouth.

The man's voice came out like uncorked champagne. "Please, Rosa! Please! I'm sorry. She came up from behind! I didn't know she was awake."

The old woman, Rosa, spoke for the first time, "If you

hadn't gone to the dormitory for your extra-curricular activities so many damn times, Mary-Joy wouldn't have been able to predict your behavior and hit you with a rock! It's not just the extra-curricular activity that you're here to be punished for...it's your stupidity."

Her voice like the sound of a graveyard. It was winter branches snickering on a chilly wind, it was the crunch of footsteps over cemetery gravel, and it was the creak of a coffin lid being opened. In short, it was the most Goth sounding thing Lainey had ever heard in her time on Earth.

It was the sound of a nightmare come to life.

"Rosa! I'm sorry, *please*. Fire me. Send me back to the mainland. Anything. Just not this. You don't have to do this."

"Of course I don't *have to* Parrish, of course I don't. I'm doing it because I want to. It will serve two purposes tonight. It will visit upon you all the agonies your idiocy deserves, and it will be instructive to the audience."

Rosa lifted her head to the root gnarled roof, "Are we on? Carla?"

A tinny voice came from a speaker high in the ceiling amongst the branches. Lainey recognized Carla. "Yes, Rosa, everything is ready."

"And Mr. Ralston?"

Lainey's heart skipped several beats at the mention of her father's name.

Carla's tinny voice came again, "I am assured by Mr. Crane that the prospective Senator is all eyes and ears."

Rosa chuckled, "Which is more than I can say for Mr. Parrish in the next few minutes."

A groan escaped Parrish's mouth, the groan of pure defeat. He'd stopped straining at his bonds, his head had fallen forward until his chin rested on his chest. His lips started moving. Lainey had to strain to hear what he was saying under his breath.

It was the Lord's Prayer.

Huey Ralston was a man for whom the bottom had fallen out of the world.

His hands could not be still, his breathing was interspersed with sobs, his chest heaved with crying. He was on the verge of throwing up over the blotter and marble fountain pen holder that sat on his desk.

Crane had come into the room, and without a word had begun closing the drapes, so that without Huey's desk light on, the room would have been in complete darkness.

Myer had taken his customary seat in the corner of the room, his whole body now in a pool of shadows. Ralston could only see the occasional glitter from his quick eyes, or sometimes catch sight of the detective cleaning out of the dirt from beneath his fingernails.

Ever since his telephone call to the island—when Huey had thought he would plan himself a nice little relaxing mini-break in the punishment bloc—everything in his life had turned to shit and that didn't even include the kidnapping of his daughter.

Huey's past trips to the island to beat up on the captive slaves who had broken whatever rules Rosa and her band of Sado-Capitalists had deemed to have disobeyed, had been the highlights of his year.

But to hear Rosa, calmly and deliberately say, "There has been a change of plans. We have your daughter. She is here with us now, and we will be holding her against your continued cooperation," had side-swiped Huey like a baseball bat in the gut.

Rosa had made it abundantly clear that unless Huey did exactly what he was ordered to do by Enchanted Holdings, Lainey would be killed. Not only killed, but tortured and raped to death.

And yet, even that was not the worst of it.

Crane turned on the desktop projector. A white screen hummed down from the ceiling on well-oiled gears and clicked into place. The picture fuzzed, rolled and then became a solid image.

Rosa's realm.

Ralston had been into the Enchanted Forest on a number of occasions when he had visited the island in the past, but never had he been to Rosa's domain beneath the central oak.

He'd seen the massive tree of course, way off in the distance, rising from the center of the manmade forest. But like everyone else, he had been told not to approach it.

To break that basic rule would make it necessary for the transgressor to be ejected from the island, never to return. Like many other visitors to the island, Huey would go only so far into the Enchanted Forest to walk among the cool trees, feeling the sweat he'd built up from his pleasures in the punishment block—dry with a satisfying sense of evaporation on his skin. He would imagine those drying vapors as his own sins leeching away from his body, leaving him pure and whole again.

Of course he had to stop on occasion to vigorously pleasure himself while he thought back to the kicking, the punching, and the breaking. The busting of a young bone, watching it appear jagged and bloody from twisted flesh, as the screams of the young person resounded in his ears was the greatest aphrodisiac Huey had ever known.

If truth be told, the succession of blond bimbos he'd fucked during his marriage and before had been all so many pieces of misdirection. In the circles he moved in: the rich, the famous, the connected, it was expected. But it wasn't Huey's true nature. No. Any fool could get pleasure from sex, but it took a special kind of man to enjoy the particular good offices of De Sade.

He'd paid to beat women many times.

Professional submissives whose masochism was such that they enjoyed selling themselves to the men, and women, who would enjoy hurting them. It always left a bad taste in Huey's mouth. Not because he didn't enjoy it, but because it was all a game. There were agreed limits, boundaries over which he was not allowed to cross. As he made more of his political career, it had also become more imperative that he kept his desires to himself. Once his face started to appear statewide, and occasionally across the nation on TV, Ralston's visits to the pro-subs had necessarily dwindled to zero.

All his desires in that direction had to be met with pornography, and compared to what Huey really wanted to do to those girls, porn was very slim pickings indeed.

And then one day, Stephen Crane had come into his life, seemingly parachuted in from nowhere, with the promise to be the best political operator Huey could ever imagine. Although Ralston could not find any evidence to back up Crane's claims, other than stupendous recommendations from well-regarded GOP luminaries, who gave Crane the most glowing references.

From the start, Crane moved through Huey's personal staff like a tornado through a trailer park, firing nearly everyone and hiring his own people, introducing him to Myer, the useful detective who was forever on hand to smooth over any legal difficulties that Huey might encounter. Whatever reservations Huey might have had about the operation Crane was setting up were dispelled, as the poll numbers started coming in, as the incandescently positive editorials appeared. And the debates with his opponents went so well, it was almost liked they'd been paid to throw the match.

They had.

They'd been paid off, and they'd been neutralized as political opponents.

By Crane.

It was only when Crane told Huey about the island—specifically *La Isla Encantada* (the Enchanted Island), and that Huey's passions were already well known to the people who ran the facilities there—that the possibilities of becoming connected with the most powerful people on the planet became a reality.

"The People behind the People," Crane had called them. "These are the real movers and shakers, Mr. Ralston. They can give you whatever you want, whatever desire you want met. For a price."

Huey had always thought that he made a good fist of being rich and powerful. He wore the trappings well and played the role even better, but he soon realized he was a small fry compared to these people. *The People behind the People.*

"I can do anything?"

"Anything." Crane said. "Anything your heart desires. And there is absolutely no comeback, guaranteed."

The very idea sent fluttery jitters whizzing around his body like pinballs. The shiver of anticipation, and the edgy pleasures to be not just fantasized about, but made actuality.

"You are to be offered membership, Mr. Ralston. Your polling numbers are so good that the Owners of the island would welcome you among their number. It's not... er...cheap."

"I can't imagine it is."

"Membership fees are twenty million dollars US per year, plus five million dollars per day for your visit."

Huey had done a quick calculation in his head, say five visits a year plus fees amounted to $45 million. That represented somewhere in the region of one tenth of his gross income in a year. Well, one tenth of what he admitted to the IRS he was earning. In that context it was $45 million to do whatever he wanted, however he liked, to anyone he chose. It seemed like the steal of the century.

"First visit is of course complimentary."

And that had been the clincher which had pushed any last iota of doubt from his mind.

That first trip had been a whirlwind of depravity and a truly life changing experience for Huey. The blindfolded trip to the airport, the three or four hour flight—watches and smart phones weren't allowed on the island so it was difficult to tell—to what he guessed was a jungle airstrip in the middle of Central America given the flight time. Then the 12-hour trip on the rusty old steamer to *La Isla Encantada* had been the most exciting journey he had ever taken. Even the grubby cabin, two decks down with the blacked out portholes and desultory bed had not dampened his anticipation.

Once within his chalet—showered, fed and ready for a night of delicious torture, the blond Columbian Amazon Carla had arrived with an iPad loaded with photographs of the children and young women who were awaiting his attentions in the punishment block.

"House rules?" he'd asked Carla after he'd chosen the girl with whom he was to spend his first night on the island.

"Just don't kill her. The death of a subject will trigger a twenty million dollar breach of contract clause, which will have to be paid into our account before you will be allowed to leave the island."

"You can keep me here?"

"You think that we can't?"

"I just thought..."

"Of course you did. *Unthink* it. We bring close to one hundred girls here a year, from every corner of the globe. Runaways, abandoned girls, those in the care of the state, those in the care of uninterested relatives, those who no one would miss from the trash cities of the Philippines, to the daughters of rich and powerful men. Disappearing a man like you would not even move the needle on our personal seismographs. So, again house rules. Do not kill the girl. Are we clear?"

"Crystal."

The vertigo of that particular danger only added to the experience for Huey; it was an engine that drove him to the punishment block heady on the rarified air of ecstasy.

It was a feeling that had only been matched by the sound of the door of the punishment cage being shut behind him by the guard, and the slowly upturning face of the girl who seemed to know already exactly what he was there for.

In the end, he didn't kill Mary-Joy.

But it had been a close run thing.

And now, a year and five visits later, Huey was in his office, looking at a screen showing Rosa, a man he half-recognized taped to a chair silently praying to himself, next to a bed to which his only daughter was chained.

"Shall we begin?" said Rosa looking directly up into the camera.

19

"**N**o!"

Passion could do nothing to defend herself but close her eyes and shout.

The trigger clicked impotently three times.

The SIG was empty.

The bulletless gun didn't bring Passion a complete mitigation to the distressing situation. If the gun had been loaded, the girl meant to kill her, that was clear. But at least Passion was alive to explain to the girl that asking questions might be a better option than shooting first.

Just an idea.

Passion opened her eyes just as the empty gun smashed with full force into her shoulder.

The girl had thrown it at her.

The pain seared in a nova of agony as the gun bounced off her body and clattered to the ground. Passion clutched at her shoulder and loped out of the restroom after the girl, who had already turned and sprinted away.

"Wait! I'm not going to hurt you!" Passion yelled as she ran past the body of the dead pilot in the widening pool of blood beneath the Gulfstream. "Stop! Come back! I'm not going to hurt you!"

The girl's feet spun across the concrete crazily fast, her arms working and her head down as if she was about to use it as a battering ram. She ran towards the open end of the hangar; the nearer she got to the bright entrance, the more of a silhouette she became.

The girl was fast.

But Passion was faster.

Not a long distance expert by any stretch of the imagination, but Passion had a skill at sprinting over short distances. She competed at city level as a teen in Canada and had done well enough in the 100 and 200m races to attract the eye of a national scout. But as academic interests took over, and her mother's work took the family abroad to several diplomatic (read: spying) postings, Passion had given up the athletics for more cerebral pursuits. But now, years later, her lithe body was still strong and her speed across the floor more than enough to reach the girl before she emerged into the bright Houston afternoon.

Passion dove at the girl and brought her down with one tackle. They spun in the dust on the concrete base of the hangar, arms and legs flailing.

"Get off me!"

The girl punched and kicked in fury, but she was no match for Passion. Within a handful of heartbeats Passion was on top of the girl, knees pinning her arms down, backside firmly pressed to the girl's thin hips and tops of thighs so she could not raise her knees or feet to kick.

The girl could do nothing else, so she spat in Passion's face.

Passion raised her arm to strike the girl across the face to calm her down, but the ragged pain her shoulder from the impact of the gun made her bring the arm sharply down. The collar bone didn't feel fractured from the impact, but it hurt like hell. She was going to be stiff and bruised from the injury for some time.

The girl spat again, but this time Passion was able to get her head out of the way, and used the hand running from her good shoulder to push the girl's head over so that her cheek was against the concrete.

"Listen to me, you little shit. I'm not going to hurt you. Whoever you think I am, I'm not connected to the people who brought you here."

"No one brought me. I escaped!"

"Whatever. Just chill okay? I'm only holding you down so you can't get away."

"If you didn't mean me any harm, you wouldn't be holding me down!"

"Excellent logic kid, but I'm not letting you go just yet. I've seen that movie a dozen times and it doesn't end well. If you promise not to spit at me again, I'll let you move your head. Okay?"

The girl did nothing to respond.

"Okay?" Passion repeated, relaxing the pressure in her arm a smidge.

The girl nodded beneath Passion's palm and so her head at least was released.

"Okay, introductions. I'm Passion, I'm a detective and I'm looking for missing girls. Are you a missing girl?"

The girl's eyes widened. "You know about the island?"

"I know nothing about any islands. So let's get the basics out of the way. Name?"

"I am Mary-Joy."

"Pleased to meet you, Mary-Joy. Hey. Do you like ice-cream?"

Passion made Mary-Joy keep her head down as they drove out of the Roman Field Airport, past Morris' security hut and into north Houston. As the girl covered her head and lay down, Passion saw the network of scars around her right elbow. At some point this girl suffered a catastrophically horrific injury. The scars told a story on the girl's skin of agony and terror. Passion could only imagine what scars there were inside the girl's mind.

Passion found a drive-thru on an anonymous strip, got them both cokes and ice-cream, which they ate in the parking lot of an equally anonymous mall. The afternoon was cooling thankfully, as the sky was moving towards twilight. The blue sky being erased into deep purples, oranges, and yellows by the rays of the horizon-bound sun.

Passion didn't want to push the girl, but she still didn't trust her enough to take the child locks off the Hyundai's doors while the girl drank and ate hungrily.

"How long since you last ate?" Passion asked, passing Mary-Joy her half-eaten ice cream.

"I don't know," Mary-Joy replied between scoops. "Days. Three maybe."

When Mary-Joy had finished eating and had settled a little more, Passion asked her who she was and where she had come from.

By the time she had finished, Passion was breathless with admiration for the child's bravery, and sick to her guts to the state of the world they'd both been born into.

———

Mary-Joy had managed to get onto the steamer unnoticed as the commotion caused by the American girl falling off the jetty had turned all eyes in a different direction.

She'd climbed the metal ladder as high as she'd dared,

and jumped across to the rusting hull of the steamer holding the butt of the gun in her mouth. While the crew was progressing down the jetty with their captives, Mary-Joy tumbled over the side of the steamer onto the deck and sprinted to the nearest tarp-covered lifeboat. There were only two, one on either side of the rusty hulk, but it would do for the journey.

Mary-Joy had waited there six hours before the steamer set off again towards the mainland. The twelve hour trip had been quiet, and she had not been discovered. They'd arrived back at the jungle port just as night was falling. The five man crew had disembarked and gone to the shack to get drunk with the Gulfstream crew who were enjoying the sultry jungle night and were in high spirits.

Mary-Joy had made it to the Gulfstream without incident and waited. It was the most intensely sumptuous space the girl, brought up digging through trash to scrape a living, had ever witnessed. She had to mentally shake herself out of the shock of seeing such grandeur and excess in one small place. The leather, the TVs, the carpets, the bed. There was a bed! A bed *inside* an airplane! It was ridiculous!

Mary-Joy had never been able to measure the true distance between poverty and privilege before as acutely as she could now.

Her hands never touched such richness, even the smell of the Gulfstream interior—warm, fragrant, and lush with the aroma of newness—had made her heart beat in both wonder and rage.

But she knew these thoughts were secondary. She had to find a place to hide within the cabin, and she had to find it soon.

The next morning, the Pilot, his co-pilot, and the stewardess arrived on the plane. They had not bothered to check the storage racks beyond the wood-paneled galley and bed area. Mary-Joy had curled herself into the mahogany cupboard, pulling the door shut behind her. She draped a fur coat taken from a hanger above her head over her body.

Mary-Joy slept only in snatches, her hand always on the gun.

The Gulfstream had taken off, climbing steeply.

Mary-Joy pushed the door open a crack so she could see the length of the aircraft all the way to the cockpit door. The stewardess, a thin brunette in a blue uniform, had curled her feet underneath herself on a cream leather seat and rested her head on the window as the plane climbed. She was catching up on sleep. The pilot and co-pilot were laughing and joking in the cockpit, their voices carrying easily down the deadened acoustics of the fuselage.

Three hours later as the plane had landed, and as Mary-Joy heard the rumbling of the taxiing wheels on the tarmac of Roman Field, she had come out of hiding. As determined as she had been to take Parrish out of the equation in the dormitory, she needed to employ the same level of ruthlessness to escape the confines of the Gulfstream.

The stewardess was still asleep, not even waking up for the landing. Mary-Joy hit her with the butt of the gun, using the same ferocious force she'd used on Parrish. The stewardess didn't even groan. She slid to the floor, blood running freely from her hairline, down the side of her face and into the corner of her mouth.

Mary-Joy didn't pause, as she moved quickly down the cabin, its deep pile carpet completely suppressing the sound of her footsteps. The pilot and the co-pilot were talking about showers, sleep, and stopovers they'd had in past jobs. Beyond them, through the cockpit windows, Mary-Joy could see the aircraft was rolling off the airstrip, heading in a wide semi-circle that would take them towards three huge, open-fronted buildings that looked like barns.

The pilots were still oblivious to her presence, steering the jet, checking in with air-traffic control with niceties and politeness which entirely belied the operation they were part of. The normality of their conversation enraged Mary-Joy. The way they were behaving as if the flights they were taking were just part of the normal run of things. Mary-Joy could feel her limbs start to shake with anger—the bottled-up adrenaline suppressed by her escape finally being allowed to flood into her system. It was only now that Mary-Joy felt the enormity and injustice of what she had been made to endure flood through her.

The pain, the brutality, the rape, and the degradation. Being sold to a life that was worse than living on a garbage heap. A life of sexual slavery, physical harm, and psychological torture.

Mary-Joy was consumed then by that inequality, the huge power imbalance, and the sheer horror of what had happened to her. She didn't need to think about what she was going to do now.

It was clear. It was the only way.

As the Gulfstream rolled into the middle of the three buildings and the Co-Pilot turned his head to call down the cabin to the stewardess Mary-Joy shot him in the face. The back of the co-pilot's head came away in a cloud of blood and brain, the bullet sounding apocalyptically loud as the cockpit window was punctured.

The pilot had raised his arms, and had flinched away from the noise like a child recoiling from a wasp. Mary-Joy pointed the gun at him. "Get up. Open the door. Get me out of here."

"We have to wait for the ground crew to arrive. We're early! They need to push the steps up!"

"I said open the door, or I can shoot you. I can always get the woman to do it...when she wakes up."

"Okay! Okay!"

The pilot got out of the seat, and raising his hands moved towards Mary-Joy. Covering him with the gun, the girl walked backwards down the cabin between the seats.

The stewardess chose that moment to scream and leap towards Mary-Joy. The girl didn't know if the woman had faked being unconscious or had awoken naturally, but she heard the scream of rage from the woman, and it was that that saved Mary-Joy's life. She sidestepped in the cabin, smashing into a dead faced TV and the stewardess stumbled past her, arms moving ineffectually in midair.

Mary-Joy shot her in the spine four times. The stewardess fell like a dolly dropped from a child's bed and lay still, blood flowers blossoming on her back.

The pilot raised his hands higher. "I'll open the door. There's an inflatable ramp for use if we're forced to make an emergency landing and we need to get out quickly. I'll operate it. You can get down that. Please. Don't shoot me."

The pilot was falling over himself to cooperate now that he was the last one alive. He moved down the cabin to the door, released the lock and operated the emergency ramp. It blew out on explosive bolts. The pilot turned around, hands held so high they were flattened against the ceiling.

Mary-Joy felt the rush in her again. The sense of power that reversing the tables on the people, who though may not have carried out the thousand abuses of her young body, had been wholly complicit in it.

"Please don't shoot me!"

Mary-Joy shot the Pilot in the mouth just to shut him up.

Passion blew out her cheeks. She'd never heard a story like it before. An island where the rich, entitled, and important could go to meet their every sick desire. Where there was no possibility of discovery, where everyone had an alibi.

It made Passion sick to the very pit of her stomach. She could almost not take it in. Her eyes were gritty with tears, her heart breaking in her chest.

Could it be true?

"Who are you looking for?"

Passion shook her head to clear it. "What?"

"Who are you searching for? I bet she was from a rich family. There were girls there from rich families. I bet their parents could afford to send someone to look for their missing children. No one would be coming for me. It's the way of things."

Passion knew that Mary-Joy, wise beyond her years and tougher than anyone could know, was right. No one would employ the Agency on the rates it charged to look for a girl like Mary-Joy.

Passion thumbed the screen of her smartphone and brought up a picture of Lainey as Pippa from the cloned phone.

"I'm searching for her. Lainey Ralston."

"She's there," Mary-Joy said simply, with hesitation. "On the island. It's because of her I was able to escape. While they were trying to pull her from the water, I made it onto the boat."

The news hit Passion like a freight train. She'd been right.

Lainey was alive.

But Passion didn't get a chance to enjoy the moment, as the glass behind them shattered, bursting apart as the air sang with gunfire.

20

Rosa held up a test tube to the camera.

"Mr. Ralston, this contains enough skin flakes and whiskers from your morning shaves in the chalet here on the island, to fix your presence here with absolute certainty. Any court in the world would convict you. Even the ones we don't control."

Rosa reached behind her to the table, and picked up another test tube half-filled with straw-colored liquid, and a sachet full of brown solid matter. "If need be, we can back that up with samples of urine and feces collected from your toilet use here."

Rosa eyed the sachet with a suspicious eye, "I'd ask your doctor for a colonoscopy if I were you, Mr. Ralston. Just a friendly piece of advice."

On the bed, Lainey had turned her head away, but could still hear the words. The nightmare flowed into her ears as easily as it did into her eyes.

"But this sample is of course the top of the shop, the piece of resistance as the French don't say."

Lainey felt a rough hand moving up her inner thigh

towards her crotch. The hand rested at the apex where her two limbs met and cupped the area beneath.

"How would you like, Mr. Ralston, for your daughter's body to be found with her...*juices*...mixed with yours?"

Rosa let that abomination hang in the air for a full fifteen seconds, as the sickness the idea dripped with, sank into the minds of everyone listening. Even still taped to the chair, Lainey could hear Parrish groaning and weeping.

"The implication being, you'd made the beast with two backs with Alaina before consigning her body to a shallow grave somewhere out on your pathetic excuse for a cattle ranch? How would you like us to ensure the conspiracy you've been involved in—the taking of a girl from the Houston streets who looked approximately like your daughter and getting your people to kill, dress up, and disfigure her body, so that she could be passed off as your daughter? Then corruptly paying off the labs which had confirmed her identity? How do you like those apples, Mr. Ralston? What would the voting public make of that, I wonder?"

"Why are you doing this? I don't understand!" Lainey's father's voice, broken with emotion, came through the tinny speaker in the ceiling—harsh and grating, the humanity stripped from it.

Rosa removed her hand from Lainey's crotch and giggled with a sound like a spade breaking earth in a wet graveyard.

"I'll admit to a small FUBAR at our end, sir. Our procurement agents—those we charge with selecting, grooming, and transporting the girls from better families to the island—picked on your daughter entirely by accident. You see, not everyone who visits the island is satisfied with poor brown flesh from the slums, shanty towns and favelas of the third world you and your kind are so busy creating,

Mr. Ralston. Some members of our little club are...*more* discerning. They enjoy white meat, girls from the rarified end of the gene-pool. Girls like your daughter. Our mistake was not thoroughly going through her background. My operatives missed that her whole...online persona, I believe it's called by the young...was a lie. A deception so that she could live the life of a normal, albeit rich, teen tear-away, without the knowledge of her parents. My team in the United States thought they were grooming Pippa Graves, a spoiled, little rich bitch Goth. When in reality they were trapping your daughter Alaina. Not an ideal situation, of course. I mean, we would have gotten to this point in the end..."

"I don't..."

Rosa cut Ralston off mid-sentence "Here, Mr. Ralston. This point was always our end game with people like you. You were being *groomed* in the same way as your daughter."

Rosa let that hang in the air too.

The underground room was sucked free of air and the temperature felt like it had raised to fifty degrees. Lainey sensed her certainties being hollowed out by Rosa's words. Hollowed and roasted in the heat. Surely being dead would be better than this? Surely that would be a blessed relief, so that Rosa's words would stop, and Lainey's view of the world could stop being torn down.

"Eventually, when your usefulness to us had been fully realized we would have had this DNA conversation. It's why the people I represent set up Enchanted Holdings, the shell companies hidden behind it, and the facility on the island in the first place. Is it becoming clearer now Mr. Ralston?"

"I...I..."

Rosa continued as if she were explaining something to a slow child. "Your daughter wanted to live the way she wanted, wanted to do the things she wanted to do outside the orbit of your controlling influence. She wanted to be away from your drunk wife's inability to walk past a bottle of vodka. Surely you can see that is why she rebelled against you. And yet, hypocritically, you Mr. Ralston, wanted exactly the same as Alaina."

There was just the ragged breathing of Lainey's father from the speaker now. He had no words.

"For you, the controlling influences were societal norms, and your drunken, fickle mother, was the electorate. You had your secret desires to torture and maim young girls to your sadistic hearts content and we offered, like Lainey's "Pippa" profile, a place for you to live them. We groomed you too, Mr. Ralston. As I said, our only miscalculation was having to move things forward, because of your daughter. But we're putting that to rest, right now."

"You can have everything I own. Please. *Everything*. Just let my daughter go, and let us walk away from this. Please."

"Mr. Ralston, we *are* going to have everything you own. That's a given. And you're not going to walk away, you're going to work *for* us. From this day forward, through to your election in November, and onto your Presidential run in twelve years' time. Mr. Ralston, from this day forward, we own the very air you breathe."

Lainey's stomach was twisting with anxiety, the heat in the room beyond unbearable. The knots in her guts hurting like kicks and punches.

And then the scream and the gurgle and the spray of fresh, hot blood across her body. She couldn't look but she could hear Parrish struggling in his chair, the wheeze of wet blood from his opened throat, and the terrible sounds of him dying.

"Shhhh Parrish, shhhh. It'll be over soon. The more you struggle, the quicker your blood will flow. If you want to marshal your thoughts. Make your peace with your God, do it now, Parrish. Death is your punishment for losing the girl, but you can if you wish to go to it without fuss. Perhaps your death will have more meaning than your life. Keep praying, Parrish. Speak to your Lord."

The struggling in the chair slowed, and Parrish eventually settled into a rough breathing, his lips pattering with prayers as his body wound down. Eventually the sprays of blood that had covered the back of Lainey's head, neck, and shoulders stopped, and she could no longer feel the droplets hitting her, just the gentle tightening as the thick fluid began to dry where it had landed on her exposed skin.

Lainey dared still not turn her head look at Parrish. The last thing she heard before she slipped into the welcome unconsciousness brought on by insurmountable fear, was Rosa saying, "And here endeth the lesson, Mr. Ralston." Then the clink of the straight razor being put down onto the tray.

———

Lainey woke from one nightmare into another.

The first thing she heard were children crying, their sobs loud and filled with distress. Lainey was surprised she could move her hands and feet. The chains had been removed at some point and she could feel she was laying naked on a mattress. She chanced opening her eyes.

Lainey saw she was covered in a thin white sheet and that she was laying on the bottom layer of a metal framed bunk bed. The room was dimly lit. There were barred windows, and through the nearest window she saw what could only be the night sky.

Lainey sat up, the sheet falling off her thin shoulders as she examined her skin. While she'd been asleep, someone had cleaned the blood from her body, tying her hair back in a ponytail. At the end of bed was a pair of functional flip-flops resting on a pile of white underwear, a cotton bra-top, and beneath what looked like a folded up orange jumpsuit.

But Lainey's nakedness and clothing requirements were not the most pressing matter for her right now. On the other side of the dormitory, along a second row of maybe ten or so bunkbeds, were two of the girls she recognized from her boat trip to the island. One was about Lainey's age, the other slightly older. They hadn't been allowed to talk on the steamer as it chugged through the waters leaving the jungle port and airstrip behind, so she hadn't been able to find out their names, or any information about them. Their eyes had met though, and those looks had bonded the girls in the shared purgatory of their situation. Right now they were clinging to each other screaming and sobbing.

There was a dragging sound, and Lainey saw two guards walking away from the girls, dragging a third girl between them. This third girl was kicking and trying to punch at the guards. They were oblivious to the attack as if this was something to be expected. The girl was dressed in an orange jumpsuit like the one that was at the end of Lainey's bunk.

Eventually the guards yanked the girl to the dormitory door. One punched a code into a pad, and it was opened from the outside by another guard. They hauled the girl out, and the door was slammed behind them.

The two girls on the opposite bunk continued their crying. Lainey thought about getting up to go and comfort them, but then she saw everyone else in the room, and they were ignoring the girls in the moment of great distress.

Like Lainey, they were either looking at the girls from their bunks, or they were turning away, their faces blank.

Why was nobody helping them?

Lainey reached for the jumpsuit and stood. She put it on without underwear and did up the zipper. The material was freshly washed, and was stiff. It was made from the kind of material that Lainey wouldn't have been seen dead in over at the clubs in Houston, but now it was just serving a purpose.

Lainey wasn't going to stand by and let the other girls cry without being comforted. She just wasn't. She took a step.

"No. *Don't.*"

Lainey spun around and saw that there was someone on the top bunk above her. A beautiful Indian girl, with black hair tied back in a braid and eyes like brown pools of liquid chocolate. She was reaching out to Lainey, trying to touch her shoulder.

"They're crying. I can't just leave them."

"You have to," the girl hissed. "We're not allowed to cross from this side to other. There was an escape from one of the other wings. Two girls attacked a guard. Stole his keys and his gun. One girl got away. So they've brought in new rules. We can only talk to the person in the bunk below or above us. We cannot go to any other bunk at *any* time. We cannot approach the door without permission, and anyone tampering with the new entry coders will be taken to the punishment block." The girl sounded like she was reeling off the items on a menu.

Lainey couldn't stand the crying, but conversely she didn't like the sound of the *Punishment Block*—not after the conversation she'd been forced to listen to in Rosa's hole in the ground, about how her father liked to get his kicks.

So she tried, against all her better instincts, to shut the sound out. Lainey sat back down on the bed, and looked along the rows of bunks on her side of the dormitory. All the other girls she could see were trying to do the same:

ignore, shut out, deny. She could see it in their faces, and she knew that they could see it in hers.

Eventually the sobbing subsided, and the girls on the other side of the aisle were reduced to the occasional sob and pathetic sniffle.

Lainey had no idea what the time was, but the windows were still showing darkness outside the building.

The ceiling lights were dim, emergency orange, or like the distant sodium glow of the highway at night. There was air conditioner whirring somewhere overhead, but the room was still too hot to be comfortable. There didn't appear to be any noise leaking in from outside, but Lainey had no reason to believe she was anywhere but still on the island.

The disgust hit her then, as the memories of what she'd learned about her father came back in sickening whirls in her guts and jagged thoughts in her head. How could she have not known that her father was like this? How could he have kept it hidden from Lainey and from her mother, Brenda? Perhaps he hadn't been able to keep it from his wife. Perhaps that was why she wanted to be drunk all the time.

For the first time in a long while, Lainey felt a tinge of remorse about the way she had always gone up against her mother. Maybe the woman was doing the best she could with the life she had been given. Maybe she only stayed around to make sure that Lainey was safe. Maybe she wasn't such a fuck-up after all.

Lainey, in that moment, missed her mom, more than any other time she could remember.

The bunk above her creaked and the face of the beautiful braid-haired girl appeared. "How are you feeling?" she whispered.

It was the first kind words Lainey had heard since

Daniel had put her into the Buick outside her home. "I don't know. It's...all too much. I just want to go home."

"Me too. But I fear that's not something that is going to be happening very soon."

"No." Lainey sat up, and reached a hand out, she suddenly felt the need to feel some warm human contact. A tight hug was what she needed right now, but in the absence of that, she'd settle for a handshake.

The girl on the top bunk seemed to understand immediately what Lainey needed, and reached out her hand too. They clasped palms in the darkness, the warmth of the girl's hand more appealing and generous than the humid heat of the dormitory. Lainey clung to it like her life depended on it. Perhaps in time it would.

"Lainey, Lainey Ralston," she offered.

"Gairola," The girl replied. "Bimala Gairola."

21

Passion ducked and pushed Mary-Joy's head down as the bullets thudded and the glass flew around them. Without raising her head, Passion started the Hyundai and stamped on the gas pedal, hoping that just going forward would help them to build up speed before anything else hit them.

The bullets started thudding again into the back spaces of the SUV, missing the tires but zinging around the metal-work with crazy sparks, "Stay down!" Passion yelled at Mary-Joy as the Hyundai gathered speed.

Passion looked up through the steering wheel and over the hood, thankful that the parking lot was not filled with more obstacles. She risked raising her head higher, as she heard the bullets smacking into the tarmac behind, rico-chets bouncing up and tanging on the bodywork of a Chevy and a Ford ahead.

Passion turned the wheel and drove diagonally across the lot, drifting left far enough that she hoped to get the Chevy between the Hyundai and whoever was behind with the machine gun. There was a break in the rat-tat-tat growl of their assailant's gun as he or she changed mags.

One shooter. That was something at least.

"Why are they shooting at us?" Mary-Joy said, her head all the way down in the foot well. After what Mary-Joy had told Passion about the island, and the fact she had seen Lainey Ralston there, there could be a hundred people with a vested interest in keeping the location and nature of the island a secret.

The strip of stores and gas stations was thankfully light on traffic, as they screeched onto the street out of the parking lot. Passion figured it was better to head out of the city right now, and turned onto the expressway, heading north.

The rearview mirror was shattered, but there were still enough crazy shards for Passion to make out if they had been followed out of the parking lot. Nothing was following as of yet. The traffic that there was, was heading into the city, not out.

Passion picked up her smartphone as she drove, "Mary-Joy, you can get up now. I need to call for help, and we need to change cars. I might be able to do both with one call."

Mary-Joy sat up in the seat, her hands moving in front of her belly with clear signs of anxiety. *Poor kid*, Passion thought as she hit the button to call Bryan. After all she'd been through on the island and beyond, to nearly get tagged like that in a parking lot was the ultimate in unlucky.

Night had not even fallen.

Someone wanted them dead and dead quickly. If whoever that was had used someone who would attack while the sun was still in the sky, that exposed a level of stupidity or confidence in the assailant that was difficult to fathom. Either way, hitting in daylight was just a no-no among the professionals. The exposure and the chance of witnesses giving an accurate ID to the cops made it the hit choice for only the desperate or the amateur. On the other hand, if the early evening hit had been called because Houston PD, FBI, and the NSA were cool with it—as the presence of Detective Myer at the meeting with Ralston had suggested—then the situation was far more dangerous than could reasonably be measured.

She had to speak to Bryan, and she had to speak to him now.

The call would not go through.

NUMBER NOT RECOGNIZED the screen flashed back at her. The shock of that almost made Passion swerve the car across the central reservation.

Shit.

The phone still had full signal, the bar at the top of the screen told her so. But the number was not calling.

Passion thumbed the contacts list for the number of the hotel where she'd been staying.

Her contacts list was empty.

As an experiment, she thumbed 911 onto the key pad.

NUMBER NOT RECOGNIZED.

Passion knew the NSA and CIA had developed a number of counter espionage virus bombs they could send as invisible push notices to suspect phones. They'd been developed when the IEDs of choice in Iraq and Afghanistan had been set off by mobile phones sending a trigger signal. The plan being that if they disabled everybody's phone in the area they'd stop the terrorist from exploding their device or having the suicide vest strapped to their body, detonated remotely by some other fucker with an iPhone.

It seemed obvious to Passion that as she hadn't taken

her cell phone through any MRI scanners recently, the chance it had been hit by a virus bomb was a good one.

"Is your telephone not working?"

Passion threw the smart phone out of the smashed side window where it tumbled to the blacktop, spinning and disintegrating as it bounced. "Well it is now."

In the same way Fake-Jake's telephone had been zeroed to the Roman Field airstrip, the phone may have led the assailant to the parking lot to attack the Hyundai. Passion judged getting rid of the machine now that it was completely useless was the best course of action.

And because the Hyundai was new, a rental, and top of the range, it was certain that it would have a tracker hidden somewhere in the chassis.

It was either the telephone or the Hyundai which had brought the assassin to the parking lot. The phone was gone, and now the Hyundai had to go.

Night fell fully as they took the 336, circumvented Conroe, headed out on the 105 towards Montgomery. Five miles from the town, Passion spied a derelict lot set back from the highway, overlooking Lake Conroe. It was a convenient place to stop, so she pulled in and ran the Hyundai around the back of what was left of the building.

The garden was overgrown, the dwelling that had once stood there, a dilapidated ranch style house had fallen to near rubble. There were chain link fences around it and signs declaring it was going to be redeveloped into a complex of featureless apartments sometime in the next year.

Passion pulled the Hyundai onto the grass behind the house so that it could not be seen from the road. If it had a tracker, it was a moot thing to do, but just in case it had been the telephone that had triangulated their position, Passion thought it was worth doing anyway. Behind the derelict house was a densely overgrown wooded area which had been left to do its own thing for a good few years.

"But I don't want to stay here, I want to come *with* you."

Passion pushed the girl back down into the grass. "There's a gas station and a motel back the way we came, half a mile. I'm going to go back there now and get us a new car. I'm going to try to call my friend from a payphone and I'll get us some food. If the cops are looking for us, they're going to be looking for an adult and a girl. I need you to stay here for now, while I try and find us a way out of this mess, okay?"

Mary-Joy opened her mouth to protest, but Passion put a finger on it. "Please."

She pointed back down the highway, "If I'm gone more than an hour, come looking for me okay?"

Passion took off her watch and handed it to the girl. "Take this. One hour. Please."

Mary-Joy took the watch and snapped it onto her wrist. "One hour," she repeated with all seriousness.

Passion went to the rear door of the Hyundai, opened it and took out her Ops bag. A Kevlar reinforced rucksack with compartments for her gun safe, flashlights, laptop, false ID badges, tactical zip-ties, handcuffs, ski mask, black tee-shirt, cargo pants, custom all-black Converse All-Stars and most importantly the kit that would help her steal a car.

Passion changed, took the Beretta Cheetah from the gun safe, slid a mag into the stock, slammed a round into the chamber and slid the pistol under her tee-shirt and into her a belt holster. Then she jogged away from the derelict house towards the half mile distant lights of the motel and gas station.

The motel had a pleasing number of late model cars

out front in the lot. Any one of them would do for the next stage the journey to...where?

Yes indeed. Where was she going?

The Agency offices where Bryan and his back up team were based was in Washington. Passion had only ever visited the nondescript boxy office building once in the years she's been in their employ. Bryan had told her it was easier if the Agency was as weightless as possible. In fact, when she thought about it, she couldn't be sure if the Agency was still where she thought it was. It had never come up in conversation, and Passion preferred to stay on the road, taking modelling assignments where she could, and dressing down when she was on duty.

So if not Washington, then where? Passion had absolutely no clue, but she knew getting in touch with Bryan had to be a priority to pass on the information about the island.

The gas station had two payphones on the wall facing the motel. Passion circled around the back of the gas station, and emerged from the shadow cast by the motel sign looking for all the world like she was coming from the motel to get some evening snacks before settling down for some serious TV. She ambled leisurely and smiled at a fat guy coming from the gas station with a paper bag stuffed with chips and a XL bottle of Mountain Dew under his arm. He was doing in reverse what Passion was trying to give the impression she was doing. His smile was full of bad teeth and Passion wished she hadn't bothered.

The first payphone had a handwritten OUT OF ORDER scotch taped to the keypad, so Passion moved to the next one. She picked up the receiver and listened for the dial tone. All present and correct. Dropping coins into the slot she dialed Bryan's number from memory.

The line fuzzed, beeped, clicked and a recorded message told her that *This call cannot be placed at this time.*

Passion replaced the receiver and the coins clanked into tray. She repeated the action twice more, with raising anxiety each time to the same result.

Shit. Shit. *Double shit.*

She went into the gas station shop, picked up some chips, Diet Doctor Peppers and a couple of ham subs from the cooler. The cashier at the counter was watching an old portable TV in the corner of her glassed off booth. Her hair was dirty blond and she was dressed like a woman in her twenties, all tight wrap over leopard print blouse, more earrings than were necessary and knuckles encrusted with fake rocks. The cashier's face wasn't one of a woman in her twenties, however. The skin was the deeply lined face of a woman who'd lived maybe thirty years more. The foundation was flaking on her cheeks and her lipstick had been put on with a trowel.

The cashier didn't smile as she rang up Passion's purchase, which was a blessing as Passion thought she probably had the same dentist as the fat guy she'd passed on the way to the payphone.

"Fifteen ninety-nine," the cashier said with a voice so flat you could have laid a brick wall against it.

Passion handed over her credit card. "I don't suppose I could use your telephone could I?"

The cashier pointed towards the door. "Payphone outside."

"Yeah, I tried those. Out of order. Please, it's really important."

The woman looked at Passion as nothing could be more important to getting back to her episode of *America's Got Talent.* "Just one call, and it'll be five dollars."

"Put it on the card."

The cashier's eyebrows disappeared into her hair. "Cash."

"Okay." Passion reached into her purse and pulled out a five, handing it over. The cashier slipped the bill inside her blouse to sit inside her bra, then reached under the counter to pass Passion an ancient cordless telephone saying, "nine for an outside line," like this gas station was the Hilton.

Passion took the cordless and thumbed nine, waiting for the dial tone before pressing in Bryan's number. Putting the receiver to her ear, Passion was dismayed to hear it doing the same shit as the payphone outside. The line fuzzed again, beeped again, clicked again and the recorded message told her one more time that *This call cannot be placed at this time.*

Passion looked at the phone like it had turned into a cockroach in her fingers. She sighed, and was about to try again when the cashier said, "Declined."

Passion's eyes snapped up. "What do you mean, declined? I didn't get through."

"Not the call, sweetheart. The card. You're gonna have to pay cash, or you can put this stuff back on the shelf."

Passion paid cash, put the food and drink into the spare section of her Ops rucksack and headed from the gas station store back towards the motel, her head fizzing to fear and anger.

Why couldn't she get through to Bryan from *any* phone? Why had her credit cards, both of them, been declined? Passion suddenly felt the same chill she had experienced in Ralston's office when she realized she was being frozen out of the investigation and was being fed pure bullshit.

No money, apart from the eighty dollars and change she had in her purse. No contact with Bryan. No chance of going to Houston PD because: Myer. Where *could* she go? What should she do with Mary-Joy?

First things first. A car.

She stopped, opened the ops bag and took out a small but heavy black cube of tech. There was a rubber keypad, a digital read out, and a short rubber-covered aerial. She turned the device on, and waited.

The device was a CIA grade keyless entry hack tool, given to field agents for the very purpose of stealing cars in this way. It would tap into the automatic RDIF proximity signals coming from key fobs in the motel room. When it had harvested two or three, all Passion had to do was walk around the motel a couple of times with the machine on, as it did its stuff. She returned to the parking lot, and the tech went into reverse, sending out the codes it had harvested, fooling the cars in the lot into thinking the keyless entry fobs were close enough to pop the locks.

Passion walked down the line, and the box did its thing. A red Nissan Versa clicked its locks as she approached.

Bingo.

Passion looked around as she put her hand on the car's door to make sure no one was watching from the motel and pulled the handle.

It was then that she heard Mary-Joy screaming.

22

"Your Aunt *sold* you?"

Bimala nodded sadly. Her head was still hanging upside down from the bunk above, but dawn was pressing at the windows, lighting up the dormitory as the girls sleeping there began to wake.

Not at all tired, Lainey had tried to get as much information from Bimala as she could. She'd heard the entire story of her parents' death, the deal with the Aunt and Uncle, the paranoid fantasies of the latter and then, unholiest of the unholy, the realization that her Aunt had sold her into sexual slavery on the island.

As the sun had come up, Lainey's mood, which was already at a low point, had dropped even lower. Even in the heat, she'd wrapped the sheet around her tightly to approximate the feeling of being hugged. She felt very small, very vulnerable and after what had happened with Rosa, truly terrified.

Even though Parrish's drying blood had been washed from her skin she could still imagine its stickiness there on her flesh. She could still hear the breathing of her father from the speaker and still taste the dirt in the air of the hole.

Lainey had to force herself to tell Bimala her story, and when she'd finished it was full daylight outside the barred windows, and clouds were building up.

"I think I saw the girl who escaped," she whispered.

Bimala's eyes widened. "Where?"

"When the boat crew guy hit me and knocked me into the water. There was a girl beneath the jetty. She had a gun and she was holding onto the ladder. She didn't say anything, but I could see in her eyes she was willing me not to give her away. I rolled onto my back, kicked away from her, and the crew guy dove in to get me. When I looked back she was gone. I guess she must have gotten onto the boat."

Bimala smiled and clapped her hands. "This is the best news ever. Maybe she'll get to the mainland and tell everyone about us."

Lainey remembered her attempted escape from the jungle airstrip and the moat full of starving dogs. She didn't feel hopeful that the girl had gotten away, but didn't want to spoil Bimala's optimism just yet. The girl was at least giving Lainey the kind of positive human connection she needed to help deal with this situation.

A trouble shared.

Two guards, perhaps those who had taken the girl in the night, appeared from the dormitory door. "Rise and shine, ladies!" the taller of the two guards said. Now that the light was better, Lainey could see his uniform name tape read "Schmidt." The other guard, a blond stocky creature with no hair on his head but a wispy goatee on his chin, looked along the rows of girls. His face unable to hide the lust that was boiling up inside him. His name tape read

"Karpov." The bloated skin of his face was pockmarked with acne scars. He was the kind of guy who if Lainey had bumped into him at a club, would immediately go to the restroom to wash herself off. Karpov looked like dirt personified, creepily made flesh.

He approached Bimala and Lainey's bunk, the sweat standing out on his forehead.

"Do nothing," Bimala whispered. "Do nothing at all."

Lainey wanted for the ground to open up and swallow her as Karpov reached up to the top bunk. His hands disappeared from view and all Lainey could hear now was the hollow in the air made by Bimala's silence.

The front of Karpov's pants were tented at the fly. Bimala didn't whimper or make any sounds of resistance.

She did nothing. Just as she'd warned Lainey to do.

Lainey's heart shivered in her chest as the guard carried out the abuse in the open, with no one to interrupt or stop him. Eventually he seemed to get bored, the front of his pants deflating, and he walked away wiping his hands on the outside of his thighs.

"Okay, ladies. Showers then breakfast. Move it!" Schmidt yelled.

Lainey filed out of the dormitory with Bimala still silent at her side. The girl's eyes were staring forward, her hands working behind her head to re-braid her hair. Bimala's lips quivered, but she did not cry. A tear balanced on the edge of one eyelid, but that was her only other outward show of emotion.

The showers were exactly as Lainey feared. They were all forced to strip off in front of Schmidt and Karpov who eyed them all with maximum avarice. Lainey tried to cover her breasts and groin, but Bimala silently shook her head and gently moved Lainey's hands away from her breasts.

"If you cover up, they pick on you," was all she whispered to Lainey as they filed past the guards into the tepid communal showers. The soap was cheap, the lather it made on the skin thin and lacking any moisturizing action. Lainey had been used to a plethora of bath oils, bath bombs, and moisturizing lotions back home. The small slivers of orange, transparent soap being passed around did the barest job of cleaning, and for a moment Lainey was almost pleased she'd been washed down after fainting.

The towels they were given to dry themselves were stiff and sandpapery, thin with age and frayed. As Lainey rubbed at her skin in silence, red scuffs and scrapes appeared along her arms and thighs. Her body was not used to this kind of treatment, and although she knew in the grand scheme of things that the rough towels and the cheap soap were the very definition of First World Problems, it didn't stop her feeling acutely homesick and very sorry for herself.

"You'll get used to it in time," Bimala whispered, obviously noticing the look on Lainey's face.

"How long did it take you?"

"Six months, maybe less."

"Six months!"

"Compared to what else they do to us here, the towels and the soaps count as luxury."

Huey looked out onto his future. It was not something that he wanted to do, but the realization that he had been made into meat tenderized and prepared to be barbequed over his own vanity by Rosa had a salutary and comprehensively odd effect on the Texan politician. One that he could not have foreseen merely 24 hours ago.

He'd awoken this morning, no longer broken and tearful, but resolved.

For the first time in his life, he was going to do the right thing. The thought was crystal clear in his mind. There was only one course of action.

He was going to go public on the island. He was going to telephone his old political contacts, the ones Crane had fired or estranged, and he was going to tell them the whole story. Blow the fuckers out of the water.

He didn't care anymore, a life in prison, even on Death Row was preferable to the snapping away of his free will and setting him on the course to be a puppet plaything for Rosa and whoever *the People behind the People* were.

Ralston could guess at who those *people* were—secretive apolitical cabals who moved behind the front put up by regular politicians and businessmen. The kind of *people* who made money through whoever was in power—the left or the right or the centrists. The ones with no political or religious affiliations. The ones who made sure arms got sold to both sides in a war, the ones who allowed the lie of democracy where it suited them, and the ones who promoted totalitarianism where it achieved their goals.

It had all fallen into place after the video conference with Rosa. A place like the island was the natural progression for *the People behind the People.* A place where they could give the lie to the great and the good that they were untouchable, above and beyond the law.

Dealing in the harvesting of vanity and hubris, collecting their DNA and other evidence to be used when the time was right. These people, those Rosa said she worked for, weren't Illuminati, Freemasons, Skull and Bones, Rosicrucians, Ordo Templis Orientis, Knights Templar or the *fucking* Bilderberg Group. They were, if they even existed as a group, just further fronts hiding behind the societal equivalent of shell companies. Deeper than the deep state, their near invisibility throwing the scent off for anyone investigating the case.

They weren't secret societies or the "twelve families" beloved of conspiracy theorists. Enchanted Holdings was just an arm, the blackmailing arm needed to keep the weak-minded, and the easily flattered on their side.

But no longer did that apply to Huey Ralston.

He'd spent his life living for himself, doing what he wanted, doing it the way he desired, and that was a habit now, not one he was willing to give up. If he was going to go down, he was going to take those bastards with him.

Huey drove himself to the La Colombe D'or, on Montrose Boulevard, a 1920's style boutique hotel where over the years Huey had more than a few excellent meetings with various extra-marital ladies. It was quiet, discrete, and the suite he always booked was pleasingly available.

He was due to meet Cal Michaels and Jerome Peterson there. They were Huey's operators from the days before Crane. They were still shakers in the Texas GOP, and at first had been surprised by his call first thing that morning, but had agreed to meet, after both expressing their sincere condolences on hearing about the death of his daughter. In fact, Cal expressed some surprise that Huey was willing to think about politics when the grief over the death of his daughter must have been so raw.

"Of course it's raw, Cal. I'm destroyed, but sometimes... public service has to come first. I can grieve later. This is big. Will you come? Do an old friend a favor?"

"Of course, Huey. Wild horses wouldn't keep me away."

Jerome had been intrigued, but was still smarting from the way he'd been eased out by Crane.

"Crane won't be there, Jerome. This is strictly outside his purview."

"Good. That cocksucker deserves to be hung from the highest gallows in the land for what he did to me and Cal. You know that I was very disappointed in you, Huey."

Not as disappointed when I tell you what I have to tell you, Huey thought.

"Crane's fingers are nowhere near this, but I've got something big. So big, I need your advice on how to get it out to the most people in the quickest time."

"Any clue before I traipse all the way downtown, Huey? Christ, it's not even 8:00 a.m. yet. Did you shit the bed?"

"I can't say, but trust me, Jerome. This is bigger than the moon landing with Dealey Plaza sprinkled on top."

"Ok. If Cal is on board, then so am I."

"He is. La Colombe D'or at 9:30?"

"Old habits die hard, eh Huey?"

"Indeed, Jerome. Indeed."

Huey was waved through by the concierge, collected his key card from the front desk and took the stairs to the first floor with a sense of righteous purpose he had never felt before.

The suite was at the back of the mansion on the top floor, overlooking a small group of palms that stopped the room from being seen from the street.

Is this what public service really felt like?

If he'd known that being civic-minded could make him feel this energized, then he wished he'd made it the central meaning of his life, rather than a succession of depraved encounters and dubious business deals around which the flotsam of his family now swirled.

He felt a twinge for Lainey.

They would surely kill her now, of that he could be sure. But what was that saying? The needs of the many outweigh the needs of the few... Was that Kennedy...or was it Star Trek? Huey could not remember, but whoever had said it was *correctamundo*.

The corridors of the hotel were deserted. He passed the occasional hotel worker pushing a room-cleaning trolley, but saw a scant few hotel residents. Perhaps most were down at breakfast, or had taken themselves downtown for business meetings or a little sightseeing. Whatever, it didn't matter.

Huey reached the suite, and keyed the door open with the card. Inside, the connected set of rooms were dark, the drapes still closed and Huey had to reach to the side of the door to turn on the main light. The tastefully concealed lighting flickered on and the extent of the suit, all curved wood with sumptuous 1920's styling came into sharp relief.

As did the two men standing there.

"Surprise!" Crane smiled, and Myer raised his gun.

"Did you really think that we don't know every move you make, who you talk to and who you plan to meet?"

Huey took a step back, the shock of the raised gun and the unexpected presence of the two men almost taking the strength from his legs.

"You've bugged my phone?"

There was a warm laugh beside him as Jerome stepped from the bathroom, followed by Cal. "No," said Jerome, "they bugged your friends."

Passion knocked on the apartment door, keeping Mary-Joy in front of her—enclosed in her arms, looking around to see if they'd been followed into the building.

Sven, bleary-eyed, which seemed to be his default state whenever Passion came to his apartment, opened the door with a puzzled look, which was followed by his hand going up to scratch his head. "Miss...Durant...?"

"I need your help."

Passion could see from Sven's reaction this was not the words he was expecting to have come from her mouth, but with a shake of his head he opened the door and let them into the apartment.

In the few days since she'd last been there, Passion could see that Sven had not made many more additions to the home. There was at least a sofa now, and a TV—men did like to get the important stuff out of the way first when making a new home—and there were bags of groceries on the kitchen surfaces waiting to be unpacked.

"What is the help you need? It is late. I am tired and to be perfectly honest with you, I am confused."

So Passion told him.

When she'd finished she thought she was going to have to pick his jaw off the floor for him. Mary-Joy had long since curled up to sleep on the sofa, her knees drawn up in a fetal position, her head protected beneath her horrifically scarred arm. This was a girl used to sleeping anywhere and any way she could. A skill forged in the Filipino slums.

"They must have tracked the Hyundai to the derelict lot outside Montgomery. That's why I never saw anyone following. They didn't need to. I left Mary-Joy there while I went to steal a car. I was an idiot. I thought they'd been tracking my telephone, but I'd dumped that miles back. Mary-Joy managed to find me in the motel parking lot, told me about the guys with guns rolling up to the Hyundai and we lost them, and came straight here."

"Why me?"

"You're the only person right now that I know who isn't in this up to their necks. They're inside Houston PD, they've blocked my access to my employers. Whatever phone I use, I can't get through. It's like the Agency has been taken off the grid permanently; all my credit cards have been cancelled, and I dare not go back to my hotel to get my stuff. Now they really can't track us, I can't risk going back there."

"I need more coffee. You're speaking so fast, I think you need less."

"Will you help?"

Sven went to the kitchen to refill his cup. "Help how?"

"Let us stay here a while. They can't track us here now. I've dumped the phone and the Hyundai, so that gives us some breathing space. I'll try to make contact with some of my mom's old colleagues in the Canadian SIS. I think I'm going to have to take this outside the US. Whoever is running the island, and the operations Stateside have octopus arms. I don't know who I can trust right now. Except you."

Sven nodded, and sipped from his refreshed cup, running his fingers through his hair.

"I have heard some sick things in my time. But this island is the sickest. It must be exposed. It cannot be allowed to continue." Svan sat down again, still shaking his head, his eyes conveying his shock. "And you are sure Alaina is there?"

"Yes. Mary-Joy saw her. For sure. Heard Lainey shouting out her own name. One hundred percent."

"We must get there. Find her. I was very foolish. I should have protected her better. I should not have thought of myself. This is unfinished business for me."

Passion could see that Sven was a proud man, one who hated leaving a job half finished, especially one he'd contributed to going wrong. Sven set his shoulders and nodded to himself.

"This I must do."

"Thank you."

As the lights went out and the frame charges blew the windows in on a gust of black smoke and glass, Passion spun away and hit the wall hard with her head. She heard the clunk of the stun grenades hitting the floor before the flashes and the bangs blinded and then deafened her.

23

They sat in a semi-circle of canvas chairs. Their wrists and ankles bound with zip-ties. Mary-Joy, Sven, Passion, and on the end of the line...Huey Ralston.

The room was wood-paneled and smelled of fresh varnish. Two huge picture windows showed the island and a sky that looked like an old bruise.

Passion could see way beyond the compound across the fields to the forest. They'd been transported there from Houston in a headlong rush that felt more desperate than planned. First they'd been hustled into the Gulfstream, which they'd met at Roman Field, kept face down on its plush carpet, covered by armed guards in their faux SWAT uniforms the whole time. Passion had not seen any evidence of Mary-Joy's murder spree in the aircraft, so either the organization had a spare, or they'd gotten this one fixed up by PDQ.

After the three-hour flight, they were picked up from the jungle airstrip by a black Bell 206 JetRanger, flown just under two hours to the island to land next to this central building in the walled compound on a helipad. Then they were dragged and pushed inside the building and upstairs to the stateroom. They had not had time to breathe, and their feet didn't touch.

The sky was glutted with clouds, and the journey in the JetRanger had been bumpy and erratic with blustery cross-winds whipping up off the white-crested waves below. In the helicopter, the SWAT team was having edgy conferences over weather RADAR readouts, looking with concern at the tumbling sky, and didn't seem at all happy to be flying in these borderline conditions. One of them, green-faced with bulging eyes, threw up into a bag. It wasn't a good journey.

The weather on the island now was worse and matched Passion's mood as she looked out at the island. Beyond the compound walls a black Humvee was patrolling between a putting green and the fields. Passion could just see through the mile of heavy rain to the wooded slopes of a mountain which rose from the center of the island.

The forest that squatted there at the base of the black rock didn't make sense to Passion. It looked *all* wrong. The woodland seemed to be comprised of broad-branched oaks and looked utterly incongruous next to the jungle that comprised most of the rest of the island's flora. It was as if Sherwood Forest had been torn away from Robin and Marion, and dropped onto a Caribbean island.

The forest had the look of artificial creation, like a film set or a theme park. It added greatly to the unreality of the situation. Nearer to the central building in which they were zip-tied and seated, Passion could see the higgledy-piggledy collection of *Olde Worlde* chalets, like an assortment of huge cuckoo clocks just as artificial and curated as the forest. Passion studied the chalets and their ludicrously quaint design, but found she had to look away as her eyes picked out two guards dragging a semi naked teen towards a chalet, up some stairs and through the front door.

For all the artifice of the Robin Hood forest and the Smurf Village chalets, there was nothing artificial about the horror of this place. That was all too real and upsetting. Passion's guts turned. If she could have gotten free she would have taken as many of these motherfuckers with her as she could. Passion tried to again quell the anger clouding her thinking. If she was going to survive the next hour, let alone the next few years, she was going to have to be prepared to move on them whenever an opportunity arose. Feeling sorry for the kid being dragged into the chalet and allowing herself the luxury of anger, was not going to get anyone saved, least of all the girl in the chalet.

Focus, Passion.

Focus.

Get back in the room. What do you see? What can you use?

Stephen Crane was there standing next to a statuesque blond woman dressed like she was attending a cocktail party. Behind them, five black uniformed SWAT guards armed with shoulder-strapped Heckler & Koch G36's.

There was an empty chair in front of the guards and the way the blond was looking at the watch on her wrist, she was expecting someone soon to fill it.

Sven's face was bloated with bruises. The fake SWAT team, who had blown the windows with frame charges and thrown in the stun grenades, had judged him to be the major threat given his background in Swedish Special Services. They had kicked and pistol whipped him into unconsciousness even as he'd tried to get up on his knees to respond to their attack.

Passion and Mary-Joy had been thrown face down and zip-tied before they'd had a chance to recover any faculties. They had been carried from the apartment block, out into the street and thrown into the back of a caged van. It had taken four of the black uniformed SWAT fakes to carry Sven given his size, and as well as being cable tied, he'd been handcuffed with his legs shackled. He was bundled into the cage beside Passion, his face bloody and swelling, one eye already closing.

Five and a half hours later, they were on the island.

Passion still had no idea how the assholes had found them. No phone, no car tracker. Unless they were psychic, they couldn't have known that she'd try to elicit Sven's help.

Passion tried to go back over the hours since they'd first been attacked in the north Houston parking lot. Trying to think about anything or anyone that could have tracked them, but she could not think on one moment where they'd been under surveillance. It was as if these people could just flick a switch and be told exactly where Passion and the girl were at *any* moment.

It was a handy trick if you could pull it off, and now she was sitting here on the island, captured all to hell, impotent and blind-sided.

The door to the stateroom opened, and an old woman, dressed like a fucking *hobbit* shuffled in. She wore a cloak, brown britches, and leather boots. Her face was straight from a Fantasy Movie Central Casting, and her white hair followed the turns of her head like smoke from a steam train's smoke stack.

Her hands were gnarled like roots, knuckles were arthritic and swollen to the size of walnuts. Her eyes though, they didn't match the frailness of her hands and body. They were not an artificial affectation like the clothes or the chalets or the forest below the mountain. Her eyes were bright and alive, her stare firm and unblinking. They were the eyes of a hunter in the pinched face of a fairytale witch. Hansel and Gretel's captor made flesh, the Childcatcher's mom. A wolf in Disneyland clothing.

The old woman sat in the empty chair, her mouth moving but no words coming out. It was the soft mouth of your grandmother, pink and dry, run with cracks and crevices, like two pink soft tortoise feet coming together in front of brown-stained teeth. There were no words coming out because the movements of the lips were like the palsied undulations of someone whose thoughts were played out on their face before they ever became communication.

Passion suspected the woman was reaching up to a shelf in her mind, choosing the jar with each correct word and then sending it towards her mouth in an orderly line. This was a woman who didn't waste a moment on ephemera that didn't matter. Her eyes showed the urgency of that.

When she spoke, it was with a sense of commanding stillness. "My name is Rosa González. I am the representative here at Enchanted Holdings, Owners of *La Isla Encantada*. It is *my* domain and I have been given carte blanche to run it as I see fit. I answer to the highest authority in this matter. Please be aware that I have the power of life and death over all of you. The island is nearly three hundred nautical miles from the coast. An inhospitable coast for jungles and swamps. Even if you made it there, you would die before you reached civilization—well what passes for civilization in this part of the world. In the 25 years we have been open, we have had one escape. Just one. Well done, Mary-Joy. You have impressed me a great deal."

Mary-Joy averted her eyes, looking down at her bare knees. She said nothing since they had arrived back on the island, her face a mask of fear.

"But as you all can see, that one escapee is back here already. Our reach is long, our resources infinite, and our revenge *biblical*. I assure all of you that procedures and security measures have all been tightened, and the method by which Mary-Joy left the island is impossible to replicate."

Rosa turned her gaze to Huey. "Oh Mr. Ralston, how you have disappointed me."

"Not as much as I've disappointed myself."

Rosa smiled, showing more stained teeth than should have been able to fit in one mouth. "I doubt that very much, indeed. Stephen and I always calculated there would be a chance that you would have an attack of conscience, even if we did hold your daughter..."

"Where is Lainey? I want to see her!"

"All in good time, Mr. Ralston, all in good time. Your daughter is here, she is as well as can be expected, and as of an hour ago she is still, shall we say a virgin intact. Only you have the power to maintain that state of physical wellbeing in your child, Mr. Ralston. I trust I shall be able to count on your continued cooperation in this matter."

Ralston strained at his bonds, standing up from the canvas chair. A guard stepped forward and punched him hard in the stomach. With a groan, Ralston fell to his knees and the guard was joined by another. They dragged the Texan politician back to the chair, where he grunted and coughed, unable to hold his stomach because his hands were still zip-tied behind his back.

"Well perhaps you'll come around eventually. I understand one of my guards, Karpov I believe..."

The blond nodded.

"...thank you Carla, yes, Karpov is particularity keen to spend some time alone with your daughter, Mr. Ralston. As I said, your continued cooperation is essential in this matter. Is that understood?"

Ralston nodded, a streamer of spit hanging from the corner of his mouth and dripping onto his pants.

"And you...you, I'm not sure about..."

Rosa had turned her attention to Sven, whose blackening, swollen face was looking ripe enough to burst.

Carla leant in and offered, "Sven Wikström, erstwhile bodyguard and butler to Ralston."

Rosa was suddenly delighted. She clapped her hands and her dry lips drew back to a wet gummed smile. "So you're Sven? I've heard about you from Mr. Crane here. You're the big Swedish lurch who was outsmarted by an itty-bitty girl. How did that feel, big guy?"

Sven said nothing, just glowered at his shoes through the bruises, and then as if to underline his anger, he spat a bloody gob of saliva onto the floor.

"Do you mind?" Rosa's indignation smashed through her delight and twisted her face into a mask of cruelty. "We've just had this fucking room varnished! If you do that again, I'll tear off your cock with my teeth and make you *fucking eat it!*"

The threat hung in the air for seconds before anyone dared breathe. Through the windows, the glowering clouds were thickening still. The weather was doing its best to match the tension and bubbling energy in the room.

Rosa breathed deeply, in an attempt to calm herself. She smoothed the material of her britches and composed her mouth back into the soft sham grandma thing it had been when she had entered the stateroom.

Rain was lashing against the windows like thrown gravel. Rosa's eyes narrowed. "Are we prepared, Carla?"

"We have all contingencies in place, Owner."

Contingencies?

Passion's curiosity immediately piqued. The clouds and the rain outside the picture window didn't need a meteorologist to tell Passion that filthy weather was coming in. The helicopter ride has been enough rollercoaster evidence too. But *contingencies* suggested something more than a thunderstorm and a few skitters of lightning. Contingencies spoke of hatches being battened down, aircraft grounded, and enough confusion to put a plan into action.

Passion had a plan. She'd been formulating it even before the windows in Sven's apartment had been frame charged. Way before she'd been zip-tied and thrown into cages by the Fake SWAT team.

It was just basic training and self-preservation. Make sure you have a plan if the worst happens and the bad guys get you. Always be ahead of the curve. Passion didn't feel that far ahead of the curve right now, but what she did know—that Rosa and the others didn't—was enough.

Rosa turned her head to the occupant of the final canvas chair. "And you, Ms. Durant. Or should I say, Valdez?"

"I answer to either on days like this."

"If only Alaina hadn't changed her identity on social media to cover up who her parents were. If only my operative Daniel hadn't mistakenly identified her and taken her to be a choice addition to the elite harem on the island. If only Mr. Crane knew of that foul up before he suggested to Mr. Ralston that the Agency would offer him the best chance to get his daughter back from the kidnappers. If only Mr. Ralston didn't need to maintain the pretense of his happy and above all voteable family in the eyes of the good people in Houston. If it hadn't been for that entirely avoidable chain of events, then you wouldn't be sitting here now, about to die. Such a shame."

"I get the impression that you never think it's a shame when you decide someone should be dead. You look the type who would enjoy that immensely. Anyone who talks about murder, kidnap, and the trafficking of children for their systematic exploitation by the rich and powerful, suggests to me someone who only has a passing acquaintance with the concept of shame."

Rosa lips pursed into a blade-thin half-smile.

Passion pressed on. "To be honest with you, Rosa, I wouldn't need the setup of the island and its evil intent to know you have no concept of embarrassment."

"Oh?"

"Yeah. Anyone who dresses like you do must be immune to shame."

The blade smile disappeared and the eyes blazed, but Rosa kept her composure.

"You think you'll get a rise from me, Ms. Valdez? No. You'll not lead me into a rage. The clothes I wear are like the chalets decked in Swiss nonsense, the forest of transplanted oaks, my little Hobbit hole in the ground. It's all for show, window-dressing for the dream we're selling. The patrons and the residents seem to appreciate the effort I put in, and the cannibals certainly love what I cook up in my cauldron for them."

Passion felt the bile rising as Rosa's tortoise feet lips worked and twisted around those impossible to listen to words.

"We're Enchanted Holdings, we don't bring the magic to you. We bring *you* to the magic."

Rosa paused and turned to Crane.

"Make a note of that, Stephen. I like it. We could put it on a letterhead or something."

Rosa fixed her eyes on Passion once more. "I can see from the disgust on your face it really wouldn't do to invite you to one of my special barbeques, would it? It would be *such* a waste of good meat."

Rosa licked her lips greedily. Her tongue was slathered

in white scum, which moved over cracks and deep crevices. It made the bile in Passion's throat rise on the wave already there, at the thought of a cannibal barbeque.

"We find that there is very little consumer resistance from customers to almost any act of depravity we can offer them. As long as we create an environment where they feel safe to indulge themselves. Isn't that right, Mr. Ralston?"

"Go to hell."

"For five million dollars a day you can set up home in hell if you want. *And* we have room service."

"Why are you telling us all this?"

"Well, Ms. Valdez, I suppose it is for a number of reasons. One, I don't get out much. I haven't left the island for 20 years, so it's nice to meet and chat with new people to tell them how proud I am of our operations. But mostly I enjoy watching the hope drain out of someone before I kill them. Do you know if you take away all hope, all chance of rescue, all sense of any possible future, a human will literally offer their throat to you to escape the horror of that hopeless thought? We had a girl recently...Macy...she ran from the compound to try to throw herself into a nearby ravine in some pointless act of suicidal rebellion. We caught her, of course. Killed her myself, and then those who paid enough ate her. I'm told she was delicious. But that's an example of what I was saying. Take away the last atom of someone's hope and they would rather die than live. I suppose you could say I'm waiting for you to offer me your throat so I can put you out of your misery."

"I'm afraid I'm going to disappoint you then."

"I doubt that."

"I'll never fucking do what you say again," Ralston spat. "I'm finished with this. I don't care what happens to me. I'm not going to be your fucking stooge in Washington!"

Rosa sighed. "Carla, we need some persuasion. I don't

think Mr. Ralston understands how much a woman of my word I am."

Carla nodded to one of the guards, he turned and went to the door, opened it and called out, "Karpov!"

Moments later a fat guard came in, his face ruddy with sweat and his shirt half undone to his white belly. Walking behind him, pulled on a neck chain, held in place by a black leather collar, was Lainey Ralston. All she was wearing was cotton underwear. Her arms were bruised and there were tears running down her face.

Ralston got up. "Lainey!"

The same guard punched him again, this time lowering Ralston to the chair in one movement. The guard stood by the Texan, his hand on his shoulder, forcing him to stay still.

Lainey's eyes were full of nothing but contempt for her father, but she seemed genuinely surprised to see Sven. "I'm sorry," she said to him.

"It's okay," he replied.

"If you've touched her..." Ralston said between sobs and coughs.

Rosa beckoned to Karpov. "Intact?"

"Completely, Owner."

"Good. You see, Mr. Ralston, your daughter is still unmolested. For at least the next ten seconds. Karpov...you may begin."

"Thank you, Owner," said Karpov pulling Lainey towards him on the chain, undoing the zipper on the front of his pants at the same time.

24

Z ip-ties are easier to get out of than people think.

There are enough videos on YouTube to show a person how to bend forwards, bang both fists down on the base of their spine and on the second or third impact the zip-ties will snap apart and the person will be free.

Ordinary zip-ties that is.

Tactical zip-ties, those in use by the Police and security forces, are a different matter entirely. They are 2mm thick, made from heavy duty plastic and a person would break their wrists before they managed to snap them apart. Even someone like Sven.

The last time Passion had been put in tactical zip-ties, it had only been the intervention of a rescuing police patrol in London that had saved her from a severe beating or worse. The Croatian gangsters she'd been investigating for smuggling people and drugs into the city, had just been too on the ball or too paranoid. She'd been blind-sided out of the blue when she'd tried her damsel in distress shtick. *Wham.* Passion's attempt to get close to the gangster's container truck to confirm the shipment had been on board, had gone south quickly and viciously. She'd been zip-tied, generally groped and thrown into the back of a Mercedes. The quick-thinking of her Metropolitan Police liaison officer had brought the team in early and she'd been rescued. But having spent some time trying to get herself out of the tactical zip-ties and failing miserably—only succeeding in scraping much bloody skin off her aching bones—had taught her a valuable lesson.

Beauty doesn't have to be just for show.

Where Passion dressed down from her modelling cover job when she was on Agency business, she always liked to keep a good set of false nails in place. Thick, self-applied Gel-nails, baked onto her own keratin by ultra-violet light and painted any color you like, as long as it was red or black. These false nails were the epitome of beauty, and yet at the same time the very essence of practicality.

Beneath each thick, easily removable resin thumbnail was a tiny, three quarter inch titanium tool. Under the covering on her right thumb was a wire that would assist picking the lock on handcuffs, and under the left, an equally tiny, but incredibly strong titanium wire saw.

Passion had been working at the tactical zip-ties between her wrists for the last twenty minutes, figuring she'd be sitting on the canvas chair for a while. While they waited for Rosa to arrive to give her Doctor Evil speech, Passion's fingers had been busy.

So, as Karpov moved in on Lainey, Passion's eyes flicked across to Mary-Joy. The girl had made eye contact several times already, waiting for the signal from Passion to begin her side of the plan.

In the car travelling to Sven's apartment, Passion had outlined what signal she would make to Mary-Joy, what she expected of her and what she would do when Mary-Joy began her diversion. She explained the risks to the girl and had not held back on what might happen if anything went wrong. Passion's sense was these people weren't playing this for fun; if they needed them all dead, they'd kill them, and they may only have a second to delay that moment.

"So, we'll only have one chance?"

"Yes. And we may not even get that. But we have to be ready, and you have to wait for my signal. Okay?"

Mary-Joy nodded. "One chance. I get it."

And now the chance had presented itself. As Karpov began to slide his hand inside Lainey's cotton bra, the tactical zip-ties holding Passions wrists together separated.

Passion winked her left eye at Mary-Joy. Twice.

Mary-Joy screamed, a piercing razor sharp sound that froze Karpov in mid-abuse and turned every other set of eyes in the room to the screaming girl.

Passion flew to her feet, her ankles still held together. She had the gymnast's sense of balance and the cheetah's sense of survival and she dove at the guard who had punched Ralston, because he was the nearest. She landed flat on her feet, still upright like someone completing a standing long jump. She didn't unhook the G36 from his shoulder, she just put her arm around his throat, and her finger in the trigger guard of the machine gun. As she applied savage pressure to his windpipe she swung the guard around, his whole body already a shield, and began firing.

The air exploded with noise as the bullets chewed across the ceiling, tearing out gusts of plaster. The line ran down the wall and then thudded into the face of the first guard. Passion swung the guard she was holding to the left and the second guard's chest burst out of his uniform, before he could even get both hands on his own G36.

The third guard's neck was torn out by Passion's wild shooting as he was bringing up the muzzle of his machine gun to fire. He went down with a yell, and Passion's continuous firing continued around to the fourth guard. This guard had enough time to get his gun ready, aim and pull at the trigger. Two bullets thudded into the chest of the guard Passion was behind before she zeroed her gun on the shooter and sent a line of bullets up his chest, through his chin and exploding the top off his skull like a tin can of rotten meat bursting open on a camp fire.

The guard Passion was holding, now mortally-wounded, slid to the floor. Passion held onto the gun and brought it to bear on everyone who was still standing.

Lainey was crouched down covering her ears, Karpov stood like Wile E. Coyote after he'd run out of ledge and was waiting for gravity to catch up with him.

Crane was laying against the wall holding his bloody shoulder, obviously caught in the crossfire. Carla was nowhere to be seen, possibly running for the door as the firing started. Rosa was sprawled on the floor; a look of complete shock on her face.

"Please don't shoot me," Karpov begged.

Passion shot him in the face.

The blast sprayed head matter all over Rosa, as Karpov's body fell across her feet. Rosa screamed in pain as the heavy body landed on her with full force.

Focus.

Focus.

The guard who Passion had used as a shield had a serrated bowie knife in a sheath on his belt. Passion took the knife, slit open the bond on her ankles and crabbed sideways to Sven, keeping the door covered with the G36. Sven had already turned onto his back and she cut his zipties.

"Thank you."

Passion passed him the knife. "Release the others."

Still keeping the door in her sights in case Carla came back with another group of armed guards, Passion approached Lainey.

The girl was sobbing while trying to pull the chain away from Karpov and cover her near nakedness at the same time. She was a wretched sight.

Focus.

Focus.

"It's ok. We're getting out of here. I promise. I'm taking you home."

Lainey looked up at Passion, her eyes brimming. "Take off the chain. Please. I don't like the chain..." It was still attached to the leather strap around her neck like a dog collar. Passion could see the girl was suffering psychological agonies she could only guess at. There were too many tears in her eyes, and her mouth was moving like someone drowning. To see this girl, broke whole pieces off Passion's heart. The kneeling girl looked up at her with terrified, fear-filled eyes.

Sven appeared, handing Lainey a black shirt. He'd taken it from one of the dead guards after releasing Huey and Mary-Joy. "Put that on."

"It's got holes in it." Lainey said, her voice cracking, hands trembling.

"It's okay," Passion said taking it from the girl's quivering fingers, draping it over Lainey's shoulders. Sven moved gently behind the girl and worked at the leather collar securing the chain to Karpov's body.

"I will deal with Lainey," Sven said, "but I think, Jennifer, you are needed elsewhere."

Sven nodded towards Rosa who had managed to crawl out from beneath Karpov and was trying to inch towards the door.

As Sven slid the knife under the leather around Lainey's

neck, Passion went to the crawling woman and stood in front of her. "I should kill you now."

Rosa looked up, her face still smeared with bits of Karpov. "It won't matter if you do. Do you think killing me will end any of this?"

"It'll will end you."

"If that's what you want, do it. I don't care. I'm 79 years old, and I've been doing this nearly 50 years. How much actual life will you be robbing me of? Very little. Kill a child, and then you're taking something *really* valuable. Kill me? Not so much."

Passion raised the G36. Rosa smiled.

Focus.

Focus.

Rosa had to live. At least for now. She might want to die, but she might provide a useful bargaining chip to get them off the island.

The sharp crack and thud of a head smashing into the floor turned Passion away from Rosa.

Huey Ralston was kneeling at Stephen Crane's chest. His hands around the wounded man's throat, smashing his head on the floor. "You fucking cocksucker! You played me! You bastard cocksucker! Die you motherfucker!"

Sven intervened before Passion could move. He reached down with one hand and lifted Ralston clear off Crane who was now coughing up blood.

"Do not be foolish, Mr. Ralston. The old woman will not tell us anything, but Crane might. He may be useful."

"I don't fucking care! We wouldn't be in this fucking mess if it wasn't for him!"

"I think you'll find..." Crane spat, "That it's what's in your pants that got you here, Ralston. I just took advantage of your weakness. If beating up and hurting women and children wasn't your thing...you wouldn't have come here to play..."

All eyes turned to Ralston, his face drained of color. He stumbled back out of Sven's grasp. "It's not like that...it's not..."

"Yes it is. It's exactly like that."

Lainey was standing, now that she was free of the chain. She pulled the dead guard's shirt around her shoulders. One thin arm was raised and an accusatory finger pointed at Ralston. "I know what you are. I know what you do. I know what you did here to girls younger than me. You're a monster."

Ralston fell back on his ass with a thud. "Honey...please...I..."

Mary-Joy held up her arm. The scars livid. "You did this, Mr. Ralston. You broke my arm and elbow because it made you horny."

All eyes in the room were on the girls facing Ralston. The man crumbled, then fell to his knees, sobbing freely. He held up his hands in a cross between supplication and begging.

"I don't care," Lainey whispered, but it was a whisper louder than a storm, "and if we get off this island I never want to see you again. And I'm going to make sure you end up in jail. Forever."

Mary-Joy crossed the room and hugged Lainey, and Lainey, her back straight, her chin high, hugged her right back.

Focus

Focus.

This family drama was all very well, but it wasn't getting them saved.

Passion raised her gun and shot out the widows.

The full force of the blasting wind outside the stateroom burst in on squalls of rain. They were on the first floor of the building with a drop of maybe ten feet onto ornamental flower beds. "Sven, go first. You can catch and steady everyone else that comes down. Let's make getting to the helipad a priority."

Sven nodded, and without a look back vaulted through the window. To an ex-man of the Swedish Special Service, a ten foot drop onto soft mud was nothing to worry about. He hit the ground with bent knees and parachute-rolled over.

Whatever alarms Carla was raising now within the facility had mercifully not brought the security forces running to this section of the building. Passion figured they were waiting outside in the stateroom, ready to meet them on the stairs or in a narrow corridor. They may only have seconds before that situation changed.

"Mary-Joy, go."

Passion pointed to the window and Mary-Joy didn't need to be told twice. Releasing Lainey she leapt for the window. Sven arrested the girl's momentum as she dropped towards him and steadied her to the ground. He did the same with Ralston and then Lainey.

"I'm not jumping," said Crane.

So Passion threw him out.

Sven easily caught the thin framed political operative and dumped him in the dirt.

That just left Rosa.

The old woman was still on her backside, but was pushing back with her heels. Passion shook her head, bent down, hauled the bag of bones over her shoulder and jumped down to Sven.

They were out of the building.

There were alarms blaring, but weirdly no guards.

It didn't feel right. Not at all.

"I do not like this," Sven said, looking around.

"Neither do I."

Rosa's brittle laugh told them that she knew something they didn't, but Passion didn't have the time to play games. "Helipad now."

Mary-Joy took Lainey's hand. Sven dragged Crane by the scruff of his neck. Ralston ran alone, his head down, his face a mask of misery and Passion carried Rosa over her shoulder like a sack of sticks.

The area around the helipad was eerily bereft of guards as well. Sven was looking around like a meerkat, Passion scanned the nearby buildings and the Swiss clock chalets. No one was to be seen.

It was as if everyone had been spirited away.

Again, Rosa chuckled.

The sky was heavy and leaden, the clouds fat with threat. They could no longer see the central mountain, it was hidden by the rushing weather.

The island's two black JetRangers sat side by side on the pad, rotors drooping idly, vibrating on the wind. Twin fuselages glistened with rain drops.

"I take it you can fly one of these, Sven?"

"Like I was born to it. You?"

"Oh yes. Ok, ghost town or not, let's do this."

But before anyone could take a step forward both helicopters exploded in gusts of flames.

25

Passion wiped mud, vegetation, and water from her face. She was lying on her back in the wet dirt. She could feel the heat from the burning JetRangers over her body. As she cleared the mud from her eyes, the conflagration came into focus.

Both helicopters were intact, but burning from the inside. Their windows blown out, both cockpits an orange rage. Some sort of small incendiary devices had been simultaneously triggered within each machine. They were wrecked.

"You didn't think we had a plan if someone tried to use the helicopters to escape? How sweet and naïve you are."

Rosa was lying next to Passion, her eyes glittering in the flame-light, cast by the burning helicopters. "If you think getting off the island is going to be easy, please try. I like a good laugh."

The others were getting up from where they'd dove for cover as the helicopters had combusted. Sven was rubbing his hands through his hair, Mary-Joy was helping Lainey to her feet. Ralston was up, and was kicking Crane in the guts.

Passion closed her eyes and shook her head. "Ralston! If you don't leave Crane alone, I'm going to shoot you my fucking self!"

Ralston moved away from the wounded man, the wind and rain lashing at his enraged face. He spat at Crane. "Fuck you."

Sven picked up Crane, and Passion dragged Rosa to her feet. She looked around. The place was still deserted. She shook Rosa. "Where has everyone gone?"

Rosa smiled and winked.

Passion felt like slapping the creepy old whore, but instead, lifted her up, slung her over her shoulder and looked around.

The wind was blasting them mercilessly now. This wasn't just a bad storm; this felt like an approaching hurricane or tropical storm. Palm trees were bending against the wind, garbage was being blown across the compound from an overturned bin. The corner of one chalet roof was flapping in the brunt of the weather.

Shit was going bad.

It was Mary-Joy who gave them the motivation to move as she pointed between the rows of buildings. "Look."

Passion saw the Humvee, but was non-plussed. "What?"

"Maybe we could use it to drive to the ravine on the other side of the forest? Take shelter? It'd take ages to walk there in this wind. But Macy said there were caves there. Safer than these buildings."

As if to underline what Mary-Joy was saying, a whole section of roof lifted off a chalet and cartwheeled through the air, smashing into the roof of one of the dormitories.

"The buildings have got to be safer, no?" Ralston ducked as a huge palm leaf flapped past his head.

Passion looked at the JetRangers, still burning.

"If these bastards would booby trap their own helicopters then I don't want to be sitting in one of those build-ings when the hurricane hits and it decides to firebomb itself. We have to assume all of the compound is wired to blow. Let's get to the Humvee, and take it from there.

Sven insisted they all stayed back from the black vehicle while he checked it over for charges or traps.

"It's clear," he said, and they all piled in.

Sven drove towards the Enchanted Forest with Mary-Joy at his side to navigate. Passion sat in the back keeping Ralston and Crane apart, while at the same time sitting next to Rosa, wedging her in tightly against the Humvee's frame so she couldn't move or cause trouble. Lainey sat with her side scrunched up to the back of Mary-Joys seat, holding her hand through the gap.

"Hold tight!" Sven yelled as the Humvee smashed through the gates of the compound, and they were out onto the track running beside the putting course—heading toward the forest over the open ground.

"Would you like me to provide an inventory of our facil-ities?" Rosa said with her coughing laugh. "I assure you I make a fantastic tour guide."

"Be quiet," said Passion as she tried to marshal her thoughts. How could an entire encampment of people disappear without a trace so quickly? They hadn't gone in the helicopters, and she hadn't seen anyone leaving through the gates before the Humvee had smashed through them.

Contingencies.

That word again. As Rosa had said, they were three hundred miles from the mainland—if they were in the Caribbean, then that was a prime path of all the hurricanes that worked their way up to the Gulf of Mexico. So hurri-cane defense and preparation would be a very smart idea to plan *contingencies* for. Right now, it was all rather moot. The storm was happening right now, and although Passion was resourceful, she had no contingencies of her own to tackle a hurricane. She was going to have to make this shit up as they went along.

So, escape. How?

Without the helicopters, they were here for the duration. The JetRangers could have flown ahead of the winds, faster than any approaching storm and got them to land at least.

Unless they could find...

Of *course!*

How could she have been so stupid?

"Lainey, Mary-Joy! You didn't come to the island in a 'copter. You came here in a boat, right?"

The girls nodded.

"And what happens when a hurricane approaches any port in the world?"

The girls shook their heads.

"All the captains put out to sea. It's the safest place in a storm, ride out the waves. Rosa, is the boat in the harbor right now?"

Rosa shrugged. "Do I look like a harbormaster?"

"Sven scratch the ravine, take us down to the coast."

Mary-Joy pointed the way and Sven followed her direction, back towards the compound and then onto the track that wound down through the jungle to the sea. The Humvee bumped around in a wide circle, shaking and vibrating, heading away from the Enchanted Forest, buffeted by wind and rain.

The track was rough and ready, but they made good progress even though the vehicle was thrown around by the uneven ground. Crane cracked his head against the chassis and groaned. His face was gray and sweaty. There were huge gouts of blood down the front of his shirt from where the bullet had clipped his shoulder. Passion thought about leaning across to Crane and applying pressure to the wound, but in all honesty she didn't care if the motherfucker died in front of her.

They burst out of the swaying jungle and back into the teeth of the wind. Leaves and twigs were blowing past them in a rushing stream. The sky was almost black with clouds. As the downward incline on the track steepened, and they ran past a wall of rock, the tires crashed and skittered over the loose stones, Passion could see past Sven to the jetty. The steamer was still there, rocking on the swell, smoke chugging from its single funnel but right now at least, the boat was attainable.

Sven pressed on, a tumble of loose rocks and stones from the cliff wall alongside them crashed and crunched onto the roof of the Humvee. Passion was deeply perturbed to look behind and see a boulder the size of a sedan drop into the road from above, and crash on into the swathe of jungle on the other side of the track.

"Christ," said Ralston. He'd seen it too.

The track leveled out and Sven skidded the Humvee around so that as they got out of the vehicle, they had only a few steps to make before they were on the jetty.

The wind tore at their clothes and hair as they made it out of the Humvee, Passion pulling Rosa out by her skeletal arm. "You gonna walk, or do I have to carry you?"

"Carry me. I can spit down your back."

"For fuck's sake." Passion hefted Rosa onto her shoulder, Sven hefted Crane and they battled the weather onto the jetty.

Waves lashed up and washed over the wood, making it as slippery as hell. Although Rosa wasn't at all heavy, she was awkward and angular. She also acted like a sail as the wind bashed into them. Passion had to steady herself several times to stop her now top-heavy body getting caught in the gale and thrown into the water.

The weather screamed down, the clouds—black and fat with their cargoes of heavy rain—rushed overhead, near enough to touch.

Twenty yards from the steamer, the wind seemed to go up three or four more notches. Mary-Joy skidded over and it was only Lainey and Sven sticking out a foot that stopped her crashing down into the waves.

Sheets of rain whipped across the surface of the jetty, and the steamer rocked. There was one wooden gangway left leading up to the deck, the others had already crashed down into the heaving swell. The remaining gangway had rope lines on both sides to steady anyone climbing its steep incline. Passion scanned the side of the steamer. There were no crew to be seen, not on the deck anyway. She thought she saw a flash of shadow behind the glass in the wheelhouse, but that might have just been reflections from the tumbling sky. Suddenly, the smokestack billowed and Passion thought she could hear the low rumble of ships' engines below the madness of the storm.

"The captain's having the same idea! Come on!"

The jetty was awash as the waves crested it. The gangway was tantalizingly close. Sven pushed the girls up it first and followed with Crane.

Ralston hobbled after and Passion, still carrying Rosa, came behind. The gangway yawed and pitched, the rope line on either side was slick with sea and rain water. Passion shifted Rosa on her shoulder, and that's when the old woman sank her teeth into Passion's shoulder blade.

The pain screamed through her like the rush of the storm, but she kept moving up towards the deck. Rosa scrabbled her hands onto the rope line, trying to arrest Passion's progress. The gangway pitched again, and slid along the jetty as the steamer's engines roared again, the smokestack belched and the boat began to pull away from the jetty.

Rosa's teeth cut into Passion's skin again and she screamed, beating at the old woman with her fist, the white shards of agony almost making her legs give way beneath her. But Passion wasn't going to leave Rosa behind. If she could get to the mainland, this woman was going to stand trial for her crimes, however much flesh she chewed from Passion's back.

The others were on the deck now. Sven was putting down Crane and was turning, his hands desperately stretching out for Passion.

She grabbed on, and he took her wrists. Sven pulled her up as the gangway fell back from the side of the steamer, crashing back down between the jetty and the hull with a heavy clang. Rosa was kicking and struggling with all her strength, biting, scratching and pulling at Passion's hair. "Let go of me you bitch!" Passion threw the old woman onto the rain slick deck.

Rosa skidded away as the deck heeled, slamming into a bulkhead. The steamer rocked and the lifeboat on this side of the ship, thudded down off its davit, rope falls spinning back and lashing out like whips. One caught Ralston on the back of his legs, pitching him over onto his back and Sven had to duck as another davit twisted on its base, swinging over his head and crunched into a wall.

"I'm going to the bridge!" Passion shouted to the others, "There must be someone up there. Sven, watch Rosa and Crane, get everyone inside!"

Sven nodded and took hold of Rosa's ankle, dragging her face down over the deck to where Crane lay, hand pressing at his bullet wound, rain falling into his eyes. Sven dragged Crane up with one huge arm, carrying him through a bulkhead door as the others followed.

Passion ran along the promenade deck to where there was a thin set of steps led up through the center of the deck, and up to the bridge wing, slinging the G36 over her shoulder.

The climb was wet, precarious and slippery as the boat was pummeled by the waves and wind. Flags hanging from hawsers from a communications mast were being torn apart by the wind, like stray fingers in a piranha pool.

Passion was battered and aching, wet and cold as she made the bridge wing next to the wheelhouse. Her shoulder blade where Rosa had bitten it was raw with pain, and the scratches on her neck were stinging as the thrashing rain spat at her like tiny needles.

She took the G36 off her shoulder, clicked the safety and opened the hatch into the wheelhouse.

Inside the bridge was only one man. He wore a captain's uniform, grubby, stained with rust and oil. He was in his fifties perhaps, unshaven and mustached, arms crazy with old blue tattoos. The name tag on his uniform declared him to be "Captain Rawlings." He was trying to do everything at once, and without any crew to help, he wasn't getting very far. His wiry frame darted around the bridge, trying to operate the wheel and the throttles simultaneously, but not having the reach to do so.

Rawlings looked up as Passion entered. He barely seemed to register that she was carrying a gun. "Thank god you're here. You can shoot me later, I need you to steer!" He pointed at the wheel as he worked at the controls for the engine.

"We're taking water. We're losing power to the engines. I'm going to try to pump out and restart the engine from up here. That means we'll be without power. I can't do that and keep the prow into the wind with the helm controls. Come on! Take the wheel. We've still got power to the rudder!"

Rawlings seemed genuinely trying to get the boat out to sea, best to give him the benefit of the doubt for now. Passion slung the gun back on her shoulder and walked to the wheel, stopping it spinning of its own accord, and keeping it steady.

Through the wheelhouse windows she could see that they'd moved some way from the jetty, but now there was little or no power. The engines had coughed and died in the guts of the ship, the steamer was now fighting to turn. If it got sideways in the water, the whole thing would be consumed by the storm. Passion fought the wheel and the wheel fought back just as hard.

Rawlings thumped the throttle mounting, and then kicked at the steel plinth it stood on. "It's no good!"

He came over and wrested the wheel from Passion's grasp—not that anything she was doing with it had much effect. The steamer was turning against the wind, the headland swinging around, the rocks looming.

As she watched, Passion saw the jetty slide back into view. There was a huge rending crunch as the boat crashed into it, tearing it up like a scab from the surface of the sea, bleeding wood and iron spars—screeching metal drowning out the sound of the storm.

As Rawlings yelled for everyone to "Abandon ship!" the steamer rolled on the waves and crashed sideways into the wind, coming down with a boom and squeal on the metal of the bridge, and slowly it rolled over on to its side.

26

Water crashed in through the hatch, the world tumbled and Passion was thrown around like a sock in a clothing dryer. As she was already drenched by the rain, she couldn't get any wetter, as the sea ran into the wheelhouse.

A clanging crunch told her that the ship was now scraping its side against the rocky seabed, and the whole vessel was grating over the rocks back to the shore.

Rawlings was floating unconscious in the water, face down. As the waves in the wheelhouse rose and fell, he was sent sliding into machinery with ever increasing ferocity. Passion threw out a hand to grab him, but she missed. She was holding onto the hatch at the opposite end of the sideways wheelhouse now. She pulled at the latch and the door fell open, narrowly missing her head.

Rawlings brushed against her legs and she managed to grab and turn him over. His face was torn and ripped along one cheek, but he was breathing.

The wheelhouse rocked as the storm battered the steamer. More glass smashed and through the open hatch

Passion could see the sky above throwing everything it had at them.

She had to get out into the open. If the ship turned completely over, she might be fully trapped. With the hatch open, she had a chance.

Passion slapped the uninjured side of Rawlings' face, "Wake up! Come on! I'm getting out of here, and I don't want to leave you!"

The steamer shifted again, and through the open hatch Passion heard another crash as something major sized and sounding like it was made of metal was ripped away from the superstructure.

Rain poured in, thunder rolled overhead, and Passion was thrown painfully back into what had once been the floor of the wheelhouse, the wounds on her back from Rosa's attack smarting with agonized fury.

Rawlings' eyes flickered open. "We...gotta...gotta get out of here."

"Yes," said Passion, waiting for the next rise in the water in the wheelhouse to carry her up to the hatchway. She launched herself up to the lip of the wall that was now an opening in the ceiling, and hauled herself up and out onto the outside.

The world was all the wrong way up. She could see the keel of the steamer half in and half out of the water. Where there had once been a prow was now a roiling mess of furious water, bursting in and out of the forward hold, and up going over the side in a white spray.

Rawlings' arm came out of the wheelhouse on the next swell in the tide rushing through the ship. Passion grabbed him and hauled the captain out of the wheelhouse to lay on the deck that had once been a wall. They both crouched back into the shelter provided by the upended low walls that had once been around the bridge wing.

Out of the wind, Passion could think. The ship was still moving on its side towards the shore. They could hear the grinding of metal over the rocks. Even if the steamer had righted itself on the swell caused by the onrushing storm, the water now would be too shallow for it to float. This vessel was staying on the island. There really was no way out.

The grinding beneath the ship abated and there came a mighty thump through the superstructure. With a final heave the ship steadied—still on its side—but enough to suggest to Passion that the steamer was fully beached on the rocky shore.

Passion put her head up and looked along the exposed side of the ship. Her heart leaped at what she saw. Twenty yards down the rusted side of the ship, Sven, Lainey, and Mary-Joy were clinging to hawsers and open portholes in the passenger decks.

They were alive.

The wind pummeled, the rain lashed, and the sky roared. But they were alive.

They climbed to the top of the steamer's hull and used hawsers and rope falls to lower themselves the thirty feet to the rocks.

They scrambled over the rocks, but as they crested them, they could see that the Humvee was no longer by the head of the now smashed jetty. It had gone.

They ran to the edge of the jungle, and hunkered down in a hollow between a tringle of trees.

"I didn't see what happened to Rosa. She slipped out of my grasp as the ship keeled over. She may have gone into the water, I do not know."

"Crane and Ralston?"

Sven shrugged, "I made it my priority to get Mary-Joy and Lainey out onto the hull so we had a chance of getting back to shore. Ralston said he would help Crane but they got washed away down a corridor. I didn't see them again."

"Good," Lainey said with conviction.

Rawlings was holding his face where it had been ripped open, it was still bleeding but not as much. "Thank you," he said to Passion.

"I'm not a monster," she replied. "Even if people like you are."

Rawlings eyes dropped, the shame in them clear to see.

"But you can pay me back in another way."

Rawlings looked up, "How? My ship is wrecked, I can't use it to take you back to the mainland, however much you want me to."

"I know. But there's something else you can do?"

"What?"

And Passion told him.

The steep climb down to the ravine on the other side of the Enchanted Forest was difficult, but once they were out of the wind, and sheltered somewhat from the rain, it was not impossible. Mary-Joy had been right; the limestone ravine definitely provided cover from the storm. And down below that they could see the cave entrances that Macy—poor dead Macy—had told her about. If Passion was right, Macy's death—squalid and horrible though it had been— was not in vain. It might actually lead to the end of all operations on the island, and in some ways that might make her death worthwhile.

Sven and Passion had left Lainey and Mary-Joy in Rosa's

lair under the central oak in the Enchanted Forest. Although the rain was still sheeting in through the doorway, it was still basically dry. They used the oil heater in the hearth to warm the girls off, and then went with Rawlings back to the compound to get the things they need, before heading towards the ravine, back through the forest again.

The hurricane, such as it was, had not dragged its eye across the island. Although it had comprehensively battered *La Isla Encantada* and destroyed the steamer—which Rawlings told them was called "The Enchantress"—the compound was battered, but mostly intact. The chalets were all so much driftwood, the low cinderblock dormitories were roofless, but the walls were sound. And once Sven had disarmed the incendiary bombs ready to go off in its doorway, so was the armory.

When Passion had thought about what the *contingencies* were if the island was hit by a hurricane or other natural disaster, she'd come up with a solution, but it was Rawlings and the information provided by Mary-Joy that confirmed it. What did the rich and famous and powerful do when things on the surface of the planet got too dangerous?

What they always did.

They built shelters *underground*.

Rawlings confirmed that there was a small network of tunnels under the island, which in days of yore have been for pirate gangs as hideouts, or smugglers dens to store their booty, or any other ne'er-do-well of the sea.

Rawlings seemed happy to spill the beans on his former employers now that his ship was destroyed. He thumped the nearest tree, anger boiling to the surface, and running over like the sea swell that had taken it down. "That bitch Rosa made me keep the Enchantress here! Wouldn't let me take her out. Didn't want the ship going down and raising the alarm with the authorities. Might bring them snooping around the island. Said they'd just appropriate another one! My ship. My blasted ship!"

Rawlings told them that they'd had news of the storm coming in the days before Passion and Sven had been brought to the island. There wasn't any firm confirmation that the storm, now a Category Two hurricane, would hit the island full on. But everyone—staff and residents—were put on high alert. "A captain doesn't let his ship die on a whim," Rawlings said. "Fuck that bitch. Fuck her and the horse she rode in on."

Rawlings' crew was already underground in the shelter when he decided to disobey a direct order from Rosa and take the Enchantress out to sea to ride out the storm.

Then when the storm changed course and rolled towards *La Isla Encantada,* Rawlings knew if the ship was still tied to the jetty, it would likely be dashed against the rocks. "And I was proved right, huh?" he said miserably. "And now I'm out of a job and I'm going to jail. Hey, will you put in a good word for me? When we get back to the main-land? I am cooperating after all."

It was as much as Passion could do to stop Sven twisting off Rawlings' head, yanking his black heart out of his chest in his fist and spitting down his neck.

Passion didn't feel any less forgiving, but she didn't save the guy just to have him offed by the huge Swede.

They'd left Rawlings handcuffed to a radiator in the stateroom in the main building—thankful that the storm was beginning to wind down and headed back through the forest to the ravine cut by a river coming down off the island's central mountain.

The wind was less harsh, and the rain less intense and with the ravine providing shelter, they reached the bottom in good time.

The cave entrance was dark, but the insides looked dry

and safe. Rosa's people hadn't posted guards outside, and that was a blessing. Passion didn't want a firefight if she could avoid one. This was strictly a no-fire if necessary operation. Bullets in a confined space was more than likely to hit the captive girls, who had been taken down there too.

Ten yards inside the cave was a metal door set into the rock with an entry coder next to it.

"Ready?" Passion asked putting on her gasmask.

Sven nodded and put on his.

The armory back at the compound had provided everything they needed. Gas masks, stab jackets, tactical belts, handcuffs, and heavy duty zip-ties. It seemed the faux SWAT team who had lifted them from Sven's place had been well-stocked from this armory or one like it.

They had everything they needed.

Sven punched in the password, given to them by Rawlings, and opened the door. Passion had already taken the pins from two stun grenades and two CS gas canisters. She threw them though the gap, and Sven closed the door.

The crump of the explosions were clearly heard behind the metal, and wisps of gas started to leak out around the doorframe.

Rawlings had told them that behind the door was a wide open area with a high ceiling that had been decked out with chairs, tables, coffee machines, and food dispensers. It wasn't the kind of luxury the clients of the islands were used to, but it was the main area when they could sit to ride out the storm, or any other emergency. Behind that were a couple of tunnels that led back into the mountain where cots and bunks would allow people to sleep or rest if the emergency went on longer than expected. The shelter wasn't a massive "survive the apocalypse" deal, but it was somewhere safe, warm, and reliable.

Until now.

Passion nodded her head behind the door as they heard dull thumps and a multitude of coughing and shouting.

"Annnnnnd now."

Sven, who had been keeping his shoulder against the door to stop anyone pushing out, stepped back and the door crashed open on a cloud of gas and choking bodies.

Twelve or so girls, men and uniformed guards fell out at once, tripping over themselves. Sven bent over, zip-tying the men, while Passion picked out the girls and began washing out their eyes from a canteen of water.

When Sven had cleared the residents and the guards he looked into the space behind them. He walked into the living area of the makeshift shelter, and Passion followed. Inside they found another fifty people in respiratory distress from the CS Gas. They went through them with no resistance. Zip-tying the men, and washing the eyes of the girls, and sending them out through the door.

They found Carla trying to crawl into a cupboard. Passion kicked her over and took great delight in zip-tying her arms around her back, far tighter than she needed too.

Within twenty minutes the shelter was secure, and everyone was accounted for.

Except for Crane, Ralston, and Rosa.

Among the coughing, zip-tied men, and the girls who were so incredibly grateful to have been rescued, one girl came forward and introduced herself politely to Passion as "Bimala."

Her eyes were red raw and her burned throat made her voice croaky. "Forgive my interruption, but you were talking about Rosa...the Owner?"

Passion looked at the girl, a young woman who had

been through so much as a captive in this terrible place, but still willing to offer whatever information she could.

"Yes, sweetheart, what can you tell us?"

"She was here. I was standing by her while she was talking to Carla, telling her how she'd escaped from the steamer."

"But when the bombs and the gas came in, I lost sight of her. She didn't come out this way?"

Passion shook her head. "No, and we've been through the whole shelter. She's not there. Are you sure she came back?"

"Yes. Very sure. She was telling Carla that they needed to activate a distress signal to...I think she said...the People behind the People? I'm sorry, I do not know what that means. But she couldn't do it from the shelter."

Passion felt her heart quickening. "Did she say how she'd do it?"

Bimala thought, "not really, but I heard her saying she also needed to go back to her house in the Enchanted Forest."

S ven hauled Carla back into the shelter and threw her against a wall. Her head bounced on the limestone and her eyes almost crossed as the concussion began to bite.

Sven picked her up and threw her again. Carla's teeth bit into her bottom lip and blood ran down her chin. She smiled up with pinked teeth. "The answer is still no."

Sven backhanded her across the cheek. Her head snapped sideways and a spray of blood went up the wall. Sven made a fist and drew back his hand.

Passion caught his wrist.

"Wait. She's not going to tell us anything."

"Perhaps not, but hitting her is making *me* feel better."

"Would you like me to book you a chalet?" Carla's shitty grin illuminated her bloody face. Her eyes wide with pure malevolence.

"We don't have time for this," Passion bit on her knuckle. "Rosa got out of here somehow, and she's heading back to her burrow. We need to get back there now."

Passion's concerns were Mary-Joy and Lainey, left in

Rosa's home beneath the central oak in the Enchanted Forest to ride out the storm, not knowing that Rosa was on her way back to them. There was no way of contacting them, and Carla was refusing to help. They'd been through the guards and residents too. No one knew where Rosa had gone, and Carla wouldn't say.

Passion's first thought had been to begin climbing out of the ravine to run back through the forest, but that would take over an hour. If Rosa had made it out through a secret escape tunnel she could already be back in her burrow. Lainey and Mary-Joy might be only minutes from death.

Something was sticking at the back of Passion's mind, however. Something was pushing up through her thoughts. She bit hard into her knuckle again. Think. *Think.*

The Enchanted Forest.

Rosa's Tolkien clothes and hobbit hole in the ground.

The Pinocchio Swiss Clock Chalets.

The Childcatching.

The Hansel and Gretel notions underpinning the whole idea of the island.

Fantasy and Fairy stories—the greatest ever told, twisted and corrupted into this...but...

Then it hit her.

They'd found Carla trying to crawl into a cupboard.

Could the answer be *that* simple?

Had the Carla the blond-maned lion been trying to follow the witch into a wardrobe?

Passion ran across the room, pulled the cupboard door open. The back surface was smooth wood. No shelves, no hangers, just an empty space. She ran her hands over the surface, feeling for a catch, a hidden control, anything...

Fairy tales. Fairy stories...

Passion took a step back. She thumped the side of her head with the heels of her hand. What would this sick fuck have done? What would have made her smile and laugh and think she was oh so clever? What would be right? What would be the perfect key to open a secret door?

Passion had only one option that presented itself, and so she tried it.

"Open Sesame."

And it did.

The tunnel was lit with sparkling LED lights which made the space look like it was full of stars.

Passion and Sven moved as fast as they could in the restricted space. It was a tunnel that hadn't been dug for people of Passion's size, let alone Sven's. She could imagine Rosa scuttling through it like a spider through a drainpipe as they lagged behind bashing shoulders, arms and knees on the rough walls and floors.

The tunnel ran upwards through the cliffs at a thirty degree angle. It was enclosed, dry and hot. As they powered on, their breathing became labored and Passion's chest began to hurt with the effort of trying to use maximum physical effort to catch up with Rosa.

Sven had already taken off his stab jacket and was carrying his rucksack against his belly. Keeping it on his back snagged on the ceiling every step, making swift progress impossible.

In some sections of the tunnel where the roof came down even lower, Passion found she could make better progress on all fours, moving forward like a dog following a scent. Sven copied her lead and they began moving faster. The rough floor cut into their hands, causing them to become slippery with blood, but Passion was determined to get to Rosa's dark fairy tale home as fast as she could.

Lainey and Mary-Joy were relying on her.

After twenty minutes of steady up-incline travel. the tunnel narrowed again and flattened out, ending in a dead end. The LED lights had gone and if it hadn't been for Passion's flashlight, they would have been in complete darkness.

Passion swung the beam up the blank rock wall, and saw there was a shaft above them. There was an iron ladder bolted to the side of the shaft, but it was the size of it that rushed a true sense of defeat through Passion.

The shaft was much thinner than the tunnel and it was going to be a struggle for Passion to move up with any speed, and for Sven it was not just possible.

"I will not fit up there."

Passion nodded, wiping the sweat from her forehead and trying to fill her burning lungs with as much oxygen as she could before attempting the climb. "Go back to the ravine, you'll have to go cross-country, back to the forest."

Sven lengthened the shoulder straps on his rucksack and passed it to Passion. "Hook this to your belt, and carry it behind you. There's magazines, a gas mask, teargas, and stun grenades."

Passion nodded, slinging the G36 across her back. Sven handed her his Bowie in its sheath. "Shoot first, but just in case..."

Okay.

Focus.

Focus.

"Let's do this."

Passion pulled herself up onto the ladder, as Sven turned around and went on all fours back down the tunnel.

There was a hatch with a wheel at the top of the fifty foot ladder. It looked like an airlock in a spaceship, or something from a freaking submarine.

Passion hooked her arm through a rung and hauled the rucksack around to her chest. She pulled a CS Gas canister and a stun grenade. She didn't know what was going to be beyond that hatch—another shaft, a tunnel or whether it would open directly under Rosa's feet, and the wizened crone would just fall through and bounce screaming down the shaft to her death. But it was a good idea to be prepared.

Passion started to undo the wheel on the hatch.

After three revolutions, she felt the weight of the hatch on her hands, and she lowered the circular steel door down to rest gently against the rock wall of the shaft.

Above, the light was dim and orange. She could see up to the rough ceiling of the burrow beneath the great oak. There were no sounds coming from the room above. No voices, not shuffling feet, no swish of cloth. Nothing.

Maybe they'd been wrong. Perhaps Rosa had another bolt hole in the shelter, one that took her back to the compound maybe... Maybe she'd announced to Bimala that she was coming back here as a diversion to send anyone who followed on a wild goose chase.

Passion was caught in at the cleft between two paths. Did she risk calling out to the girls, or did she throw the stun grenade into the hole and mop up afterwards?

Still no noise. No movement. Where were the girls?

No choice then.

She took the pin from the grenade and threw it up into the hole. The three second fuse ticked down, Passion covered her ears as best she could and closed her eyes.

Two.

Three.

Four.

Five.

Passion opened her eyes.

No flash. No bang. Just the fat black and yellow end of a Taser pointing down at her. Then the click and rattle as the trigger was pulled, the wires shot out, the barbs bit into her flesh and the 50,000 volts they carried made every muscle in her body go rigid, made her feet slip from the ladder, and her body to drop.

Passion lay panting on the floor of Rosa's hole in the ground.

The vibration in her muscles from the Taser jolt still coursing through her frame. As the barbs had attached to her skin, the energy from the Taser's power packs had lanced through her. Her body arched with electrical inflexibility.

The only blessing to save her from falling completely from the ladder was that her arm was still hooked around one iron rung. Her feet dangled, but the crook of her elbow had left her suspended, as the stiffening power shot through her.

The jolt of her bodyweight hitting her elbow and shoulder joint at once wrenched the muscles and almost tore the arm out of her socket.

As the voltage subsided, and her muscles relaxed, Passion had swung on the hooked elbow and managed to grab the ladder with her free hand.

With immense effort. she put her feet back on a rung. Her body was not working in the way it normally did because of the Taser shock, but she was aware enough to cling onto the ironwork. Rosa said, "Climb up, or I'll zap you again."

Passion forced her limbs to work in their confused and disorientated state, but managed to climb the last few feet of the shaft. She slithered out of the hole and collapsed exhausted on the dirt covered flagstones.

Rosa handcuffed Passion's hands behind her back and left her there for a few moments, while she spoke to a tinny voice that replied from a speaker in the ceiling.

"I'm sorry. It got away from me. Just got away. But it's all under control..."

"It's not under control!" the man's voice came back. It was filled with anger and threat. "We've got twenty governments wondering what's happened to their politicians. They're screaming because they can't contact them. There's rage out there because of this fuck-up, Rosa, and you're the architect of it!"

"I'm sorry. It won't happen again."

"You bet your life it won't, you stupid mongrel. I'm shutting down *La Isla Encantada* as of now. You're relieved of duties."

"But..."

"No buts. The Nicaraguan forces will be there within the hour. You will surrender to them, and report back to me here at the earliest opportunity. Is that understood?"

"Yes, Owner. It is understood."

"Cut the transmission."

There was a hiss of static from the ceiling and then silence.

"Sorry you lost your job, Rosa, but I must also decline to give you a reference for the next one."

Passion received a kick in the face for that. Rosa hauled her up into a sitting position and sat her against the muddy wall. "I am going to enjoy making you dead you mulato cunt."

Passion looked up at Rosa. "I have no doubt that you will. But I can die knowing your island is history and you're a no-mark pariah."

Rosa's face creased with the agony of this previously unknown humiliation. Her fists clenched and unclenched, for a moment she looked like a toddler about to stamp her feet and have a tantrum.

Passion pressed on, if the old woman was going to kill her, she might as well say what she liked. "Awww, diddums. Did daddy give you a spanked bottom?"

Rosa's eyes flickered and rolled back in her head. She reached onto the table and picked up a long thin-bladed stiletto knife, its blade glinting dully in the meager light of the room.

Passion wasn't giving up her tirade. "That's it. Cut my throat out. I don't care, you bitch. I've ruined your life's work. My *work* here is done."

Rosa took a step, but not towards Passion. She moved to the bed instead, theatrically pulling back a blanket. Passion saw who was there, and her heart smashed like dropped ice.

Lainey and Mary-Joy, duct taped by the ankles, knees and wrists. Across their mouths more tape, tightly wound around the bottom half of faces covering their lips, only leaving their nostrils free to breathe. Their eyes moved in panicky jerks as they became accustomed to the light outside the blanket.

"It's okay. It's okay." Passion said as their eyes settled on her.

Rosa snickered. "It's far from okay, as you put it, Ms. Valdez. The three of you are going to die, and I'm going to get away. So, on balance, I think it's going to be okay for me...you three? Not so much."

"You don't have to kill the girls. They're no threat to you."

"I know. But I'm going to kill them anyway. If I let them go, that would leave you with some hope, Ms. Valdez. Hope that they'd get away and tell the world what happened here. Now, we've had the hope conversation, haven't we? I like to drain all of it. Every last drop. I see that you've accepted that you're going to die, but you think you can persuade me to let these girls go—so that you don't die in vain. Am I right?"

Passion said noting.

"But I want you to know that you died *absolutely* in vain, and that even at the last you were a failure. You failed to save the girls. They are going to die first, and then I am going to kill you."

Passion's mind raced.

If she could keep Rosa talking, she might, just might keep them all alive long enough for Sven to get there and affect some sort of rescue. Passion knew she was running out of options and the next words out of her mouth sounded as lame as they did in her head before she said them.

"What happened to the stun grenade?"

"What?" Rosa looked like she was deciding which girl's heart she would cut out first, and genuinely seemed irritated by the question.

"I threw a stun grenade in here. It didn't go off. What happened to it?"

Rosa tutted, shook her head and reached to the table. She picked something up and threw it at Passion's feet where it rolled a couple of times until it was still.

It was the stun grenade, but smothered in a length of duct tape.

"You should have waited two and a half elephants before you threw it really. I simply re-depressed the spring and held it in place with tape. Next time...wait longer."

Passion had to be impressed by someone who was as insane as Rosa still having such presence of mind.

"Nicely done."

"Your praise is not necessary. I didn't survive this long by not knowing how to get out of a tight spot."

"Ok. But there's also something else I'd like to know before I die. Please indulge me..."

"Alright, who am I to give up an opportunity to gloat? Continue."

"The grenade was good, but I still haven't worked out how you found Mary-Joy and me at Sven's apartment. You weren't tracking my cellphone. I'd dumped it. It wasn't the rented car because I'd dumped that too. How did you do it?"

Rosa wagged the stiletto at Passion. "You really want to know?"

"Yes."

"Are you sure?"

Come on, Sven. Come *on*.

"Yes, I do. Please."

"Well, it's easier if I show you."

Rosa leaned over the bed and pulled up clump of Mary-Joy's hair between her fingers. Then, as Mary-Joy screamed behind the tape and struggled against her bonds, Rosa used the knife to saw a piece of flesh from the side of her skull raised up by the pulled hair. Blood splashed from the new hole in the side of Mary-Joy's head.

"Stop! Stop!" screamed Passion as Rosa dug her fingers into the open wound, her face a puzzle of concentration.

"How's the hope faring?" Rosa asked Passion as her fingers came away, sticky with blood. She was clutching a small square of metal. She held it up to her mouth and licked it clean.

Between thumb and forefinger Rosa presented a small circuit of glittery copper. "We chip and pin all the girls you see, but don't tell them what we've done. Usually after they've been beaten unconscious, so that when they wake up they're in so much pain anyway they can't tell what we've done to them. Mary- Joy's was inserted when Mr. Ralston snapped her elbow for his kicks."

Passion's head was swimming with grief and horror; just when she thought the island and its practices couldn't have upset her more than they already had, there was *this*.

"It's a low level passive signal," Rosa continued like she was giving a product update seminar. "Our receivers have to be within a kilometer or so to pick up. And it's not terribly discerning; that's how Mary-Joy managed to get away from the compound while we thought she was still inside. *Inside the wall. Outside the wall.* It's a fine line. By the time we started looking outside the compound for her, she was already on the Enchantress. But regardless, once we knew she was in Houston and we could use the more powerful trackers available to us on the mainland, we found you both. Still impressed, or wish you hadn't asked?"

Rosa threw the chip onto Passion's lap while Mary-Joy writhed and bled on the bed, screaming beneath the duct tape.

"So. Any more questions, or can I get on?"

Passion was destroyed. There was nothing left to say or do. Sven was not coming, and she'd exhausted all her options.

"Please. I beg you. Don't kill them. Kill me. But not them. *Please*."

"I do love it when they beg." Rosa moved in on Lainey, pushing her chin up and pushing the stiletto against the skin of her windpipe.

"This is my favorite bit..."

As the engine growled, the exit from the burrow out to the Enchanted Forest shuddered as an enormous impact shook the whole burrow. Lights came down from the ceiling, a wall caved in. Rosa was thrown back off her feet, and the bed was pushed aside on a blast of hot metal and grinding gears. The Humvee crashed through the doorway and forced its bulk into the hole.

Rosa was screaming.

The old woman had been thrown across the room and smashed against the wall. She was pinioned there by the oil radiator, which had fallen onto her chest, and the heavy oak table which had upended during the Humvee's egress, crushing her legs against the stone floor.

Passion got to her feet, made sure that Rosa was going nowhere and set about freeing the girls.

She tried not to look at the Humvee. As it had crashed through the doorway she'd caught a fleeting glimpse of the driver.

It had been *Huey Ralston* not Sven.

Sven didn't make it to the burrow until ten minutes later, when it was all over.

Ralston in a fit of anger or need for revenge had driven the Humvee straight at Rosa's burrow. The impact had sent him bursting through the windshield. The crumpled metal around the windshield tearing open his neck and chest. Passion could see immediately there was nothing she could do for the man who was transfixed on the hood of the Humvee, copiously bleeding out.

As Passion had used her still handcuffed hands to release first Mary-Joy, and then Lainey, Huey Ralston's head lifted once. His mouth was a froth of blood and gurgling breath. As the light gradually went out in his eyes, Passion was sure she heard him say, "Sorry."

Lainey clung to Passion in the tightest hug imaginable, not looking at the wreckage of her dead father in the Humvee.

Passion hugged her back, burying her face in the teenager's hair.

It was then, looking over Lainey's shoulder, she saw Mary-Joy standing up from the stabbed out eyes and slit-throated corpse of Rosa. The old woman's foot trembled for three seconds, her arm fell lazily from her face, and blood gushed down her waistcoat.

Mary-Joy's fists were covered in gore. Her eyes were blazing and her chest heaving. She put the stiletto down on the table and said simply, "I said that I would."

EPILOGUE

Mumbai baked under an oven sun.

Passion and Bimala rode the *Tuk Tuk* to the university, and walked into the grounds at the appointed time. Since he had left his wife Chaaya, Bharat had moved into faculty lodgings on the campus.

He came from the building at a run, sprinting in the way older men often do, arms flailing, legs pumping, mouth open and closing on a flapping jaw. Bharat was not a man who was used to moving this fast, but he was not going to waste a second by not running towards his niece.

Bimala ran from Passion's side too and the Uncle and niece met in a crush of arms and yelps and tears. Heads turned in the quadrangle, looked at the pair initially with suspicion but then seemed to catch the infection of their happiness.

"I did not think I would see you again."

"I didn't think I would either, Uncle Bharat."

"Tell me everything!"

Bimala hesitated, her shoulders stiffening momentarily.

"No, Uncle. Tell me about the flowers."

Lainey sat on the end of her bed, back in her room at the Ralston residence.

"Will you go to the funeral?" asked Passion.

"Yes." Lainey was emphatic. "Not for him. But for mom. She needs me and...and I guess...I need her."

Passion hugged the girl who she had promised to find and to bring home. She couldn't put it down as a success, not with everything that had happened to Lainey. Perhaps she would heal in time, perhaps she would take over her father's company one day and make a real success of it.

Right now however, Lainey needed time to rebuild her life and her relationship with her mom.

Passion tried to let go, but Lainey's face was buried in her chest, her arms encircling and squeezing. Holding on for dear life.

"Will I see you again?"

"Of course, Lainey. You try and keep me away."

"I thought...I thought *they* might try to stop you from seeing me. I thought...*they* might keep us apart."

"They can try, Lainey, but I think they're going to need some time to get their act together. The whole island thing might not be out in the open yet. It might be dismissed as another conspiracy theory, but their stock has dropped a long way. They operated the island on the premise they could keep everyone who visited, safe. We proved them wrong."

"Yes. Yes we did."

"I need to go to Washington to sort a few things out with Mary-Joy, but I'll be back after the funeral. Okay?"

"If you don't...I'll come looking, I'll find you and I'll bring you home."

The next hug went on for the longest time.

The Washington monument pierced the russet sky as the sun moved toward the horizon. They sat on a bench eating ice cream. The adoption procedure had been completed and Mary-Joy was now legally part of Passion's family.

"You don't have to call me mom."

"I don't want to," Mary-Joy said adjusting the brim of the Redskins cap she was using to cover the dressing over her headwound.

"Oh."

"You want me to?"

"No...maybe...I dunno."

"Maybe in time I will."

They sat in silence, licking at their cones.

"I booked the tickets."

"Thank you."

"We fly out on Thursday."

"The chances of Benjie being alive are small, but I want to try. He'll be the same age I was when I left now."

"Oh wait. I got you this."

Passion bent over and pulled the book from her bag, brushing some crumbs off the cover and handed it to Mary-Joy. The girl's eyes sparkled with tears as she read the title. "The Very Hungry Caterpillar."

"I thought you might like a new one, seeing as the old one got...well, you don't have it anymore."

"Thank you. Thank you...mom."

Once they'd finished pushing each other and laughing they embraced, both ice cream cones falling to the pavement and the book's pages flapping in the breeze.

Mary-Joy stayed back at the hotel while Passion went to where the Agency offices used to be. The flattened, half-demolished building was surrounded by police tape and chain-link fencing.

A gas leak had blown it up the same afternoon Passion had found she was unable to contact Bryan. That might have explained the inability to contact Bryan by phone, but Passion was pretty sure a gas leak and subsequent explosion wouldn't have cancelled her credit cards.

"There's not even gas to the building. Can you believe that?"

Passion turned to see Bryan, leg in plaster, arm in a sling, stitches all over his face, getting out of a taxi. Bryan was a short, chubby, gray-haired man in his early fifties and he was finding it difficult to juggle a crutch, a satchel, and a large brown envelope. He managed to squeeze himself out of the taxi and onto the sidewalk, while at the same time dropping all three things to the pavement.

Bryan tried to get his wallet out of his inside jacket pocket, but failed because his broken fingers were in splints.

Passion paid the taxi driver and helped Bryan to a Starbucks across from the Agency building. She got them both coffees. When she returned to the table, Bryan held out the envelope.

"No sign of Crane on the island. He could have drowned in the wreck of the Enchantress, or he could have crawled away into a hole to die..."

"But..."

"A credit card signed to him for campaign expenses from Ralston was used in Managua, Nicaragua, six days after the events on the island."

"Daniel?"

"Nothing. Wherever he is, it's not in the United States."

"And Detective Myer?"

"No trail at all. Last seen at work in Houston two days after what happened on the island. Officially listed as missing. No one knows where he is, not even his wife."

There was a rack of newspapers on the wall of the Starbucks. Passion could see every front page. Today, like every other day there was absolutely *zero* news about what had happened on the island—to the girls they had rescued or the rich, famous and powerful people who had been spirited away by the Nicaraguan security forces.

Nothing on the internet, nothing on radio, TV nor in the newspapers.

The People behind the People may have suffered a blow with the take down of their blackmail facility, but in the grand scheme of things it was only a minor irritation. They had regained control of the narrative pretty quickly.

"What shall we do?"

"Well, Passion, there's no Agency anymore that's for sure."

"But you're still getting intel."

"I have my sources, it's true."

"Are you going back to England?"

"That rather depends on you."

"Oh?"

"These bastards blew up my job and they tried to kill my favorite employee. I think we have unfinished business, don't you?"

Passion put down her coffee and fixed the plump, stitch covered Englishmen with her sharpest stare.

"I couldn't agree more, Bryan."

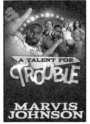